LINCOLN WAR BRIDES

BLUE Aster

LILY ROBISON

This is a work of fiction. Similarities to real people, places, or events are entirely coincidental.

BLUE ASTER

First edition. January 3, 2026.

ISBN: 978-1970614015

Written by Lily Robison.

Hunted

Henrietta

May 1878, Colorado Territory

Henrietta darted between luggage racks and disembarking passengers, seeking an escape from the man in the checkered suit. He'd pursued her across ten states and three different railroad lines in her flight from Philadelphia to La Junta, always present, always hunting. She'd first spotted the garishly dressed man in Dodge City after she'd overheard two ladies gossiping about a detective on a case. When she'd asked, the old biddies had regaled her with a sordid tale of burglary, kidnapping, and a missing woman. But Henrietta wasn't missing.

She knew exactly where she was, and she was in danger of being captured.

The detective had been easy enough to identify in his worn tan and blue suit, his beat-up bowler hat, and a black-and-white striped necktie. She only hoped that he didn't have an accurate description of her appearance and couldn't easily pick her out of the throngs heading West. Even so, very few young women traveled alone.

She would stick out if she didn't quickly join another group. Swinging her head from side to side, she quickened her step while surveying the crowd for an unsuspecting family to latch onto.

Dismissing single gentlemen and affectionate couples, who would wonder at her presence should she attach herself to them, she focused on parents with small children and older couples. Henrietta spotted her targets climbing out of the second-class carriage two railcars down, exclaiming about the heat, the crush of people, and the arduous journey to New Mexico Territory. The portly, elderly couple clearly needed a capable young woman to guide them to the stage depot, and Henrietta was all too eager to be that person. She adopted the blank, angelic smile she'd perfected through hours of receiving visitors in her mother's parlor and approached the weary travelers.

"Ma'am, please let me help." Henrietta reached for the woman's leather valise.

"Thank you. That's quite kind of you. I was just saying to Mr. Martin how I wish one of the children were here to assist with the baggage."

Mr. Martin was loudly directing a porter who wrestled with a large trunk. If the weight of the valise was any indication of the couple's packing habits, two strapping men would be lucky to manage it down the railcar's steps. She winced in sympathy when the sole porter shifted the trunk onto his back, a groan escaping his throat. Mr. Martin's help consisted of rapid-fire, confusing directions which the porter ignored.

The woman lowered her voice conspiratorially, "My husband is not as young as he once was."

Mr. Martin looked askance at his wife. "What was that, Berta?"

"Not a thing." She smiled at her husband, then turned to Henrietta. "And his hearing is quite gone. It is a trial, but the good Lord only gives us what we have the strength to endure."

"Quite right," Henrietta said with a sympathetic nod.

"What's your name, dear?"

"Um..." Henrietta spied the Pinkerton agent approaching. She fidgeted and glanced around the platform for inspiration, settling her gaze on a young woman holding a bouquet of asters and baby's breath. "Aster."

"That's lovely. And your surname?"

"Blue," she blurted out the color of the young woman's dress.

"Never heard of such a name." Mr. Martin gave her a quizzical look.

"My given name is Aster Bluvoroskaya."

There was no sign of comprehension on their faces. "It's a patronymic," she said as if this would explain everything.

Noting their blank stares, she knew they had not had the pleasure of reading Tolstoy. "It's Russian, but nobody could pronounce our name, so my father had it changed."

"Ah, well, it is a delight to meet you, Miss Blue."

"It's lovely to meet you as well, Mrs. Martin, and whereabouts are you traveling to?" she asked, despite having heard their destination earlier.

"Fort Stanton. Our son is stationed there. Do you know it?"

"Is that near Lincoln?" Henrietta asked. She knew it was—her uncle had been the commander at the fort before his death, but it was best to feign ignorance just in case the Pinkerton agent questioned them later.

"Quite near. Oh dear, it is hot here." Mrs. Martin stopped in the middle of the platform and fumbled in her handbag for a handkerchief.

Henrietta bit back her impatience as Mrs. Martin slowly dabbed at her forehead and neck. Henrietta shifted between both feet, laden with the Martins' luggage and her own hastily packed carpetbag, as the detective moved ever closer.

"You'll be taking the stage then? May I ask what brings you through such inhospitable country?" Henrietta asked, longing to set down the cases and wipe the perspiration off her face.

"My husband is a vicar, and we are on our way to see our son and his lovely wife, who is expecting their first child."

Henrietta exclaimed her pleasure while leading the couple away from the detective toward the platform steps. The couple dawdled along behind her, as she'd hoped they would.

"Tell me, where are your parents?" Mrs. Martin stopped again, to Henrietta's dismay, to peer at the various people milling about.

Henrietta bit her lip and ducked behind the plump woman as the Pinkerton man approached. She stifled a sob and said, "I last saw them in the churchyard."

"Poor child, are you quite alone in the world?"

Henrietta nodded vigorously.

"Well, no more." Mrs. Martin patted Henrietta's arm lightly, as one might a well-behaved terrier.

"Thank you. I can't tell you how much that means to me."

"Oh, and you are engaged to be married!"

"What?" Henrietta started and almost dropped the bags. She scanned the platform for her fiancé, but he couldn't possibly be there, could he?

"Your ring," the woman said, admiring the bauble on Henrietta's gloved hand, the outlandish pearl ring she'd tried to pawn to no avail.

"Yes..."

"Is that why you're on your journey?"

"Um..."

"Oh, are you one of those mail-order brides heading West? Our neighbor's girl answered the call, didn't she, Arnold?"

"What was that?" Mr. Martin said.

"A mail-order bride." Mrs. Martin's voice was loud enough to turn the heads of every passerby. Henrietta winced.

"Bright? Yes, it is a very bright day today," the vicar bellowed.

"You *must* be a mail-order bride. It's quite the rage these days."

"Yes," Henrietta said absentmindedly as the Pinkerton agent sidled up next to them, his eyes fixed on her. She set the bags down on the dusty road in case she had to make a run for it.

He was not a large man, barely an inch taller than she was. His eyes were black beads, his hair was slicked back, and she struggled to tear her eyes away from the thick droplets of sweat and hair pomade coursing down his forehead.

"Sir, ma'am." He nodded his head to the vicar and his wife. "I'd like to ask you a few questions."

"How can we be of service?" Mrs. Martin faced the weasel of a man.

"Are you together?" The agent nodded his head toward Henrietta.

"Yes," Henrietta said before Mrs. Martin could respond. "Yes, we are."

"What's this about?" Mr. Martin shouted.

"We have reports..." the Pinkerton agent began.

"What? I'm hard of hearing, man, speak up!"

"We have reports of a missing woman," the Pinkerton agent said loudly.

"Oh no!" Mrs. Martin covered her mouth with her hand.

Henrietta mimicked the gesture, gasping aloud for greater effect.

The agent studied Henrietta as if she were a specimen under a microscope. "Her name is Henrietta Beedy from Philadelphia. She's about your age."

Henrietta swallowed loudly, her throat suddenly parched. She opened her mouth to say she was from anywhere other than Pennsylvania, when Mrs. Martin saved her.

"I've never been to Philadelphia, though I've always wanted to see Independence Hall. What happened to the woman? Was she taken?"

"I'm not at liberty to say, but she may or may not be traveling with a companion either willingly or unwillingly," the agent said, his gaze fixed on Henrietta's bodice, but not from desire she was sure, covered as she was in her high-collar shirt and jacket. She fought the urge to squirm.

"That's not much to go on, is it?" Mr. Martin asked.

The agent's obsequious smile slipped from his face. "We believe she may be headed for New Mexico Territory."

"Isn't that a coincidence? We ourselves are on our way—"

"We shall be on the lookout for her," Henrietta said, cutting off the vicar's wife. "And how should we reach you, Mister...?"

"Jameson. Steven Jameson. You can send a telegram to the office in New York City. They'll find me." The man handed her his card. "Wherever I am."

"Wonderful." Henrietta considered the card, batted her eyelashes and offered the sweetest smile she could muster.

Jameson nodded, then frowned. "You'll recognize her. She has a hideous scar." He pointed to the side of his neck and his shoulder.

She bristled at the insult, but managed to keep her composure. As soon as he was out of sight, she crumpled the card and dropped it to the ground, then kicked it under the platform for good measure.

"PURE PROVIDENCE," MRS. Martin said for the tenth time that morning. Now that they'd emerged from the sweltering heat under the prairie schooner's bonnet, it was only years of decorum training that kept Henrietta fixed next to the couple when every fiber in her being urged her to seek out a cool, quiet place to plan her next move.

"What?" Mr. Martin bellowed.

"It's providential we found each other, don't you think, my dear?"

"Oh, yes, yes. Providence is a fine city!"

Henrietta smiled wanly. She was infinitely grateful she'd found the couple, but after more than a week of traveling with the woman's continuous chatter and the poor vicar's deafness, her nerves were frayed. But that was all behind her. She'd finally arrived in Lincoln without a Pinkerton agent in sight. Of course, he could have taken another stage or hired a guide. She shook off the concern, imagining her mother's voice in her ear. *Don't borrow trouble.*

The town of Lincoln was just as Henrietta had imagined, boasting a dusty dirt road stretching straight as an arrow, flanked by two-story wood-framed buildings and the occasional adobe structure—tan, pink, and brown like the sea coral she'd once seen in a book in the Philadelphia library. She snapped her mouth shut to keep from gawking at Tunstall's store, her cousin Rosalie's workplace, and the scene of all that trouble months earlier.

Sweat beaded on her forehead and on the back of her neck. She longed to unbutton the high collar of her shirt to allow the breeze to cool her skin, but that would mean exposing her scar to her new friends and everyone else in Lincoln. If only she'd bought a fan in Santa Fe at the little market by the hotel they'd stayed in. At least she had had the foresight to buy a wide-brimmed straw hat with a yellow ribbon to keep the sun from burning her already freckled nose.

She longed for a cool lemonade and a place out of the beating sun. Murmuring a desire for shade, she picked up her carpetbag and entered the store. How she'd missed Rosalie. It had been only a little over a month since she'd seen her cousin, but her life had changed so drastically during that month! If it hadn't been for the incident—she refused to call it theft—Henrietta might have been on her honeymoon in Saratoga Springs. Shame consumed her for abandoning her fiancé and her parents on her wedding day, no matter the circumstances. She shook her head in a vain attempt to shake away the guilt. She was not the rash one in the family, not the one to do something so foolhardy, to dash off without a word, to run away from responsibility.

And yet, she had.

"Wait for us, dear. We want to meet your intended," Mrs. Martin said, following close behind.

"Oh, there's no need. I'm sure you want to continue to Fort Stanton to see your son," Henrietta said, captivated by the bustling scene before her as farmers, ranchers, and children mingled with gunmen and even Indians in the busy store.

"Nonsense. We wouldn't think of leaving you here alone." Mrs. Martin looked askance at two men assessing an impressive assortment of weaponry. "What's your man's name, child? I've quite forgotten."

Mrs. Martin couldn't have forgotten because Henrietta had never told her. She could confess the truth. There was no man here in Lincoln—her entire story had been a fabrication to hide her identity and cover her escape. She almost did. The words were on the tip of her tongue when the checkered-coated Pinkerton agent stepped into the store.

Henrietta slipped behind neatly stacked crates of tomatoes, eggplants and squash. The vicar was across the store studying a plow blade, barking questions at a thin, gray-haired man behind the counter. Mr. Martin would be of no help. Oh, where was her cousin Rosalie when she needed her?

Henrietta wasn't quick enough to evade Jameson. He spotted her easily and headed her way. There was no escape. Her shoulders drooped, and she prepared for the end of her wild adventure. It was time to turn herself in, to face her family, to try to explain herself. Perhaps the agent would allow her to see Rosalie before escorting her back to Philadelphia if she gave herself up willingly. She sighed and took a step forward, determined to meet her fate.

Then her salvation strolled into the store in the form of the only other person she knew in Lincoln. Tall and lanky with thick brown hair streaked red by the sun, Duke Gildownie could have stepped out of the pages of a Wild West dime novel, looking every bit the cowboy from his worn hat to the dust on his boots.

"Um, Mrs. Martin, there's my fiancé now." She gestured at the somber man, ducking his head to avoid striking the lintel.

"Oh, yes?" Mrs. Martin's face lit up with excitement.

Henrietta had to convince the man to go along with her scheme long enough to shake the Pinkerton agent, which meant she needed to get him alone, out of earshot of the Martins and Jameson.

"Duke!" Henrietta waved to the tall man.

He glanced at her with a blank expression. Goodness, did he really not recognize her? She felt a prickle of irritation. They'd only spent a few moments together in Philadelphia, but surely she was not so forgettable as that.

She rushed past the Pinkerton agent, certain Mrs. Martin couldn't keep pace. "Duke," she sang.

He stood stock-still as she came bounding toward him, his eyes squinting as if trying to see her better. *In for a penny, in for a pound.* She stood on her tiptoes, threw her arms around his neck, pulled his head down, and kissed him.

Duke

HE TRIED TO EXTRICATE himself from the crazy woman, but her grip was tight on the back of his neck. Her lips were soft and supple and tasted of sweet, fresh berries. He should have pulled away immediately, but it had been a long time since he'd been with a woman, and she felt so good in his arms. His hands slipped around her waist, and he pulled her closer, molding her body to his. In some distant, rational part of his mind, he wondered who she was and why she was kissing him with such fervor in full view of the townspeople of Lincoln.

It might have only been thirty seconds, but he was lost in the embrace. A loud whoop and a whistle brought him back to his senses long enough to disentangle himself from the stranger. He stood there bewildered and tried to absorb the frantic, whispered words she threw at him. It was a complete jumble, but there was something about trouble, and he'd never been one to leave a lady in distress.

An older woman practically shoved the young woman out of the way to gather him into a fierce bear hug. Then he was surrounded by an older man yelling inane questions at him and another man in a jarring checkered suit with squinting eyes assessing Duke for some particular purpose, all their voices raised at once. He slipped from the woman's embrace and stepped back, forgetting just how close he was to the front door of the establishment. He knocked his head on the door frame, ensuring a headache was well on its way.

The noise and the people closed in on him, stealing the breath from his chest. Panic seized him. He grabbed the doorframe and raced out into the street, to the relative safety of the traffic. He'd almost made his escape when the pretty young woman circled his wrist in a vise. *She could have been a wrangler with such a powerful grip.*

"What's this all about?" He peered into her pale blue eyes, wide with fear.

"It's me. Henrietta." She glanced at the couple following her, then hissed, "But you need to call me Aster. Aster Blue."

"Who?" Duke tried to place her, but came up woefully short. She was striking, with sky-blue eyes, chestnut-colored hair, and full, lush lips. He cleared his throat and looked away.

The older woman dodged horses, wagons, and a braying donkey as she deftly crossed the busy thoroughfare, followed closely by a man Duke assumed was her husband.

"No escaping us, sir, we're practically family," the older woman said between wheezes as she caught up to them. "Dear Aster has told us all about you."

"Why—"

The young woman cut him off by jabbing her elbow into his side.

"Duke, may I introduce you to the lovely people I've been traveling with? Mr. and Mrs. Martin. They're on their way to Fort Stanton to welcome their first grandchild into the world. Can you imagine it? A beautiful baby."

A pit formed in his stomach at the mention of the child, and he inhaled deeply to maintain his composure, desperate to keep the memories at bay. The young woman, Aster, continued chatting amiably and then said the words that stopped him short.

"And may I present my betrothed, Duke Gildownie." Her voice was loud enough to draw the attention of everyone in town.

"What? No..." he stammered as the older man clapped him on his back, hard. Between the ache in his head, his injured side, and now the bruises he was sure would appear on his back, he was desperate to break free of these people.

The young man in the bizarre getup arrived just in time to hear Aster's declaration. "How long have you been engaged?"

"Who are you?" Duke asked. The question could have been directed to all four of the people, but only the small man answered.

"Detective Jameson at your service, sir."

"Detective?" Duke narrowed his eyes.

"From the Pinkerton Agency. My card."

Duke stared at the business card in Jameson's hand but made no move to take it. Detective, deputy, or agent, he had no love for any man who made their living chasing after other men. He'd seen the worst of the law when they'd arrested his adopted brother, Shaw, six weeks earlier.

"What do you want?" Duke asked.

"Only to speak to the girl, to ask her a few questions." Jameson's smile didn't reach his eyes.

"The *lady* may choose to answer as she will."

"I've already told you everything I know." Aster gripped Duke's arm tight enough to leave a bruise.

"What's this about?" Duke asked.

"It's about a crime, sir, and a missing woman." Jameson's beady gaze was fixed on Aster's face.

"And you believe she is hiding the woman? Have you searched her luggage?"

The detective smiled wider, his snake eyes appraising. "I believe *she* is the missing woman."

"Ah. That is a serious matter." Duke considered the lovely woman on his arm, her eyes wide and beseeching. "Are you missing?"

Mrs. Martin chuckled, covering her mouth with her hand. Agent Jameson bristled, all pretext of courtesy slipping away.

"Why, no, Duke, I am not." Aster tugged on his arm to leave. Despite her innocent stare, he knew she was lying. The question was why.

"Well, if that's all," Duke said to the Pinkerton man, "you'd best run along home." *Or to whatever hole you crawled out of.*

Trapped

Henrietta

She didn't release the breath she'd been holding until Jameson was out of sight. It was harder to lose the Martins, who were intent on knowing all about their relationship, the mail-order bride program, and their future plans. Duke, for his part, did not contribute to the conversation, leaving her to spin a web of lies entirely on her own.

"You must visit us at the Fort as soon as you can." Mrs. Martin raised a handkerchief to her eyes. The woman was actually crying.

"There, there, my dear. I'm sure they'll have forks," the vicar said, then, in a loud whisper to Henrietta, "she does love her cutlery."

Henrietta nodded and wished them Godspeed as they climbed into their transportation. Once the couple's hired buckboard was well on its way out of town, she released Duke's arm and prepared herself for the anticipated onslaught. But he simply bade her farewell and sauntered off.

"Wait!" She ran to catch up. She was a tall woman, but even so, he outpaced her easily.

He sighed and turned back to her. "I don't know who you are or what trouble you've gotten yourself into, but I have no intention of being dragged into it further."

"You really don't remember me?" she asked, allowing her irritation to creep into her tone.

"Aster Blue?" His lips twitched. "Nah, I'd remember that name."

"But you know *me*." She patted her chest.

He peered at her, then shrugged. "If you say so."

"I met you in Philadelphia. We spent the better part of an afternoon together."

"Don't remember." He turned away from her again.

She pursed her lips. *Unbelievable.* She grabbed his arm before he could slip away. "Where is she?"

"Who?"

"Rosalie? I came halfway across the country to see her."

"My sister-in-law?" Duke asked. "I reckon she's in Santa Fe."

"I've just come from there." She couldn't face another trip bouncing around in a prairie schooner. She needed a bath, clean clothes, and a comfortable night's sleep. Her dress was stained with dirt and sweat, and torn in at least three places. Even with an accurate rendering of her description, the detectives would be hard-pressed to identify the respectable daughter of one of the most prominent families in Philadelphia.

"Must have just missed her." He tried to pry Henrietta's fingers from his arm, but she held firm.

"When will she be back?"

"Two weeks, maybe more," he said, "after the sale."

"What sale?" She couldn't imagine Rosalie on a shopping excursion. Unlike Henrietta, Rosalie had always fought against a trip to the modiste.

"Cattle sale."

"Cows?" She scrunched up her nose.

"Yes," he drew out his words as though speaking to an imbecile. "Cows."

She frowned. "Why is Rosalie buying cows?"

"Not buying, selling."

"Interesting," she said though it was anything but. She looked over Duke's shoulder at the Pinkerton agent who continued to stare at the two of them. "Well, there's nothing for it. I'll have to stay with you until she returns."

"No, you won't!" He flinched, and if it hadn't been for her tight grip, he would have yanked his arm loose. "It would be completely inappropriate."

She tossed her head dismissively. "I trust you."

"Why? Why would you trust me?" He closed his eyes and shook his head. "No, don't tell me. It doesn't matter. I don't have time to babysit."

"Babysit? I'm twenty-one years old!" She released his arm and fought to wrestle her annoyance into submission.

"And evidently a criminal."

"About that, it's not what it seems." She laughed nervously and offered him an innocent, wide-eyed gaze.

"Then what's it about? Why's a detective looking for you?"

She leaned forward and said, "I can't tell you."

"In that case, good day to you, Miss Blue." He tipped his hat and strode away from her again, rubbing his arm. This time she didn't follow. She'd have to find some other place to hide until her cousin returned.

She could throw herself on the Martins' mercy, or she could seek out Cousin Rosalie's friend Selestina, if Henrietta could only remember the woman's last name. The stress of the past few weeks struck her. She was alone, practically penniless, in a foreign land surrounded by strangers. She sniffed back the tears threatening to fall and peered around her for anything familiar. The entire town could have fit into a single Philadelphia block and was as unlike her home as a cheetah was to a house cat.

The dirt road reeked of manure; there was no grass to speak of, not like the lush lawns and gardens in her neighborhood, and the people! It was impossible not to stare at the men who passed by in their scuffed cowboy boots and leather chaps, laden with weapons—knives, rifles, and revolvers. Why would anyone need that much protection?

Her family had traveled often, but she'd always been under the watchful gaze of her mother, a nanny, and even her cousin Rosalie. When they went shopping, there was always a servant waiting nearby. The only time she was truly alone was when she was riding in the park, and that was only when she slipped the groom sent to accompany her. The sheer need to find Rosalie had driven away all her natural fears, but now that she had reached the end of her journey, she had nothing to show for it but a weary body, a pocketful of cash that wasn't hers, and a secret she couldn't share.

Carpetbag clutched to her body, she walked along the arcade and searched for a hotel. Jaunty music drifted out of a building half a block away, compelling her forward. Once upon a time she'd dreamed of being a musician, a famous pianist traveling the world, playing before crowds of thousands, but what used to bring only joy had become another disappointment. She'd failed to master Liszt's "Le Rossignol," not even considered his most challenging piece. Her fingers still ached when she remembered how long into the night she'd practiced, repeating trills and runs, until she faced the realization that she would never be able to play the music as the composer had intended. She'd shut the piano lid that day, never to open it again.

Still, the music, full of gaiety, beckoned her through the open door of the saloon. The piano at the back of the dim room was a common spinet, but when played by a true musician, even a crude instrument could produce a melody to make the soul weep. The man seated at the piano was no master, but the tune was lively and fun, tempting her foot to tap in time and the tightness in her chest to ease.

She moved forward through the crowded space, mindless of the men and women she passed, until a flinty voice broke through her reverie.

"Well, looky here, boys, we got a new filly in the stables," a gruff one-eyed man called, swaying as he took to his feet.

Henrietta dismissed the man who was clearly in his cups, then returned her attention to the piano player, who had begun to play a ballad, sweeping and hypnotic. She'd missed listening to just one person at a piano with no supporting orchestra, no opera singer taking center stage, and no grand audience attending only to be seen by society. For the first time in years, her fingers itched to touch the keys, to slip into a familiar song and drift away from the world.

"What's your name, honey?" A woman with a painted face and an impressive show of bosom sidled up to her.

"H...Aster," she said.

"Hester?" the buxom woman asked. "Well, that's a fine name." She looked over her shoulder to a tall red head with a painted face. "Gina, we have a new gal."

"What?" Henrietta looked between her and the redhead whose crimson skirts were tucked up to display dingy petticoats. "I...I think there's been a mistake."

The drunken man lurched toward her and grabbed her arm.

"Unhand me, sir!" Henrietta tugged her arm free and looked around her wildly at the rough men eyeing her as though she were the blue-ribbon winning pie at the county fair.

"Now, listen here, Missy, my money's as good as the next man's," he said as he slipped off one of his suspenders.

"Get away from me!"

"If he ain't good enough for you, then I'll take a turn." A large man with a black, bushy beard lunged toward her.

Henrietta shrieked and stumbled back, reaching behind her for the door, unwilling to take her eyes off the men.

Duke

DUKE HAD JUST FINISHED loading the last of the goods when a scream pierced the air. He froze, lost in another time, when another woman had called out his name, when he'd sat idly by while she fought a losing battle. But it wasn't Judith's sweet voice he heard. His wife was long gone, buried beneath the live oak tree next to the little stream she loved so much.

The second wail roused him from his stupor and spurred him forward, running past men and women alike who scurried away from the woman's calls for help. He didn't blame them. Cries in Lincoln generally led to gunfire and blood in the streets.

The saloon loomed in front of him, normally a place of gambling, revelry, and willing company. Not today.

Aster stumbled onto the arcade, swinging her carpetbag wildly at a black-haired giant and a stumbling drunk with a patch over his eye. The men laughed as they grabbed at her, dodging her makeshift weapon, while making lewd comments about her figure.

"That's enough," Duke said, stepping between Aster and her assailants, only to be struck in the back by the carpetbag.

"Oh, my goodness." Aster rushed toward him.

He held up one hand to the men and the other to keep the woman at bay. "Stay back." He wasn't sure whether he was speaking to the men or to the woman swinging her makeshift weapon.

"Is she your gal then?" the one-eyed man asked, his face twisted in a sneer.

"When did you give up horse thieving and start assaulting ladies?" Duke pushed aside his jacket to reveal the Colt revolver in his holster.

Eyeing Duke's weapon, the giant raised his hands. "No offense. Didn't know she was spoken for." He nodded as he backed into the saloon, pulling the drunken lecher with him.

"I told you we were engaged!" Aster called after the retreating men, hands on hips, as if she had won the battle and had not been crying for help moments earlier.

Duke whirled on the woman. "We are not engaged. I don't even know who you are."

"I told you who I am. I'm—," she dropped her voice to a whisper, "—Henrietta Beedy, Rosalie's cousin."

He rocked back on his heels and considered the woman in front of him. She was stunning; there was no other word to describe her. Her eyes were a startling pale blue, like the color of the sky on a crisp winter morning. Her hair was a rich brown, lying in thick waves down her back, and she was tall, coming up to his shoulder. Rosalie was blonde and quite petite and, well, looked nothing like this woman.

He frowned in disbelief.

"I *am* her cousin!"

Duke pushed his hat back and scratched his head.

"We met in Philadelphia less than two months ago."

"I remember Philadelphia, but I don't remember you." He rubbed his back, then twisted to relieve the ache.

"You came to *my house*."

He squinted at her, then shook his head. "You don't look much like Shaw's wife."

She reached forward to grab his arm, but he sidestepped her. She pursed her lips, then closed her eyes and inhaled deeply, fighting to control her temper.

"My cousin Rosalie married your brother at a church near my home on Rittenhouse Square. You wore a brown jacket and an ugly black vest at the wedding. That vest, in fact," she said, pointing at the offending article of clothing.

He looked down at his clothes and then back at her, struggling to recall what he'd worn to the wedding, but he'd never cared much for what he threw on in the morning. "I can't say I recognize you, but I guess I can put you up for a few days until Shaw and Rosalie come back. But if you're lying about who you are—"

"I'm not lying, well, I'm not lying *now*...but it would be best if you didn't mention my real name to anyone."

She licked her lips, and he had an intense desire to taste them again. What was wrong with him? That kiss must have sucked the wits from his head. He stuffed his hands into his pocket, suddenly afraid they might betray him by reaching out for the young woman.

"Rosalie and Shaw can work it out when they get here, but you gotta stop telling people we're getting hitched," he said, looking anywhere but at her.

"Those men tried to accost me!"

He rounded on her. "What did you think was gonna happen if you strolled into a brothel with your luggage in hand?"

"Surely, no one would believe I was...looking for employment?" she sputtered.

"I reckon they did." He winced as he picked up her bag.

"Did I hurt you?" She reached out to him and he jumped back.

"I'm fine."

"I am sorry," she said quietly as they walked back to the waiting wagon. "I was scared."

He stole a glance at her and, for the first time, noticed the dark circles under her eyes, her pale cheeks, and the mud on the hem of her skirt. Her beauty had first captured him and then terrified him, prompting his desperate need to escape from her. He hadn't noticed how worn and weary she was. He cursed himself for leaving her on her own, an innocent in this town, exhausted after a long journey across rugged terrain. She might not be Rosalie's cousin, but she clearly needed a helping hand.

"Rosalie never mentioned anyone assaulting her." She shuddered, and he fought the urge to wrap his arm around her.

"Everyone knows she's Shaw's woman," he muttered.

"So?" Aster cocked her head. "Why should that matter?"

He steered her out of the constant stream of people walking along the arcade and lowered his voice, "My brother's a gunman."

"Yes, there was that business with the sheriff a while back, but I'm sure it was a misunderstanding." She waived her arm dismissively.

Was she naïve enough to believe his brother had shot the sheriff by accident? He opened his mouth to tell her exactly what Shaw's line of work had been, then grimaced when he saw a small, red-headed woman with a scowl on her face stalking toward him. He would have hidden if he'd had any idea *she* was in town. As it was, he slumped down and tried his best to disappear. No luck.

"Duke Gildownie, ye'd better stay right where ye are," she called as she pushed past two farmers complaining about wolves attacking their livestock.

"Good evening, Ma." He hung his head when she approached.

"Good evening, my foot! What's this I hear about ye getting married and nary a word to yer ol' Ma?"

"Oh, ma'am, it's not what you think—"

"It's right fine to meet ye, lass." Ma pulled Aster into a fierce hug. "I canna tell ye how happy I was to hear the news." She released a bewildered Aster and turned back to Duke. "But ye have some answering to do, boy. I've been on ye for five years to remarry and here ye go an' do it all on yer own."

"Ma," Duke said, "it's just a mistake—" he was cut off by a sharp pain as Aster stomped down on his foot. He shuffled uncomfortably and glared at Aster, who was looking past his Ma to a man striding their way.

That damned Pinkerton agent angled toward them. *Why the hell was he back?*

There was no choice. He wasn't going to let any young woman, criminal or not, be dragged away by that snide little man. He'd deal with his mother later. An idea struck then, a wild idea that might solve the problem of his Ma turning up out of the blue.

"You're quite right, Ma." Duke linked arms with Aster. "I should have come to you straight away, but I didn't know you were here in Lincoln."

His Ma sniffed and stood up straighter. "Well, I suppose I can overlook it, this one time. But dinnae think ye can be hiding from me anymore. I'm fed up, I tell ye, and I'll have no more of it."

"Yes, ma'am." He ducked his head as he had done when he was just a lad.

"Well, are ye going to introduce me to yer bride?"

"Aster Blue." Aster pressed against Duke. "I'm pleased to make your acquaintance, ma'am. I've heard so much about you, I feel like we're already friends."

"Is that so?" Ma squinted at Duke. "And what exactly has my boy been spouting off about?"

"Mr. Jameson," Duke called to the man approaching their small group. He'd never been so grateful to see a detective, if only to gather a few moments to gather his thoughts and plan his next steps while the others spoke.

He settled back and watched as the agent interrogated the two women. If Aster wasn't a stage actress, she'd missed her calling, inventing elaborate stories of their love affair through mail correspondence. Occasionally, his Ma threw him a disbelieving glance, but otherwise, was completely enthralled with the vivacious woman clinging to his arm.

Jameson slithered up next to him and hissed, "And this is all true?"

Duke sighed. "Every word."

A House of Lies

Henrietta

Marigolds, verbena, and yellow mallows covered the fields on the ride to the Gildownie ranch, but an occasional lilac-colored thistle appeared. Such a delicate flower topping a thorny bush. Rosalie's painting of a cactus rose came to mind, bringing with it a wave of homesickness. She'd come here for her cousin—every step, every decision she'd made had been toward that aim alone.

Now she sat here between two strangers, jostled back and forth between the Gildownies, with every bump and dip on the road, spinning one fantastical lie after another. She'd expected Duke to tell his mother who she was as soon as they'd left Lincoln, but he continued calling her Aster and occasionally threw in a helpful word like 'letter' or 'Matrimonial News'.

"And then yer family came here, to America?" Bridget asked.

"Yes, that's right."

"How long ago was that?"

"Um. Well, before I was born," Henrietta stammered, trying to keep track of the many lies she'd told.

"And do ye speak Russian?"

"Only a few words, I'm afraid. My parents believed in a clean break from the old country."

"Ach, that's a pity that. I'd like to have learnt a new language." Bridget shifted on the seat. "Say something."

Henrietta's eyes widened. "In Russian?"

"Aye, Russian."

Henrietta's mouth dropped open, and she struggled to remember any Russian words from Anna Karenina.

"That's the house up ahead." Duke pointed to a two-story wooden structure in the distance. As they neared the house, she could make out a covered porch boasting three large rocking chairs. There was a fenced-in vegetable garden, abundant in the early days of summer, barns and outbuildings, and a clearing for a new structure. The sun hung low behind the buildings, painting the sky a brilliant vermillion.

"Red sky at night, sailor's delight," Henrietta said.

"How do ye say 'tis a fair night in Russian?"

"Um, is this your ranch?" Henrietta sat up straighter and looked around for a property line separating this land from the neighbor's. They had passed no other homes since leaving Lincoln three hours earlier. Unlike Philadelphia, where every home was distinctly separated from its neighbor on Rittenhouse Square by gardens and walls.

"We've been on the ranch for the past two hours. I hope to buy more land once we start turning a consistent profit," he said with an apologetic tone.

"But it's wonderful." The fields were no different from the ones they'd traveled through—rough and rocky with patches of tall grass, cactus and wildflowers, and cows in the distance, but near the house, more than a dozen horses grazed and dozed in an enormous paddock. There were bays and chestnuts and several with spots on their backs.

"Why do those have freckles?" She pointed to the distinctively colored horses.

"You've never seen an Appaloosa?" Duke said.

"Is that what they're called? They're beautiful." A foal nuzzled against his mother who was grazing next to the fence.

"I suppose it's not a surprise you don't recognize them. There's not many of them anymore, not even in New Mexico Territory."

"My boys are breeding them." Bridget said with a smug grin on her face.

"That's the idea."

"Amazing." Henrietta had always loved horses, much to her cousin Rosalie's chagrin. Riding had been the one part of the day entirely her own, though her freedom had been confined to Fairmount Park. In New Mexico Territory, she was constrained only by mountains and streams. She itched to get in a saddle and ride with nothing and no one to call her home.

Duke reined in the horse near the house and climbed down. It was a simple, two-story, white-washed building with none of the fussy turrets and ornate woodwork so common back East. Practicality over ornamentation. There were barns and outbuildings scattered about the property, partially hidden by live oak, pecan and spruce trees. An enormous vegetable garden lay to the left of the home. She'd wondered earlier at the lack of produce when she'd seen the many sacks of grain and feed loaded in the wagon bed.

Duke jumped down and offered a hand to Henrietta and then to his mother. When Bridget grabbed her arm to lead her into the house, Henrietta begged off, saying she wanted to help Duke unload the provisions.

"Nonsense, there are three strapping lads here to do the work."

"Oh, I don't mind." Henrietta threw Duke a furtive glance. She needed to talk to the man alone before she was introduced as his bride to all his relatives.

Bridget sighed and pressed her hand to her heart, completely misinterpreting Henrietta's hesitation. "I remember being young and in love. Ye take yer time, lass."

Henrietta smiled weakly and waited for the small woman to enter the house. Once Bridget was out of earshot, she turned on Duke. "What are you doing? Why would you lie to your mother and drag me into it?"

He took off his hat and rubbed the back of his head, wincing, before placing it back on his head. "You started this, and you haven't even told me why."

"I—" Henrietta hesitated as she clutched her reticule and the secrets it held. "I was in trouble and needed to slip away."

"What kind of trouble?"

"I don't think we know each other well enough to be sharing secrets."

He arched an eyebrow. "According to you, we've been involved in a torrid love affair for the better part of a year. I'd say that gives me the right to know."

She gnawed on her bottom lip and avoided his gaze. "I may have taken something which didn't exactly belong to me."

"So, you stole something?" Duke crossed his arms and leaned against the wagon.

"I wouldn't characterize it quite that way."

"And how would you characterize it?" he asked.

"I think of it more as borrowing." She should have gone with Bridget, if only to avoid this conversation.

"Without permission?" He raised an eyebrow.

"Perhaps." She looked at the door longingly.

"What did you borrow?" he asked.

"Nothing important."

"If it wasn't important, why is a Pinkerton agent searching for you? And why did you drag me into your elaborate ruse?"

"I wish I could tell you, I do, but I would be betraying a confidence." She wrung her hands together, eager to end the conversation. How could a man she barely knew understand what had driven her to this madness?

"But you are a thief?"

"In a strictly literal sense, yes, but I was justified," she said.

"And you refuse to tell me what you stole, why you stole it, and why it's important enough for a detective to be tracking you?"

She nodded. "Yes, exactly."

"Then you'd better carry on as you are, Aster, or whatever your name is, until you choose to confide in me. All it would take is a quick ride into town for your house of lies to come crashing down." He pushed off the wagon and started to turn away from her, effectively ending their conversation.

"You would betray me?" Her stomach roiled, and she clutched the sleeve of his jacket.

He peeled her fingers off his arm, his mouth set in a terse line.

"I don't know you. I'm not even convinced you are related to Rosalie."

"I met you in Philadelphia, in the garden at my house."

"So, you say."

"Because it's true." She threw up her hands in exasperation.

"So far, all you've done is lie. Why should I believe you now?"

"Fine. You don't trust me. I accept that, but why do you insist on deceiving your family? Tell them the truth, and they can decide for themselves if I am who I say I am."

"Well, I've been thinking about that." He looked down at his feet. "I work the ranch all day, and I haven't had a lot of time for cooking and cleaning and the like. My Ma's bound and determined I find a wife and settle down. To be honest, it's starting to get under my skin. If you could pretend we're getting married, she'd be more likely to focus on my sister Martha or one of my brothers for a while."

"She won't notice when we don't actually exchange vows?" Henrietta arched an eyebrow in disbelief.

"Well, normally she would, but Martha's fair bursting with a babe in her belly. Ma will run along back to Roswell in a week or two, and I can get on with my life without an interfering woman in it."

He sniffed and looked away from her.

She considered her options. She couldn't leave without seeing Rosalie, and her experience in town had been shocking and slightly terrifying, though she would never admit that to another soul. He held her future in the palm of his hand, but if they could strike a bargain which suited them both, then she might make it through this adventure unscathed.

"So, one could surmise you need me?"

"Only for a bit of cooking, cleaning and—"

"Keeping your mother occupied?"

He smiled and nodded. "Yep."

"She seems a kind-hearted woman. She will be so hurt when she finds out."

"By then she'll be with Martha and the baby. She won't have time to spare a thought for me."

Henrietta wasn't so sure, but she was too tired to argue about it, and she could not let him turn her over to Jameson. "I suppose I dragged you into this in the first place. If you think it's best, I'll go along with it, but only until Rosalie comes back. And then, whether your mother is here or not, we come clean."

"Deal," he said and held out his hand.

She looked at it for a moment, contemplating the bargain, then shrugged and placed her hand in his. His grip was firm and sure, so she swallowed down her unease. "Deal."

No sooner had the word left her mouth, the door slammed open, and a tall young man with strawberry-blonde hair came bounding out of the house. He would have caught the eye of every lady at a party, with his twinkling blue eyes and devilish grin.

"Hiya Aster! Welcome to the family!" The man rushed up to them and picked her up.

Henrietta was too shocked at his forwardness to protest. He twirled her around and around until the world spun. When he set her back down, she wavered and reached out blindly, grabbing hold of

Duke. She pressed a hand to her stomach, already threatening to heave from the dizziness.

"You always go too far," Duke said under his breath.

"Shut your trap, man. I'm the one who should be spitting mad at you, running off and getting married without telling a soul."

"We're not married."

"Good as," the young man said. When he reached again for Henrietta, Duke shoved him away.

"Enough. She's had a long journey and needs her rest."

"I'm completely well, thank you." Aster took a deep breath. "Pleased to meet you." She held out one gloved hand while keeping the other firmly gripped around Duke's arm.

"Well, hell, I'm pleased to meet you too, Aster. I'm Cash, the smart, good-looking one. Don't know why you settled for this lump." He shook her hand so hard she thought it might fall off.

Taken aback by his rude remarks, Henrietta wasn't sure how to respond. Fortunately, she was saved by another man who emerged from the house. Like his brothers, he was taller than most men, but where Cash was fair, this man was dark, and he was older than both if the faint lines around his eyes were any judge. His skin was deeply tanned, his hair was dark, and he had deep brown eyes, so dark it was like looking into the bottom of a well.

"Wyatt, ma'am. I'm pleased to meet you," he said with a solemn expression.

"It's good to be here." Aster smiled tentatively.

"Best go on inside and take a load off. I'll help Duke with the provisions." Wyatt threw a questioning look at his brother, then grabbed a bag of flour and hoisted it onto his shoulder.

When Cash darted back toward the house, Wyatt called to him, "You're gonna help too."

Cash threw her a cheeky smile, then turned back to his brothers. Henrietta hugged herself as she walked alone through the open doorway, as if preparing to face not Duke's mother, but a fire-breathing dragon determined to burn the truth from her.

Duke

HE HAD INTENDED TO fess up to his brothers. They'd never kept secrets from each other in the past, but as he opened his mouth to tell them all that had happened, he was cut off by his younger brother. Cash was no baby at twenty-five years old, but he sure acted the fool most of the time.

"You old dog, I can't believe you went and got yourself hitched. At least you picked a pretty one, though she is a tad young for you."

"I'm twenty-eight, not fifty."

"Leave him alone, Cash." Wyatt had already dropped off the bag of flour inside the house and was halfway down the steps again. "He must have had a hankering to have someone warm his bed again. Can't blame him for that."

"There are less permanent solutions to that particular problem." Cash climbed into the back of the wagon to pass down the goods to his brothers. "Did you get anything good? Whiskey or tobacco."

"There's some in the crate nearest the wagon bench," Duke said.

Cash clambered over the sacks of flour, grain and feed, grinning. "We can celebrate your nuptials!" He picked up a bottle of rye and mock-toasted Duke.

"We're not married yet."

"It's probably for the best you found yourself a gal. You've been a bear to live with. Maybe she'll soften you up a bit." Wyatt leaned against the wagon wheel and looked Duke up and down. "I understand why you chose her, but how the hell did you get her to agree?"

"Funny." Duke threw a bag of feed on his shoulder and headed around the side of the house to the horse barn, Wyatt keeping pace with his own sack.

"What I can't figure is when you had the time to do your courtin'. You work from dawn to sundown. Hell, I didn't think you even knew how to write a letter. That's how you nabbed her, right? She's one of those poor mail-order brides who don't have any other choices?"

"Why don't you focus on your own love life? Can't believe Ma's always on me when you're practically forty."

"Ha!" Wyatt said. "Besides, she's given up, which is fine by me. Now that you're passing on the family name, the pressure's off me for good. What I can't figure is why you changed your mind? After Judith and the baby..."

Hearing his late wife's name spoken aloud after all these years was like a punch in the gut. He'd never said he wouldn't talk about her or their baby boy, yet no one ever had. They pretended she'd never even existed in this family, and that pain was worse than her death.

"If you're going to chew the fat, we'll never get the wagon unloaded," Duke said.

"Cash will do it."

"Not in this lifetime," Duke snorted.

Wyatt grabbed him around the shoulders as they strode back together. Duke could have told them then, but he didn't. Cash never could keep a secret, and Wyatt? He'd make him squirm a bit. With Duke safely married off, Ma would naturally turn to her oldest son. His oldest brother was a loner, living most months in the hunting cabin up in the mountains. It wasn't a life for a young wife, and Wyatt was too set in his ways to change, but when Ma had a hankering to do something, she sure had a way of seeing it got done, no matter the agony it caused.

An Unexpected Kindness

Henrietta

She grinned as she finished scraping off the last of the peel with a paring knife. When she presented the clean potato to Bridget, the woman nodded as though it were no more than she expected. Rosalie had regaled her with stories of cooking side by side with this woman, of sharing intimate secrets while bonding over cakes, pies, and jams. Perhaps Bridget would not become Henrietta's mother-in-law, but that didn't stop her intense craving for the small woman's approval.

Henrietta continued to peel and chop each potato into perfect cubes, ready to drop into the pot simmering merrily on the large cast-iron stove stop. Despite the burn scar covering a good part of her body, she'd never feared the stove or fire. Accidents happened—not to say she was eager to show her scar to just anyone. Quite the opposite.

"Ouch." Pain flared in her finger as the knife slipped out of her hand, cutting her. Henrietta stuck her finger in her mouth.

"Did ye cut yerself, lass? Here, let me have a look."

Henrietta dutifully passed over her finger for the woman's efficient ministrations. Bridget wrapped a clean cloth around it and then returned to the turnips. The triumph Henrietta felt moments earlier eked away. Why had she thought she could step into a kitchen and cook a meal well for the first time?

Bridget didn't notice her dismay, for which she was infinitely grateful. As soon as the bleeding stopped, Bridget directed Henrietta to the stove to stir the stew while she added the vegetables.

"What set ye on this path, lass?"

"Which path is that?" Henrietta asked, stalling.

"A mail-order bride. Must have taken a fair amount of courage setting off on yer own."

"I suppose," she said, reminding herself to keep as close to the truth as possible. "The train portion of the journey was quite easy, enjoyable even. We passed through some amazing country. The Adirondacks were stunning, though I confess the heights gave me a bit of a fright."

"I'll get my boy to take you to see Sierra Blanca. It stands taller than any of those wee Eastern hills." Bridget sniffed, and Henrietta bit back a smile at this woman's clear prejudice for her own land.

"It is lovely here. I've heard about it, of course, from Ro—reading."

"Books canna do it justice. Seeing a place with yer own two eyes and walking a path with yer own two feet will give ye more joy than reading a hundred of 'em."

"I think you're right. I've experienced more in the past three weeks than I have in a lifetime."

"And it's just the beginning." Bridget peered at her with the assessing gaze of a hawk. "How long have ye been alone in the world?"

The lie was on the tip of Henrietta's tongue, but she closed her mouth, and shook her head, unable to speak. She didn't want to lie to this woman, Rosalie's mother-in-law, who her cousin loved and admired above all others.

"Ach, I'm awfully sorry, lass." Bridget said gently, then pointed a knife at the pot. "Keep stirring or it will burn up and we'll have no supper to serve the boys."

Henrietta focused on stirring the stew in even, steady, circles. They continued to chat about the wonders of New Mexico Territory, but Henrietta was careful to keep the conversation focused on what she'd seen and done over the past few days on her journey. As kind as Bridget was, Henrietta would need to be on her guard. This woman was sharp. It would be far too easy to slip again.

BRIDGET SLAPPED CASH'S hand as he reached across the table for the yeast rolls. "Mind yer manners, boy."

"How long are you planning on staying this time, Ma?" Wyatt asked as he ladled stew into his bowl.

"Why? Do ye want me to leave already?"

The three grown men clamored, talking over each other, eager to assure their mother that in no way were they encouraging her to go. Henrietta fought to keep the smile off her face. How different it was here, sitting at the dining table surrounded by three boisterous men reaching, grabbing, and shoving each other while plying their dishes with food. In Philadelphia, she dressed for dinner, was served food from silver platters, and was expected to behave with proper decorum. Conversation was muted, focused mainly on the weather and upcoming social engagements.

Sitting amongst the Gildownies, she understood her cousin Rosalie's intense desire to break free from Philadelphia society and to return to New Mexico Territory. How freeing it must be to say what she wanted to say, to reach across the table for another yeast roll, and to banter with a houseful of siblings.

The beef stew was thick and rich, with potatoes, turnips, and carrots. It was sweet and tangy with a hint of spice from red peppers called ancho chilies. The fragrance wafting off the serving dish enticed her to fill her bowl to the brim. She fought the urge to lift the bowl to her mouth and drink from it as she had with her milk when she was young.

The men had no such compunction, though their mother berated them, reminding them that there was a lady present. Henrietta grinned as the grown men deferred so readily to the tiny woman seated at the head of the table. A pang of longing struck her deep in her belly. She yearned to know this family and to feel the ease they had with each other. She stole a glance at Duke, seated so close he brushed against her every time he reached for his glass.

He was handsome in an outdoor, rugged sort of way. His nose was slightly crooked, as if it had been broken years ago. His brown eyes were rich and warm, flecked with gold, like embers in a fire. As if he could sense her staring, he grabbed her hand under the table and gave it a squeeze. Such a simple gesture. An unexpected kindness.

After they'd finished dinner and cleared away the dishes, it was only natural for the engaged couple to take a stroll outside in the cool evening. When Duke offered his arm, she took it, grateful for the support as they wandered the property. He guided her to a live oak tree, its limbs so large they could have been trunks on any elm tree at home. They swept so low they almost touched the ground. Duke lifted her up and set her on the branch, then clambered up to sit next to her.

"The stars are brilliant here," she said. "I've never seen so many before. It's like looking into the heavens."

"That's my favorite. Cassiopeia. It's faint now, but in the winter the constellation shines like a diamond necklace in the sky." He pointed at a cluster of stars, but she didn't know the names and couldn't find the ones he meant, hidden amongst the millions of twinkling lights.

He wrapped his arm around her and lifted her hand to point directly at the stars he'd mentioned, his breath warm on the nape of her neck. She shivered despite the pleasant evening, grateful for the high neck of her jacket and the arm around her shoulders. As he leaned in closer, she smelled wood smoke and horses and sweet pine.

"It's so lovely. Have you been here long?" she asked, letting herself relax into him, exhaustion from the trip catching up to her.

"About ten years. It was my Pa's dream to have land of his own, but he passed away soon after he bought the place."

"I'm so sorry." The warmth of the night, Duke's low voice in her ear, and the promise of a haven from her pursuers made her drowsy, and she fought a yawn.

"Ma would say life isn't meant for the weak, and I suppose she's right, though sometimes..."

"Sometimes?" She struggled to keep her focus on the conversation, but she was weary, and it was so peaceful sitting here in the stillness, listening to the singing crickets and the occasional hoot of an owl, miles from civilization.

"It doesn't matter. You're tired. Let's go in," he said, then jumped down from the limb and raised his arms.

He wrapped his hands around her waist, and she fell forward into his embrace, her breath hitching as her breasts brushed against his chest. He released her and stepped back, murmuring an apology.

It was only later, with her covers pulled up to her chin, that she realized they hadn't discussed the lie even once.

SHE FELT AS THOUGH she'd barely closed her eyes, but it must have been hours later when a loud noise shattered the silence. Her first thought was Jameson had discovered her, had come here, brandishing his gun, to drag her back to Philadelphia. She sat upright in the bed and listened for another sound. Sure enough, voices, quiet but insistent, drifted through the open window.

She climbed out of bed and winced as the floorboards creaked under her feet. She tiptoed to the first-floor window and peered out into the night, certain whatever was happening outside was not meant for prying eyes.

Two men propped up a third, limp as a scarecrow, with his arms draped across their necks. In the moonlight, she could see his shirt was soaked crimson. She stepped back and held her hand to her mouth to prevent the sound of her gasp from reaching the men. Inching closer to the window, she strained to hear the conversation.

Duke's deep voice floated through the window, "Shaw's not here, and if he was, he'd tell you the same. We're out of the fight."

"You're siding with Murphy and Dolan, then?" The stranger spat on the ground.

"You know we're not, Charlie. We're with you. But I'm no shooter."

"We ain't askin' you to join the Regulators, just to give a little help. You can see the man's bleeding out," the ruddy-faced Charlie said.

Duke sighed and glanced at Henrietta's window. She shrank back and counted to ten before creeping forward again.

"Sorry, I can't risk it, not with Shaw just getting out of jail. The law's itching to pin something else on us."

Was he really going to let a hurt man bleed to death on the doorstep? Without conscious thought, she flew out of the room. The men had returned to their horses by the time she raced out the door into the night.

"Wait!"

"Aster, get back in the house," said Duke, his tone firm and commanding.

"He's hurt." Henrietta pointed at the man struggling to mount a horse.

"He's a Regulator."

"I don't know what that means. All I see is an injured man who needs our help. What if it were Cash or Wyatt who was in pain?"

Duke ran his fingers through his thick hair, then shook his head and gestured for the men to come inside.

"Thank you, ma'am," the injured man said. "God bless you."

She nodded. "None of that. Let's see you're taken care of." She rushed ahead of the men to the dining room where she cleared the table of candlesticks, discarded hats, and the salt cellar.

"What do you know about stitching up wounds?" Duke hissed once the man was laid out on the table.

She swallowed loudly as she forced herself to look at the gaping hole in the man's side. "Nothing, but I know how to treat an injury." She'd had enough experience as the patient. Now, if only she could recall how the physician had tended to her. "We'll need clean water, bandages, and an antiseptic."

"Will whiskey work?" Charlie said.

Would it work? It was alcohol after all. "Um, yes?"

"Maybe you should wake your Ma?" Charlie said to Duke with a concerned expression.

"Yes, I think that's a splendid idea." Henrietta blanched as she pulled the man's shirt away from his side. Blood oozed out of a hole the size of her thumb. "What caused this?" She looked at Duke in confusion.

"Gunshot." His voice was low and quiet.

"It's gone straight through," Charlie said. "Look at that, Arthur, you'll be up and about in no time."

Gunshot. Henrietta swallowed hard and focused her attention on her patient.

"The bleeding's good," she said. "It will help to remove any debris. But we'll need to stop it soon, before he loses too much blood...and we'll need needle and thread." She wiped the blood away to better see the opening. "I suppose we should clean it too."

"Right ye are, lass," came Bridget's comforting voice from behind her. "I'll see to that, and ye can do the stitching, my eyes being what they are."

Henrietta nodded jerkily and stood back as Bridget hastened forward with a bowl of water. She watched the older woman flush the bullet hole first with clear spring-fed water. Duke handed his mother a bottle of whiskey, which she poured generously over the man's gaping wound. Charlie clapped a hand over the patient's mouth to muffle his cries, and tears welled in Henrietta's eyes in sympathy. She knew better than most the strength it took to remain silent during a physician's ministrations, no matter how gentle or well-meaning the caregiver.

Henrietta found a mending kit in Bridget's sewing box next to the rocking chair in the living room and returned to the makeshift operating table in the dining area. Bridget offered her an encouraging smile as she threaded the needle with trembling fingers. Henrietta held her breath as she pushed the needle into the man's flesh on one side of the hole, then through the other, pulling it tight.

"It needn't be perfect, but it does need to be done quickly," Bridget said.

Henrietta bent low over the wound and worked as efficiently as she could, sewing uneven stitches which would have made her mother frown if they had been on a new handkerchief or pillowcase cover.

She took a moment to roll her shoulders and stretch while they turned the man onto his back for easier access to the exit wound. She focused on the task at hand, poking and pulling the needle through, wiping blood, until her fingers were cramped and wet and sticky. When Bridget handed her the shears to cut away the excess thread, she felt a measure of pride in her handiwork.

Duke handed her a damp cloth to clean the blood off her hands. Only then did she realize she stood among them with nothing but a flimsy nightgown on, her scar visible for all the world to see. She felt the familiar urge to cover up, to run, to hide, fearing the disgust and pity she would see in their eyes when they saw the ruin of the left side of her body. As she turned to flee, Charlie grabbed her hand and pumped it vigorously. If she'd been a man, he might have slapped her on the back. She escaped his grip only to be caught by Bridget.

"'Twas a fine job, lass. I couldn't have done better myself. Now, get yerself cleaned up. Ye look a right mess."

Henrietta hid her scarred arm behind her back before she realized the woman meant her nightdress covered in blood. "Yes, ma'am." She turned away from the men and scurried to the washroom only to step out again and run straight into Duke.

"What is it?" he said as he caught her.

"I don't have a second nightdress. I packed in a bit of a hurry, and I haven't had the chance to purchase another."

"Stay here."

He was gone and back within minutes, holding a neatly folded bundle of soft cotton. When she reached for the clothing, he seemed loath to let it go. Their earlier conversation echoed in her mind. His mother wanted him to remarry. This must have belonged to his late wife.

"This is too precious. I'll find something else," she said, pushing the bundle back to him.

"No." He dropped his hands. "Keep it. She'd have wanted someone to get use out of it. She was practical that way."

Henrietta waited for him to say more, but he was far away, lost in a memory.

A Deal Made

Duke

He traced his fingers over the photograph of his wife, dead five years, twice as long as they'd been married. He'd met Judith on a church picnic when he was twenty years old. When she'd offered him a slice of pecan pie, he thought he'd died and gone to heaven and told her so. She'd blushed and admitted her mother had made the pie and sent her over with a plate for the sole purpose of making his acquaintance.

They were ill-suited from the start, but they had loved each other and believed it would be enough. She'd be alive today if he had never taken that first bite of pie, had never danced with her at a party the following week, and had never married her.

He placed the picture frame back on the piano and returned to the dining area to deal with the group of outlaws he'd invited into his home. Aster's words had resonated with him. His brother Shaw had been in a similar situation not even two months earlier and had relied on his wife Rosalie and her friends to nurse him back to health despite the risk to themselves. He was grateful, but years ago, Duke had chosen another path. He'd decided to follow his Pa's dream to work the land, to build a life, a future, in New Mexico Territory. He'd stayed out of the various disputes that flared between his neighbors, content to focus on the few hundred acres surrounding the house he'd built himself.

Now the violence had spilled over into his world. Charlie and the other Regulator—Duke thought his name was Frank—sat vigil over their friend Arthur, still stretched out on the dining room table. The

Regulators were a group of gunmen and shooters who stood against Jimmy Dolan, the wealthiest rancher and landowner in Lincoln County. Dolan ran the town, ran the county, practically the whole territory with an iron fist and a crew of cutthroats eager to do his bidding.

Shaw had been a member of the Regulators, and it was only his desire to live peacefully with Rosalie that drew him away from the group. Duke thanked God for Rosalie every day for saving Shaw's life.

As if thinking of one brother summoned the others forth, Wyatt and Cash ambled into the dining room.

"Coffee?" Ma didn't wait for an answer before thrusting a cup into Duke's hand.

He nodded his thanks and took a swig of the strong brew.

"They can't stay. Dolan's boys will track him here as soon as the sun's up," Duke said under his breath.

"How about one of the outbuildings?" Cash gestured toward the back of the house.

Duke considered it, then shook his head. Dolan would find him there for sure. "Can we get him up to the hunting cabin?"

"Maybe in a few days." Wyatt knew every trail into the mountains. He was more at home in the untamed wilderness than he'd ever been inside four walls.

"Ye picked a fine lass this time," Ma said. "She dinnae even blink at the sight of blood."

Duke bristled at the implied comparison to his sweet Judith, but he refused to rise to the bait. "They'd be less likely to look in the house than in the outbuildings, especially with the ladies here," he said, changing the subject, but his mother was, as usual, undeterred.

"We should put them in Aster's room." Bridget tapped her lower lip with her index finger.

"What? No. Where would Aster go?"

Three heads swiveled toward Duke.

"Ain't she your intended? Or would you rather she bunk with me and Wyatt?"

"No, but—"

"We can fetch the preacher in the morning if you're worried about your virtue," Cash said, barely holding in a laugh.

"She can sleep with you, Ma." Duke threw his mother a pleading look.

"In that tiny bed?"

"I'll give you my room," he said.

"Is it yer bride then? If she dinnae have a Ma, I can have a little chat with her, explain what goes on between a man and a—"

"Absolutely not." Duke tried unsuccessfully to rid himself of the image of his mother and her detailed, earthy descriptions of relations. He ran his hand through his hair, then shook his head. "I'll speak with her."

As he walked away, he heard his Ma say, "Ye'd think he'd be eager to welcome her to his bed. I never knew him to be a shy lad."

Duke would have to confess the whole sordid affair to his family, but he wouldn't do that without consulting Aster first. She might have dragged him into this, but he'd certainly perpetuated the lie.

He rapped his knuckles on her door and listened for a sign of movement, but only heard the lonely cry of a coyote. He knocked again, louder.

Footsteps approached, and the door opened a crack. Aster peered at him suspiciously through the narrow opening.

"Yes? What's happened?"

"Can I come in?" he asked, placing his hand on the door.

Aster's eyebrows shot up and her mouth fell open.

"No, I didn't mean that. We need to talk in private."

She stuck her head out and peered up and down the hallway. "Seems fairly private to me."

"Aster, I am not going to attack you." He held his hands up and stepped back from the door.

She considered him for a moment, then nodded. "One moment." As he moved forward, the door slammed in his face, followed by the distinctive click of a lock being turned.

He leaned against the opposite wall, crossed his arms, and waited. He drummed his fingers on his arm and sought patience. Five minutes later another coyote cried in the dark, and he wanted to join the beast in its lament.

When the door swung open again, Aster appeared in Judith's white, lacy nightdress under a pale blue housecoat and slippers. Her thick brown hair was freshly braided and slung over a shoulder. Despite being completely covered, she clutched the collar of her robe closed at her throat.

He followed her into the bedroom, crossed to the window and propped himself up on the windowsill, and tried to look as non-threatening as possible. She stood near the door, and he swore she had her hand wrapped around the doorknob behind her back, poised to escape if needed.

He frowned and rubbed the back of his head, still aching from the day before. "You claim to be Rosalie's cousin."

"We *are* cousins."

"Fine, I'll take your word for it."

"Thank you. Now, can I go back to bed?"

Duke struggled to keep his eyes on Aster and not on the mussed bed and the thought of her lying in it.

"How much has Rosalie told you about the men who came here tonight, the Regulators?" He shifted on the sill.

She shook her head and shrugged.

"What do you know about my brother Shaw?"

"I had barely met him before they married."

He arched an eyebrow, and she continued quickly, "I know Shaw was wrongfully accused of murder."

"Anything else?" he said.

"What could be more important than that?" She released the knob to fidget with the sash tied around her waist, leaving one hand still gripped on her collar.

"Nothing, but Shaw was a Regulator, and so are these men."

She remained silent. She really had no idea what she'd stumbled into. He looked out the window and searched the night as though the stars and moon would lend him the words to explain the danger she'd welcomed in. He heard her soft footsteps approaching.

Without turning, he said, "The Regulators are shooters, outlaws, guns for hire. Whoever shot Arthur will be looking for him, and they won't stop."

"And you think they'll come here?" Her voice was quiet and near.

"There's no doubt. The sheriff knows Shaw is my adopted brother and they'll reckon the Regulators would come here for help."

"I'm sorry...I didn't know," she said, her voice shaking.

"It's done. The thing is...we can't move Arthur until he's stronger, and there aren't enough rooms to put everyone up." He turned to face her and rushed through the next words. "My Ma thinks we should give them this room since it has the largest bed, and you and I should bunk together."

She released her death grip on her collar and stepped forward. "Have you lost your mind? There is no way I am," she dropped her voice to a whisper, "sleeping with you."

"And so," he continued as if she hadn't said a word, "I suggest we tell them everything."

"And you won't run to the Pinkerton agent?"

"Nah. I never would have anyway," he said with a sheepish grin.

"Then why did you let me believe you were ready to turn me in if I didn't cook and clean for you?"

He shrugged. "Ma has been on me to remarry, and I thought, hell, if we're already play-acting, I might as well make the most of it."

"That is quite duplicitous of you."

"Not sure what that means, but thank you?"

"It wasn't a compliment." She paced the small room, arms crossed in front of her.

She was exquisite in the pale light drifting through the window, highlighting the gold in her hair, the handful of freckles sprinkled across her nose, and her tall, lithe body. When she whirled to face him, he dropped his gaze, embarrassed to be caught watching her so intently.

"Did you see it?"

"What?" He looked up sharply. "See what?"

She swallowed and clenched her fists. "My scar."

"The one on your shoulder?"

"Of course you noticed it. Everyone does. It's the first and only thing they see." She wrapped her arms around herself and blinked rapidly.

He shuffled from foot to foot and prayed she wouldn't cry. No such luck. Tears spilled out of her big blue eyes and down her cheeks as she hugged herself. Damn. There was nothing for it. He ambled over and patted her shoulder lightly.

She threw her arms around his neck and broke into full-throated sobs. Duke stumbled back, but she held fast. He wrapped his arms around her and whispered soothing nonsense in her ear. He could feel every curve of her body through the thin fabric of her housecoat. Her breasts pressed against his chest, rubbing against him, reminding him how long it had been since he'd lain with a woman. He pulled away before it became apparent to her and anyone else who might have walked through the door.

"Sorry." She sniffled, oblivious to his discomfort. "It shouldn't bother me. Pastor Peter says it's only my vanity which causes me pain and that if I embraced God more fully in my life, I wouldn't care how hideous I appear."

"You're not—"

She held up a hand. "Don't say it. I'm well aware of how I look. It's my burden to bear, and I must accept it, as difficult as it may be."

Duke scratched his head and wondered if he'd missed something. He'd seen the scar, a bit of shiny red skin on her shoulder and her arm, but he hadn't given it much thought beyond that. He certainly didn't think it would cause this much distress.

"Anyway," he said, dragging out the word. "About our deal. I say we tell them the truth and let the chips fall where they may."

"No!" Her eyes flashed.

"What?"

"Absolutely not," she said.

"My family would never betray your secret, especially with you being Rosalie's kin and all."

"Those men, those *Regulators*, saw my scar! If they mention it to someone in town, that horrid Pinkerton man will come here and arrest me."

"What would Jameson do if he knew you were the thief he's been chasing?"

She gnawed on her lip. "He'd drag me back to Philadelphia for starters, and that's unacceptable. I can't leave until I see Rosalie. Maybe if they believe I really am your wife, they won't remember much about me."

"Fiancé, not wife."

"Either," she waved her arm. "I'll fade into the background, and I bet they won't even notice me."

"You're hard to forget," he said before realizing how true the words were. She'd looked so angelic, with her nimble fingers and her long, thick hair streaming down her back as she'd worked tirelessly on her patient.

"Really?" She clutched the collar of her robe again. "I hope not. Oh, Duke, what am I going to do? I can't let them discover who I am. You have to keep my secret. Promise me."

"If that's what you want, you'd best pack your things. Looks like we're moving in together.

Wedding Plans

Henrietta

Henrietta tossed and turned, unable to shake the terror that she was about to be dragged back to Philadelphia. She was strong enough to face the consequences of the faked kidnapping and the theft, no matter how harsh the punishment, but she hadn't yet succeeded in her mission. She was desperate to see Rosalie. A life hung in the balance. Henrietta cracked an eye and spied her reticule, and the stolen property within, on the nightstand.

She was grateful Duke had insisted on sleeping on the floor. His regular breathing should have been a comfort, lulling her to sleep, but she was unused to sharing a room with anyone, let alone a huge man sprawling less than a foot from her. She pulled the quilt up to her chin to cover her scar, then reminded herself he couldn't very well see her with his eyes closed. She threw off the covers and propped herself up on her elbow, intent on looking out the window. Eager to see the sunrise, she gave up all attempts at sleep, ready to meet the day and whatever it might bring.

Her eyes drifted from the open window to the man on the floor below. His arm was thrown across his face to block the early light from shining into his eyes. His brown hair was streaked with red. His skin, though not nearly as dark as his brother Wyatt's, was deeply tanned, and his bare chest was covered in auburn curls. She'd never seen a naked man before and couldn't resist the urge to study every visible inch. His muscles were lean and taut. He had the body of a cowboy who worked tirelessly on the ranch, and she could almost see him standing in his stirrups as he tossed a lasso high into the air.

Her eyes trailed down from his chest to his navel, and she imagined the form beneath the blanket slung across his hips. She blushed and sank back into the pillows. If she'd wanted to know the more intimate details of a man's nude form, she should have married Jonathon.

What must her fiancé think of her, running away without a word? She had wanted to get married, and he was a good enough match. She'd known him for years and had danced with him more times than she could count. When he'd proposed, she finally showed him her disfigurement. He'd tried to hide his discomfort, but she knew him too well not to see the hint of fear and disgust cross his face. When he'd said it didn't matter, she'd known in her bones he was lying. She should have broken off the engagement then, but she'd wanted to be a wife, to be a mother. It's what she was raised to be and what would give her mother the most pleasure. That was paramount.

Guilt threatened to steal her breath away as she imagined her mother's disappointment. Henrietta flopped onto her side and pulled the covers over her head, trying to burn the image out of her mind.

"Have you slept at all?" Duke's deep voice intruded upon her thoughts.

"No," she said in a small voice from beneath the covers.

"Do you want to talk about it?"

She thought about sharing her secret with him. He already held her fate in his hands. What could it hurt? No, it wasn't her secret to share, even though it would be so much easier to unburden herself, to pass her duty off to Duke. "No."

"Then tell me something else."

"Like what?" She peeked out from beneath the blanket to find Duke sitting on the floor, leaning against the wall with his knees bent. His blanket was casually draped across his legs, doing little to hide the sharp planes of his body.

"Tell me about your childhood."

"What about it?"

"Aster, it's not supposed to be this hard. Tell me anything," he said. "We're supposed to actually know each other, right?"

"But everything I've said has been a lie. I'm not even Russian."

"You don't say." He grinned, and she felt the tension that she'd held tight in her chest ease.

"Tell me about *your* childhood. You said you moved here ten years ago. Where did you live before?" she asked.

"Lincoln, but of course it wasn't called Lincoln back then. It was La Placita del Rio Bonito when I was a boy."

"That sounds nice. What does it mean?" Henrietta popped her head completely out of the covers.

"The place by the pretty river."

"And is it?" she asked.

"Is it what?"

"A pretty river?"

He was silent for so long she thought he hadn't heard the question.

"Some think so," he said. "Shall I take you there?"

"I'd like that, but first, I want to see the ranch."

"You saw a good bit of it yesterday on the ride in from town," he said.

"I'm only keeping my side of the bargain. You don't betray me, and in turn I will care for the place. I can't do that if I haven't seen everything."

He smirked. "Not sure what cattle ranching has to do with taking care of a home."

"A new bride would like to see what she's marrying into." It was true, but it wasn't her primary motive. She longed to stretch her legs, to climb into one of the funny saddles she'd seen the men using, and to race across the wide countryside.

"I suppose." He drummed his fingers on his leg. "But we have other problems on our hands and," he hesitated, "you're not marrying me."

The smile slipped from her face. It wasn't just play-acting, not with an injured man in the next room, the lawmen searching for him and the other Regulators, and her own sticky problem with Jameson.

Duke

THE BUTTERY SCENT OF warm biscuits lured him into the dining area. Normally he would grab a slice of bread or a piece of jerky before starting work on the ranch. That was one good thing about his Ma—she sure knew how to cook.

Cash greeted him with a wink and a grin as he entered the room. Wyatt was no better, asking him if he got any sleep at all. It would do no good to explain they weren't married, and he'd spent the night on the floor. They wouldn't have believed him. He couldn't fathom what secret was so important a woman would risk her reputation to keep, but he didn't have time to dwell on that particular mystery. The immediate problem was his mother and her insistence that they fetch the preacher.

"And what about the man bleeding in the next room?" Duke asked.

Ma jutted her chin out. "I'll no have any busybody saying my boy didn't do right by a lass."

"You're the one who insisted she stay the night in my room."

"I'm trying to light a fire under ye. Ye've dragged your feet for five years and now ye're fussing about sealing the deal with this lass. Now ye listen to me—"

As soon as her finger started wagging, he stopped listening. There was no arguing with his Ma. He drained his coffee, nodded when she paused to breathe, and glared at Cash, who covered his mouth to keep from laughing.

There was a perceptible shift in the room when Aster entered.

"I reckon the day got brighter now you're here." Cash knocked his chair back in his eager bid to be the first man to greet her.

"Good morning. Is that coffee I smell? And biscuits?" Her face lit up. "Oh, I have heard about your biscuits, Mrs. Gildownie."

Ma's shrewd eyes focused on Aster. "And who have ye been hearing that from? My boy here's been avoiding me for years."

"Um." Aster's eyes darted between Duke and his mother. "He was telling me last night how much he was looking forward to breakfast."

Cash's eyebrows shot up. "That's what he was looking forward to?"

Duke glared at his brother, then said, "Aster, after you've had a chance to eat this amazing breakfast Ma has cooked for us, would you like to go for a ride? It will give you the chance to see the place."

"I'd love that."

"And while ye're out and about, stop in and see the preacher. If ye won't have the wedding here, ye'd best be doing the deed in town. I'll no have a bairn come into the world without his Ma and Pa properly wed."

Aster blanched and set the half-eaten biscuit down on her plate. She looked to Duke for salvation.

Duke took a long swallow of coffee. "We'll think on it, Ma."

"Oh, ye'll think on it, will ye? If ye dinnae find the preacher today, I'll drag ye by yer ears doon to the kirk myself, dinnae think I won't."

"What's this I hear about church? It ain't Sunday." Charlie sauntered in as though he were an invited guest and hadn't stumbled upon them in the middle of the night covered in blood, carrying an injured man.

Aster stood, mumbled something about checking on her patient, and rushed out of the room.

"Was it something I said?" Charlie swiped the half-eaten biscuit off Aster's plate.

"She didn't get much sleep last night," Duke said, then cringed when the men exchanged grins.

"Ye think on what I've said." Ma said to Duke before turning on Charlie while handing him a cup of coffee. "What are yer plans then? Ye surely canna stay here."

Charlie wiped his nose with the back of his sleeve. "Well, that's the thing, ain't it? Arthur's not going anywhere real soon. Frank and I can take off and come back for him in a week or so."

"In a week? What the hell am I supposed to do with him when the law comes looking? What even happened last night?" Duke sloshed more coffee into his own cup.

"It was nothin', just a skirmish with some of the Dolan men. Got one of 'em too. He ain't gonna bother no one no more."

Duke shook his head. He'd believed with Shaw free from the Regulators' clutches, their family would make it through the range war unscathed. Now it came banging on his door in the middle of the night.

"I can take him to the mountains in a few days, but not until he can ride," Wyatt said.

"I'll go with Wyatt. Watch his back." Cash's face was serious for once.

"All right. We'll head into town and check on things there—see if there's a posse forming," Duke said, thinking of the saloon and the loosening effect of a good bottle of rye on men's tongues.

"I'll come with ye," Ma said, wiping her hands on her apron.

He rubbed his head, which still ached from knocking the doorsill the day before. "Ma, you should stay here and watch over that man." Duke nodded in the direction of the bedroom Aster had retreated to. "Cash, Wyatt, spread out. Watch the place."

His Ma gave him a glare to set his feet moving at a trot out the door and to the stable to saddle the horses. The preacher was a good sort and all, but Duke wasn't sure the man would go along with their scheme. The last thing he needed was his Ma insisting the marriage contract be signed in front of her.

Truth In Lies

Henrietta

Henrietta leaned low over the horse's neck as they raced, two beings as one, across the wide-open plains beneath the New Mexico sky. All her thoughts, her worries, and the fears of the past few weeks flew behind her as she focused on the path and the horse beneath her. Riding astride, she experienced a freedom she'd never known. She sensed every movement in the mare's flanks, anticipated every leap, every turn.

She glanced over at Duke, matching her stride for stride and urged the horse faster. Duke called for her to slow down, but she was determined to win their race to the river, a shimmer of blue peeking out through a grove of pecan trees in a glade no more than one hundred yards away. Almost too late, she spied a fallen log hidden in the brush. If it hadn't been for his warning call, she might have missed it. She leaned lower, gave the mare her head, and sailed across, laughing.

Henrietta reined in the horse as they neared the river, breathing hard, her heart beating wildly in her chest. She patted the mare's neck and slipped out of the saddle easily. The water looked so refreshing; she considered removing her worn boots and wading in.

"What the hell are you doing? I told you to slow down!"

She laughed. "I'm fine. Better than fine. You're just upset you lost."

"You could have been killed, running off like that across new terrain, on a horse you don't know." He slapped his reins against his leg before dismounting.

"I trust her. She's a good girl. What's her name? I didn't think to ask."

"Because you were too much in a hurry to race off without so much as a word." His voice was calm and controlled, but his eyes flashed in the sunlight.

Her smile slipped.

"You could have injured the mare, did you think about that? If she'd stumbled and broken a leg, would you be the one to put the bullet in her head?"

"I'm sorry," she whispered. "I wasn't thinking."

"You always race off without thinking, Judith!" His eyes widened as he realized his mistake. "Aster." He turned away from her.

"Judith? Was that your wife's name?" she asked softly.

He nodded but didn't turn to face her.

"I'd like to take the horses down to the river for a drink. Will you tell me their names now?" She took the reins from his hand.

His chest rose and fell rapidly as he struggled to control himself. "The mare is Ginger, and the stallion's named Dapple."

"They're fine names. Thank you for telling me." She led the chestnut and the Appaloosa down the path to the water's edge. Sunlight rippled across the water, and the scent of pine and loam and the sweet smell of primrose wafted on the breeze. Arranging her skirts, she sat down on a log and waited as the horses lowered their heads to take a drink.

She heard Duke's slow approach but kept perfectly still, as though he were the spooked horse who might bolt at a moment's notice. He squatted next to her and watched the horses as their breathing eased. She should have felt awkward, this close to him, but perhaps a night spent together erased any discomfort.

"Do you want to talk about her?" Aster kept her voice steady as she looked straight ahead.

"No...yes...I don't know."

"I understand."

"You do?" he asked, clearly surprised.

She turned to him, his face so close she could smell the sweet scent of pipe tobacco on his breath, and said, "My aunt, Rosalie's mother, died when I was very young, and my mother lost three children. It's not my grief to claim, but I do have some experience living with people who have had everything torn from them."

"That's a heavy burden on its own."

"I am far stronger than I may appear."

"I know," he said, rubbing his arm. "I should hire you as a ranch hand with a grip like yours."

She turned back to the river, smiling as a warm and comforting sensation filled her chest. He didn't want to share, and she wouldn't push. The offer had been made, which was the important thing.

"It's so peaceful here, beneath the trees, listening to the rushing water as it tumbles over the rocks. Is this the place you mentioned? La place 'de' something?"

"La Placita del Rio Bonito. It's one of the places. Do you like it?"

"I do," she hesitated. "And I am sorry for riding away so quickly. I'm not normally so rash. The past few weeks have been...difficult, and the temptation of running with the wind was so appealing, especially on your western saddle. It's so much more comfortable that a side saddle."

"You've got a good seat. I'm surprised." He picked up a flat stone and rubbed it with his thumb.

"Why?"

"You're a city girl. Where did you learn to ride?"

"In Fairmount Park." She twisted her mouth in distaste. "Though it was so controlled. Ever since I fell, my parents have insisted that my instructors keep me at a trot. But I confess, I didn't listen."

"When did you fall?"

She waived dismissively.

"Years ago. I had a bit of a headache; the world twisted and turned in a most unusual fashion, and I had to stay in bed for a few days, which was the worst punishment possible. I've always loved being out of doors."

He rose, threw the stone, and watched it skip across the surface of the water until it finally sank right before it reached the far bank.

"Oh." She clapped her hands together. "Will you teach me?"

He nodded and offered a hand to help her rise. When she placed her hand in his, he laughed and said, "Probably should take off the gloves."

She looked down at their clasped hands and frowned, then pulled her hand away and hid it behind her back.

"What are you doing? I thought you wanted to learn?"

She bit her lip and looked down at her feet. "You'll see the scar."

"It's your choice, of course, but if you're worried about that little mark on your arm, I've already seen it, and I'm still here."

"You didn't see it in the light of day," she said.

"Let me judge for myself."

Despite her misgivings, she allowed him to slip the ever-present four-button glove off, finger by finger. She closed her eyes to shield herself from the revulsion she would inevitably see in his face. The warm breeze brushed against her bare skin as its covering was removed, and still, she kept her eyes firmly shut.

He brushed his thumb across the inside of her wrist and up her forearm, tracing the outline of the burn which had forever separated her life into two parts—the time before the accident and the time after. She shuddered as a tremor ran up her arm. When she opened her eyes, she searched his face for disgust but found only tenderness in his gaze.

"Did it hurt very much?"

She nodded, not trusting her voice.

"And now you hide beneath your long gloves and your high-necked dresses?"

She nodded again.

He considered the red, angry scar that circled her arm, then leaned low and kissed the inside of her wrist. Tingling shivers radiated through her body. "You're beautiful," he whispered.

"I'm not."

He smiled. "Then you're a bigger liar than I thought."

"What?" She pulled her arm out of his grasp.

"If that's what you tell yourself, you're the biggest liar I've ever met."

She looked down at the damaged skin, smooth and shiny, and although she knew he only said the words to make her feel better, she did. The sky and water and earth around her appeared brighter, cheerier than before, promising a better tomorrow.

"I'm ready to learn how to toss those stones now."

"All right then, the trick is in the wrist. You hold the rock with the flat side up, like this." He placed a stone in her hand and wrapped his arm around her so he could swing her arm back and then at the last moment, he flicked her wrist forward and said, "Release."

"No!" she cried as the rock plummeted into the water with a thunk and a splash. "Show me again."

So, he did.

Duke

THEY RODE SIDE BY SIDE in silence, each lost in their own thoughts, far from the well-traveled road leading into Lincoln. His mind darted between Judith and his failure to protect her, and the lovely, unaffected lady he'd attached himself to through fate and circumstance.

It was reckless to imagine their make-believe romance could be anything other than what it was—an agreement born of necessity and fear. Yet he'd felt more alive in the past day than he had in years. He spurred the horse faster and sensed Aster next to him urging her horse to match his pace. She was a talented horsewoman, so different from Judith, who had been timid and unsure.

Intent on his musings, he didn't register her words until she raised her voice and repeated them.

"Are you certain the pastor will play along?"

"As much as I can be," he said off-handedly as they approached the outskirts of town.

"What does that mean?"

"He's a good man, but maybe we should play it by ear."

"I do, you know, or at least I used to." She reined in her horse to a trot and then to a walk as they neared the edge of town. Armed men on horses and wagons laden with everything from store goods to furniture to people passed by on their way to their homesteads, spewing dust clouds in their wake.

"What?" he asked, eyeing a particularly fine Appaloosa ridden by a Mescalero Apache man.

"I can play by ear. The piano, I mean."

"We've got an old spinet in the parlor. You'll have to try your hand at it, maybe play a jig tonight."

She shifted in her saddle. "I don't play anymore."

"Why?" He tore his eyes off the horse to focus on Aster.

"Is that the church up ahead?" She pointed at the white clapboard building trimmed in hunter green paint, starting to peel under the harsh sun.

"I reckon it is," he said, trying to maintain a light tone despite the ache in his heart he felt every time he rode past the building.

"You reckon? Don't you know?"

"I don't have much cause to go into town." He steered Dapple toward the church.

"Why? You don't live far. Surely church services are reason enough to venture a few hours each week."

He shrugged and slid out of the saddle. By the time he looped the reins around the hitching post and went to offer her a hand down, Aster had already dismounted and was fidgeting with her skirts. He didn't say a word as he offered her an arm, which she took readily. Her face remained placidly neutral, but her hand was clenched tightly on his arm.

"Nervous?"

"Aren't you?" She looked at him sharply.

"We're not actually getting married," he said, trying to calm himself as well as Aster.

"Well, of course not. I wasn't thinking that at all. It's just that this is the second time in a month I've gone to church to not marry someone."

He stopped short of the door and turned to stare at her. "You're engaged?" He had a lump in his throat and a pit in his stomach, though he couldn't imagine why he should care one way or the other.

"Maybe?"

"Don't you know?"

"I am—I was. It's hard to say." Her eyes darted around them as if searching for someone.

He turned around and scanned the people bustling by. "Who are you looking for?"

"Jameson," she whispered.

"Ah. Well, I don't see him, though he might be hiding underneath a rock."

"Or in a hole."

He chuckled, the tightness in his chest easing slightly. "Shall we?" He gestured toward the church.

She inhaled deeply, pressed her hand against her stomach, and nodded.

He pushed the door open and stepped into a space he hadn't been for over four years, not since the funeral. It had been held in town so Judith's family wouldn't have to travel to the ranch, leaving him and his brothers to cart her coffin back home, the longest three hours of his life. He'd buried her holding their baby boy in her arms, together forever.

A Church Welcome

Henrietta

Duke left her seated on a narrow, backless, wooden pew near the back of the dimly lit church while he searched the building for the preacher. She folded her hands in her lap and forced herself to study the scattering of paintings while attempting to steady her breathing. She was not prone to flights of fancy, yet her mind raced. The preacher would insist they marry in truth; he would rush directly to Jameson and betray her, or he would name her a liar, a sinner, a strumpet. The longer she sat there, the more she questioned every decision she'd made since venturing West, ashamed of all the lies she'd told over the past few weeks. Her mother must be so worried, and her father—could he forgive her for causing Mother such distress?

"Hello, I don't suppose you've seen the pastor?" A woman's voice called from behind her.

Henrietta whirled around in her seat to discover a truly striking woman, older than herself, and far more worldly. Her thick black hair lay across her shoulders in gentle waves. Her olive skin was exotic and sensual, like a mythical Roman goddess.

"No," Henrietta stuttered.

The woman glided up the aisle and sat down next to her on the pew, prompting Henrietta to slide over to give her room. "Shall we wait together then?"

Henrietta nodded and clutched her stomach to ease its churning.

"I'm Susanna Grimaldi."

The woman waited for Henrietta to respond, but the words stuck in her throat. She offered a faint smile, imagining her mother's disapproval at her lack of courtesy.

"I arrived in town only this morning, and I confess it's a bit overwhelming. I saw the church and thought I could have a chat with the minister while I'm waiting to meet my uncle." Susanna withdrew a handkerchief from her handbag and lightly dabbed her forehead.

"Oh? Does he live here in town?"

"Close by. How quiet and cool it is here, away from the dust and the horses and cattle. My God, I've never seen so many cows in one place, driven right down Main Street, as though we were in a prairie and not the middle of town."

Henrietta's tension lessened as she listened to the woman chat amiably about her journey from New York City to stay with her uncle.

"And you are?" The sudden change in the conversation caught Henrietta off-guard, and it took her a moment to answer.

"H—Aster."

"Hester?"

Henrietta grimaced. "Aster. Sorry, I'm a bit flustered."

Susanna's eyes grew wide, and she patted Aster's arm. "Oh, here I am nattering on about myself. I hope everything is quite well with you."

"Um," Henrietta bit her lip and peered into the woman's eyes. She seemed so genuinely concerned, and Henrietta was tired of keeping up the façade. How lovely it would be to share all she'd been through with a kind soul.

"Aster," Duke said as he strode toward the two women. "No luck. The preacher is out of town for a few days. We'll have to come back later." He glanced at the dark-eyed beauty seated next to her and nodded. "Ma'am."

"Susanna, please. I was just chatting with your...?"

There was a moment of silence as they each waited for the other to respond. Duke cocked his head and arched an eyebrow at Henrietta's discomfort, but made no move to answer.

"Fiancé," she said finally.

"That's marvelous. Congratulations to you both. When are you planning to hold the ceremony? I do love weddings." Susanna clapped her hand over her mouth. "Oh my goodness, I can't believe I've invited myself to your big day. Forgive me, I'm so weary from the journey, I've completely forgotten my manners."

"Please don't concern yourself, though we weren't planning on having a party, just a quiet, private service."

"Oh, certainly not. We must have a celebration." Susanna's brow furrowed as she gave the idea some thought. "The hotel where I'm staying is not ideal, but I'm sure they could host a few close friends and family. How exciting."

"Thank you for the kind offer, but that won't be necessary," Henrietta said firmly. "Duke and I are very private people."

"Very private." He smiled tightly, but hid his eyes from Henrietta. She had a sudden and unexpected urge to comfort him, though she couldn't imagine why.

"Forgive me," Susanna said, standing up. "I've intruded where I'm not wanted."

"Not at all. Duke, Susanna has come all the way from New York City."

"Never met anyone from New York. What brings you out here?" he asked, his tone flat and neutral.

"My uncle," Susanna said. "I've come for a visit."

He nodded and looked away, as if considering her words. "Interesting. A young lady traveling all this way—by yourself, you say?"

"Why, yes, I am quite capable."

"I've no doubt," he said. "Grimaldi? I'm not familiar with that name. Your uncle lives here in Lincoln?"

She smiled tightly. "No, he lives out beyond Fort Stanton."

"In the Reservation?" He raised an eyebrow in clear disbelief.

"Oh heavens, no, how delightful you are," she said, standing up. "Well, it has been such a pleasure to meet new people." She offered a hand to Henrietta. "I do hope we'll be friends. I'm staying at the hotel if you'd care to join me for a cool drink while your man is doing business in town."

Henrietta looked at Duke, then mentally kicked herself. She didn't need his permission to make a friend. She didn't need anyone's permission. And he was being rude to the one lady her age she'd met since arriving.

"I'd love that," she said, lifting her chin.

Duke

DUKE STALKED OUT OF the church and straight for the saloon. He needed a shot of whiskey, more than one, truth be told. When he was teaching Aster to skip stones at the river, he'd lost himself in the moment and in her sheer joy at discovering something new. He'd been happy spending the idle time with her, and that was a problem. She wasn't his wife, his fiancé, his anything. She never would be. One quick visit to a church reminded him what he'd once had and lost.

When he'd spilled the last of the dirt onto his wife's grave, he'd made a promise to Judith, to God, and to himself. He'd never again impose his life and his dreams on a woman, so he'd worked from sunrise to long after sundown, creating a cattle and horse ranch from nothing. He'd built the house himself—he'd felled the pine trees, hauled them to the site, slept rough for months as he worked with axe, mallet, and planer to turn the logs into smooth straight planks for the floorboards.

His brothers had come and gone, had helped with framing and lent their backs to raise the roof, but none of them shared their father's dream of making a living off the land. Shaw had fallen in with a rough bunch, more interested in rustling than breeding a herd. Wyatt was content to live alone high in the Capitan Mountains, hunting and trapping. Keith had turned his love for gambling into a love for banking and had been the first after Duke to marry. As for their sister Martha, she'd been all too eager to move as far from Lincoln as she could, leaving her rowdy brothers behind. And the youngest, Cash? Hell, he rarely left the gambling halls and saloons long enough to do a lick of work.

It had been Duke alone, with a strong back and a stronger desire, to make their father's dream a reality. Until Judith. More than anything, he wanted to forget her, but her ghost clung to him closer than any shadow.

He went into the saloon and ran straight into a bluecoat. The man scowled at him as whiskey sloshed down the front of his US Army uniform.

"Sorry, Mellon. I'll get you another," Duke said.

The captain nodded curtly, then collapsed into a chair near the door. Trudy, a yellow-haired woman with an unnaturally white face and an ample bosom, approached the officer, but he waved her off with barely a glance.

"How 'bout you, cowboy? You look like you need a ride." She puckered her rouged lips and ran her hand down the front of his jacket. Duke snatched her hand before she could continue rubbing down the front of his trousers.

"Not today, Trudy," Duke said.

The woman pouted and flounced away, her hips swaying in a silent reminder of what he was missing. Duke retrieved two glasses of rye from the barkeep and joined Mellon at the table, his gaze flitting back to the voluptuous woman. Maybe Cash was right. He shook his head. If he started taking Cash's advice, he might as well call the undertaker right then to carry him away.

Duke slammed the whiskey back and waited for the familiar numbing to take hold. Mellon took a small sip and placed the glass on the table, holding fast to it as though it might be ripped from his grasp at any moment.

Duke waited for the man to speak. They weren't friends exactly, but Mellon was decent enough. After a few minutes of watching the man stare at his glass, Duke finally asked, "What's weighing on you?"

Mellon looked up, startled, as though he'd forgotten Duke was there. "Lot on my mind." He took another sip, then continued, "Have you seen your brother lately?"

"Which one? I got a few."

A smile flickered across the man's face. "McPherson."

"I assume you mean Shaw and not Keith?" Duke was itching for another swig of rye, but he had a hard and fast one drink rule when there was work to be done. And there was always more work to do.

Mellon nodded. "And Rosalie. Are they around?"

"Nah, they're in Santa Fe. Cattle sale and a honeymoon of sorts."

Mellon grimaced and took another swallow.

"What's it to you?" Duke asked, his eyes narrowed. Mellon had helped Shaw and Rosalie in the past, but Duke had never really trusted him or anyone else in the army.

"Man came by today, said he's looking for Rosalie. Her cousin's gone missing, and he thought the woman might be here in Lincoln."

Duke drummed his fingers on the table. "Missing, huh? She run off or do they think someone nabbed her?"

"I don't know. But Rosalie should be told. She might be able to help the detective. You got a way to reach her?"

"No, but I reckon they'll be back in a week or two. Sale should be done by then, and I need Shaw at the ranch. I've got to get started on the new horse barn before the snows come."

"You met her, right?" Mellon asked.

"Who?" Duke looked into his empty glass, stalling.

"The cousin. When you traveled to Pennsylvania after Shaw was released, you must have met her."

"Don't remember," Duke said. "Don't recall much of that trip, truth be told. Spent most of my time looking for investors."

"Any luck?"

Duke scowled. "Nah. That East Coast bunch is more interested in railroads and oil than horse breeding. And I don't have enough cattle to compete with the bigger ranchers for the beef market, not that I would go up against Dolan for the Indian Agent contract."

"Good man, you don't want to get cross-eyed with him, especially now."

"Why?" Duke looked at the man sharply.

"Things are heating up between the Dolan gang and the Regulators. Those idiots even took a few shots at the army last night, and my Colonel is just itching to go after them." Mellon dropped his voice to a whisper. "He and Dolan are old drinking buddies."

"Thanks for the warning. I'm glad Shaw is out of that for good."

Mellon looked thoughtful. "Now that you mention it, maybe he and Rosalie should stay gone. I got a feeling in my gut this place is about to explode." His eyes widened, and he pushed back from the table hard enough to spill his drink.

Duke swiveled to the open door to see what had Mellon all hot and bothered, but he saw only an attractive, very petite, Hispanic woman on the other side of the street.

"Thanks for the drink," Mellon said as he knocked over his chair in his haste to leave. "Damn."

"I got it." Duke righted the chair and stole another glance at the bar and the bottle of whiskey, but contented himself to slouch against the wall and listen to the man at the piano plunk out "Goodbye Liza Jane." It wasn't quite the same as listening to it on the fiddle, but the man's enthusiasm got Duke's foot tapping along with the cheery tune.

As he ventured out of the saloon and down the street to the hotel, he wondered if Aster knew how to play that song.

Spirit Walk

Henrietta

Susanna's onyx-colored eyes were fixed on Henrietta as she said, "And so you answered the call to be a mail-order bride."

Henrietta shrugged. "With my parents gone and no one to turn to, I had very little choice. Besides, I needed a way out of..."

"Rhode Island?"

"Where? Um, yes, right, Rhode Island."

"Forgive me, but you don't sound quite so sure." Susanna smiled to take the sting out of her words.

All the lies were piling atop each other in a jumble. Henrietta was unused to dissembling, and despite weeks of telling fanciful stories, she was no more comfortable with the story than when she'd begun this journey.

"This is a lovely room," Henrietta said, changing the subject. They were seated at a small table in the back corner of the hotel restaurant. The walls were adorned in a faded rose chintz paper, and the floors were covered in a silk carpet any woman in Philadelphia would have been proud to display...twenty years ago. Even so, it was pleasant to be out of the sun. She'd never get used to perspiration dripping off her nose.

"And this is delicious, absolutely delicious. There's a spice I can't quite place." Henrietta took a tiny bite of apple cake.

Susanna slid her plate across the table to Henrietta. "You should have mine too."

"Oh, I couldn't."

Susanna's eyes widened. "I'm sorry. I wasn't thinking. Forgive me."

"Forgive what?"

"You're worried about your dress, but you needn't be. You're quite slender."

Henrietta scrunched up her face in confusion. "Dress?"

"The wedding dress, silly."

Henrietta pushed the plate away, suddenly queasy. "That's right. Of course."

She needed to leave this place before her lies tripped her up completely. Henrietta stood, then grabbed her head as the room spun around her in a most dizzying fashion. She blinked rapidly, and the room slid back into focus.

"It's been so wonderful finding someone my age here in town, but it's getting late." She made a production of looking at the clock on the opposite side of the dining room.

Susanna rose slowly, smoothing her turquoise skirts, the jeweled color striking against her darker complexion. For a moment, Henrietta imagined Susanna sparkling like a sapphire. The image was so vivid Henrietta had to shake her head to clear it from her mind. She wavered and grasped the back of the chair to steady herself. Her thoughts were so scattered. Could she have a fever? No, she was never ill. And yet her mind was muddled, and she was unstable on her feet.

"I need some fresh air. Shall we walk for a spell while you wait for your man?" Susanna cocked her head and gave Henrietta a probing look. "Are you quite yourself, Aster?"

Henrietta nodded and stumbled in her eagerness to leave the room, which had become increasingly stifling with every lie that tumbled from her lips.

"Isn't that your reticule?"

Henrietta pivoted, blanching as she spied her handbag on the table next to her empty coffee cup. She snatched it and tied it tightly onto her wrist, mumbling her thanks.

"Are you feeling well, dear?" Susanna grabbed her elbow as they stepped onto the arcade running alongside the building. If she hadn't, Henrietta might have tumbled to the floor.

"Yes." Henrietta took a deep breath, then coughed at the fresh air laced with the distinctive odor of fresh manure. "Quite well," she squeaked.

Susanna lowered her voice and patted Henrietta's arm. "If you need a friend, I'll be staying at the hotel through the end of the week. You've made no decision which can't be unmade."

Henrietta's eyes widened as she realized just what the woman was intimating. "Oh no. I'm quite happy with...." She almost said Jonathon's name.

"Duke?" Susanna prompted helpfully.

"Right. Duke."

"Either way, I do hope you will come back for a visit. It's been such a trial these past weeks, venturing alone on trains and stages and all sorts of strange carriages, even though I am quite accustomed to travel since my family is so spread out."

Henrietta half-listened to Susanna as she tried to make sense of her thoughts. The sky was streaked with pink clouds, and she imagined taking a paintbrush, dipping it in crimson, and stroking it across the horizon. So absorbed in her reverie, she didn't at first notice the tall, handsome man who approached her. His mouth was open as if he were speaking to her, but with Susanna's voice buzzing in her ear, Henrietta struggled to focus on his words. He strode toward her, his face a mask of concern.

"Isn't that your man?" Susanna shook her arm and pointed at the man approaching.

"He looks swell." Henrietta giggled and covered her mouth.

"Aster," he said as he drew near.

"Who?" she asked.

He narrowed his deep brown eyes. She mimicked him, squinting in return.

"Are you sick?"

"I think she must be. I thought some fresh air might do her good," Susanna said to Duke. The dark-haired woman leaned forward, kissed Henrietta's cheek, and whispered, "Remember I'm here if you need me."

"Why would I need you?" Henrietta said loudly. "Is something wrong?"

"You tell me," Duke said as he took her by the arm and led her away from her new friend.

Henrietta gave a wave to Susanna, swayed, then toppled forward. Duke caught her. The day was bright and welcoming, and she could hear music floating in the air like a brisk breeze, ruffling her skirts and tempting her to dance a jig.

She caught Duke's hand in hers and skipped and hummed a bit of the tune. "I do so love to dance. Do you?" She glanced at his somber expression, then frowned and lowered her voice. "Or are you too serious for dancing and music and such?"

"I like to dance as much as the next man." He leaned close enough for her to feel his warm breath on her cheek. Her heart lurched in her chest. She puckered her lips, lowered her eyelids, and eagerly waited for him to kiss her. But he just took an exaggerated sniff and straightened. "Are you drunk?"

She considered the idea. "I don't think so." She leaned heavily on him, mesmerized by the intensity of his gaze. "Your eyes are the exact shade of bark. Did you know?"

"Bark? Because they're brown?"

She nodded and lifted her hand to touch his cheek, but swatted his nose instead. "Duke?"

"Yes?"

"I think there's something wrong with me." She smiled. "And I like it."

Duke

SHE DIDN'T SMELL OF whiskey or any other liquor they might have served at the hotel. He was tempted to follow Susanna and ask her what they'd had to drink, but Aster could barely stand. It wasn't until she was mounted on her horse, spouting nonsense about the intense beauty of a cawing crow, that it dawned on him what must have happened.

"Aster?"

"Who?" Her eyes lit up. "Who, who, who."

"Aster, that's your name. Do you remember?"

She shook her head violently from side to side, then leered at him. "But I remember *you*."

"Good. That's good."

When it became clear she was not going to mount the horse, he reached down and grabbed her foot to place it in the stirrup. She fell forward onto his back, and he thought he could hear her neighing softly. It was all he could do to lift her into the saddle.

"Was anyone smoking in the hotel?"

She wrinkled her nose. "Men are always blowing smoke in my face."

"Did the smoke smell funny to you?" he asked.

She inhaled deeply as if trying to smell the smoke, and then coughed and laughed, then coughed and laughed again, nearly falling off the mare. Peyote—it was the only thing he could think of that would cause this reaction. Why the hell were they smoking that in a closed space? He had half a mind to storm into the restaurant and demand answers from the damned fools.

He put his hand on her leg to steady her in the saddle as she wavered back and forth. It was no good. She'd never make it back to the ranch. Ma had sold the house in town, and the hotel was out even if he'd wanted to venture back to the drug-laced building. People might believe they were engaged, but they were not married, and he wanted to retain as much of their reputations as was still possible.

Pink and orange already mottled the twilight sky, promising nightfall within the hour. They could ride together for a spell, but the distance back to the ranch was too great to travel. He moved her foot out of the stirrup and mounted behind her, holding Dapple's reins in his hand. She pressed her bottom against him, and he groaned at the sudden contact. It was going to be a long night.

HE STOKED THE FIRE before laying his duster coat on the ground for Aster. She'd gone from chatting incessantly to long moments of hollow silence. When he handed her a piece of hardtack, she turned up her nose and chucked it back at him. She accepted the canteen, though, gulping and sloshing water down the front of her bodice.

When she started to unbutton her blouse, he placed his hand over hers and told her to stop.

"But it's uncomfortable." She pouted and plopped down on his coat.

"Try to get some sleep. You'll feel better in the morning."

She stretched out on the coat and closed her eyes obediently. He contented himself with sitting next to her. Though he was dead tired, there was a chance she'd walk away in the middle of the night if he wasn't vigilant. He'd never tried peyote himself, but Keith's wife, Mary, was Mescalero Apache, and she'd told him stories of communing with her ancestors while under its influence. The last thing he needed was Aster deciding to go on a spirit walk in the middle of the night, far from home and miles from town.

He settled back against the trunk of an elm to wait out the night, listening to the fire crackling, a foot away from Aster's still form. She was so lovely with the glow of firelight dancing on her hair. Too lovely for the likes of him. He wrenched his gaze away from her, focused on the stars, and fought the pull of sleep.

DUKE WOKE WITH A START to find Aster's face inches from his own, the sweet smell of grass and lavender wafting from her hair.

He cleared his throat. "Is something wrong?"

She smiled slowly as she traced a finger down his cheek. "Not a thing."

"What are you doing?"

She touched the tip of his nose. "How did you break it?"

"Lost a wrestling match when I was a kid."

Aster laughed and sat back, straddling him. "Do you want to wrestle with me?"

He swallowed hard and put his hands on her hips. "You need to move."

She rubbed against him, and an involuntary moan escaped his throat. She giggled and leaned over him so her breasts brushed against his chest.

"Aster...," he said, but she silenced him by pressing her mouth against his and splaying her palms on his chest. He tried to push her away, but she seemed intent on deepening their kiss. When she thrust her tongue into his mouth, he froze, his hands still on her hips.

She threaded her fingers into his hair and pulled his head up, darting her tongue deeper in her exploration. This was wrong. The rational part of his mind screamed at him to push her off, that there was nothing between them but an insane plot to keep her pursuers away, but the voice of reason was drowned out by the pounding of his heart and the heat of her body on top of him.

When she pulled back for a breath, he struggled to wrangle his desire into submission. He tried to sit up, but she pushed him back against the tree.

"Aster, please," he said breathlessly.

"Don't you like me?" Her pale eyes glistened in the dim firelight.

"You're not yourself tonight."

"All the men in Philadelphia profess their love for me," she said in an oddly formal voice.

"I've no doubt." He licked his lips. With her hair tousled and her lips bruised from their kiss, she looked more like a French courtesan than a socialite from Pennsylvania.

"But they don't."

"They don't what?" he asked, trying desperately to focus on anything but her mouth.

"They don't love me. They only love my name."

"Aster?"

"You know that's not really my name."

"Henrietta," he breathed.

"Henrietta Beedy. Men only flock to me because my father is...." She looked up into the night sky.

"Aster, Henrietta, whatever your name is, you need to move."

She smiled and rubbed against him again as though she were not a virgin but a woman who knew exactly how to make a man desperate with need. He felt his own urgent need pushing against her through his trousers.

He closed his eyes and sighed. "If you don't want to make this a marriage in truth, you need to get off me...now."

"You don't want me," she whispered as she crawled back to her makeshift bed.

"Not like this."

"Because I'm ugly?"

"What?" He peered at her in the dark, but shadows obscured her face. "No. You are perfect."

"I try to be, but I always mess up."

"What are you talking about?"

He waited for her to answer, but she turned her back on him. He wanted to reach out to her, to wrap his arms around her, to comfort her, but he held himself back, afraid of just how much he wanted to be with her. Instead, he said, "I've never met anyone like you. You have more courage than most men I know. You're smart and funny and the most stunning woman I've ever seen.

"Do you really think so?" Her voice was so soft he could barely hear it over the whisper of the breeze through the trees.

"I do." As he said the words, he realized the truth of them and the sure knowledge that they would bring him only pain.

There was no way on this Earth he would allow himself to get close to another woman.

Confessions

Henrietta

She ran her thumb across the stone, relishing in the silky smoothness wrought from years of being beaten by the rushing water. It was thin and flat and fit just right in her hand. She pulled her arm back as Duke had shown her and swung forward, flicking her wrist at the last moment. *Whish and a plunk*. The stone had been the right shape and the right weight, and yet it hadn't flown across the water, hadn't skimmed the surface as it was supposed to.

Henrietta scanned the water's edge for another specimen and spied one a foot into the river. Without a thought, she plunged her hand into the cold water and fished it out. She angled her body toward the river and ran through the motions in her mind, imagining a steady, even swing and the whish, whish, whish as the rock skidded across the surface of the water.

She nodded to herself and swung again, confident she'd done it perfectly. Her face lit up at the first skip, the second, and then fell when the rock sank again. She clenched her hands so hard her trim fingernails bit into her palms. *Breathe, relax*. She waded further into the frigid water, sleeves rolled up above her elbows, mindless of her drenched skirts. She'd removed her boots, stockings, jacket, and gloves an hour earlier.

A faint sound called to her from a distance, but she was intent on the slippery floor of the riverbed, scanning and rejecting rocks as too small, too round, too large, too heavy. She waded deeper, ignoring the current buffeting her calves. There, a few feet to her right, was the perfect stone. She took a step and slipped when a rock dislodged beneath her foot. She crashed into the water. Her skirts dragged her down, and she had a moment of panic as the river seized her in its grip. She pushed up onto her knees but was knocked down again by the rushing water. Her head went under. She fought to regain the surface only to slip and fall again.

"Aster," she heard as she tried to push herself off the riverbed.

She scrambled and flailed, desperate to keep her head above water, but the force of the current knocked her down again and again. Her mouth filled with water, and she swung wildly with arms and legs. Suddenly, tightly corded arms wrapped around her, yanked her up, and hauled her out of the river.

"I'm fine," she sputtered as Duke dumped her onto solid ground.

"What the hell were you doing?"

She sucked in a gulp of air and pushed her wet hair out of her face. Duke sat next to her, soaked to the waist, his eyes flashing gold in the early morning light. She opened her palm, displaying the perfect stone: smooth, flat, not too thin, with just enough weight to sail across the water.

"Have you lost your mind? I thought the peyote would be out of your system by now."

"The what?" Her smile faltered.

"Do you remember anything from yesterday?"

"Skipping stones." She jutted out her chin and held up the perfect rock for his inspection.

He snatched the stone from her palm.

"What are you doing?" She grabbed his arm, but he shook her off and threw the stone clean across the rushing river.

"You almost drowned!" he said.

"I did not."

"All for a damned rock?"

She opened her mouth and then closed it again, and let his words sink in. "I was practicing."

"Fine. Practice all you want. But why did you have to wade through fast moving water? Do you even know how to swim?"

She looked down at her scratched, now empty, palms in her lap. "I don't."

"Then why—" he closed his eyes and sucked in a deep breath. When he spoke, his voice was calm and controlled, "—then why did you try to cross the river?"

"I wasn't trying to cross it. I was looking for a stone."

He looked at her with a blank expression, his mouth gaping open like a fish. He gestured all around them. "There are rocks *everywhere*."

"They're not..." She sniffed and looked down at her sodden, muddy skirts.

"They're not what, Aster?" His voice was so unexpectedly gentle that she snapped her head up to stare into his eyes, so warm, so open, so understanding.

"They're not perfect."

He looked at her in confusion. "A rock's a rock."

"I thought...I thought if I found the perfect rock, then I could skip it across the water as well as you. I saw one of yours hit the surface six times before it fell."

"And I've been skipping stones since I was knee high to a fencepost. Besides, what does it matter? It's supposed to be fun, to pass the time. It's just a game." He shook his head, clearly at a loss.

She opened her mouth, then snapped it shut. "You wouldn't understand."

"Try me." He reached into her lap and laced his fingers through hers. He brushed his thumb across the back of her hand, skirting the edge of the scar.

She snatched her hand away and wrapped her arms around herself to hide the burn.

"What is it? What did I do?"

"Nothing," she muttered and searched the shore for her discarded clothes, spying them a few feet away, near the water's edge. She tried to scramble to her feet, but her skirts weighed her down. So, she crawled to the pile instead.

"If you put that on now," he said as she tried to stick her wet arms into the safety of the long-sleeved jacket, "you'll be wet all day. Let me build back the fire so you can dry off properly."

She knew she was acting the fool. He'd already seen the scar that snaked up her arm, and it wasn't as if he was interested in her. She shrugged the jacket off and turned to face him.

"All right," she said.

Duke

HE PLACED ANOTHER SMALL branch on the dying fire and crouched down to blow life into the embers. Aster sat across from him with her chin on her knees, watching him with wide eyes, blue as the river which had pulled her under. Her arms were wrapped around herself, almost as though she was hiding from him. Hell, she had no memory of last night and how much of herself she'd already exposed. He shook his head as he recalled how his body had responded to her, how much he still wanted to touch her soft skin, to tangle his fingers in her thick hair, to pull her onto his lap and to make love to her.

"Duke?"

He jerked his head up. Had he said his thoughts aloud? But no, if he had, she wouldn't be watching him with such an innocent gaze. And she *was* innocent. Despite her drug-induced advances, he was sure she'd had little experience with men. Hell, she wouldn't even let him hold her hand. Shame coursed through his veins, cooling his ardor.

He grunted a response and wrenched his eyes away from her and back to the sticks which refused to catch a spark.

"What's peyote?" she asked, elongating every syllable.

"It's a cactus." He blew again, harder this time, until a brilliant orange flared in the coals.

"Why did you mention it?"

Holding a thin piece of wood to the ember, Duke blew until a small flame appeared. He cupped his hand around the flame and blew a steady stream of air, adding another shaving and then another until he thought the fire might survive the addition of a small twig.

"Duke, tell me about the cactus." Her voice was soft, but firm and demanding.

He sat back on his haunches, his gaze fixed on the tiny fire burning between them. He didn't look at her when he said, "What do you remember about yesterday...besides skipping stones?"

She considered, then said, "I was in church...and you were there!"

He nodded. "What else?"

She scrunched her eyes as though trying to remember a distant, foggy memory.

"The preacher wasn't there, but I met a friend. What was her name...Susie, Susan, Susanna—that's it, like the song. I heard another song too, Goodbye, Liza Jane?"

She broke into verse then, her lilting voice singing a song he'd heard his entire life, but somehow, she made the jaunty lyrics twist with melancholy.

"I'm going away to leave you. It's goodbye, goodbye, I'm going away to leave you. It's goodbye, Liza Jane."

"Why do you sing it like that? Like it's ripping your heart out?" he asked, peering at her through the flames.

"I hate saying goodbye." She rested her forehead on her knees, hiding away completely.

"I don't think anyone enjoys it."

"But I've said it more than most. And my goodbyes are forever."

He nodded, then realized she couldn't see him. "Mine too."

She unfolded slowly, her face ashen. "I'm sorry. That was thoughtless and cruel of me. Her name was Judith, right?"

His heart was in his throat. "And my son, George, but it was a long time ago." The words sounded weak, even to him.

"Goodness." Tears sprang to her eyes. "I didn't know about your child."

He shrugged. "How could you? No one speaks of him. It's as if he never existed, but he did, he was as real as you or I. And he's gone, forever, but there's not a day goes by that I don't think about him and wonder what he'd be doing if he was still here."

"How old would he be now?" Aster asked.

"He'd be five. You could teach him how to skip stones."

"I bet he'd be amazing, like his father."

Duke nodded. "It helps, somehow, to imagine him still here. But my Ma, my brothers, even my sister Martha—they don't understand. If I remember him and talk about him, he's not really gone." He sniffed and wiped his nose with the back of his hand. "I'm not mad. I know it's not real, that he's dead and buried and in Heaven with his mother."

She was silent for a long time, letting his words resonate. When she spoke, her voice was quiet. "My mother lost three babies after I was born. The last was when I was nine years old. I think of them every day: who they would be, what they'd be doing. Would they like music and riding like me, or would they love to read like my mother? Or would they be like my father, fascinated by all the wondrous innovations in industry?"

"That's it exactly. My family looks at me like I'm morose, thinking about them all the time, but it's comforting to keep them alive, in here." He pounded his chest.

"Tell me about them." She inched closer to the fire, still a small and fragile thing, the flames flickering as though they might go out at any moment.

He described meeting Judith for the first time: her dark hair streaming down her back, laughing as she chased her younger brothers around a huge live oak tree, darting one way and then the next, always missing them by inches. She'd been so happy, so alive. He smiled at the memory and wondered why he had focused all these years on the pain and not the joy.

He didn't notice Aster's gradual approach until she rested next to him, on his side of the firepit. It felt natural when she took his hand and squeezed it, giving him silent encouragement to share more than he'd intended, until memory after memory spilled out, leaving him empty.

"Thank you," he said, gazing down at their locked hands. Hers was so small, and yet her grip was firm and strong and comforting.

"It's nothing." Her eyes shone with unshed tear.

"It's *everything*."

"I..." She lowered her gaze. "I have a confession to make."

"Let me guess. You told everyone you were a mail-order bride engaged to one Duke Gildownie of Twisted Oak Ranch?"

She smiled and bit her lip. "No, it's worse than that."

"What could be worse than that?" he asked.

"About yesterday." She covered their joined hands with her other hand.

"Yes?"

She peered up at him through half-closed lids. "I remember—"

Her words were cut off by a loud crash in the woods and the sound of heavy footsteps.

Henrietta

DUKE JUMPED UP AND reached for the rifle propped against the saddle before she even registered the disturbance. She scrambled to her feet and ran to him and searched the ground for a weapon.

"Get behind me," he hissed, his gaze fixed on the woods beyond.

"I can help." She grabbed a branch and thrust it out in front of her.

"You can help by getting behind me." He held the rifle loosely in his hands, but his body radiated tension, like a cornered animal ready to strike when its home was threatened. She ducked behind him but kept the branch firmly in hand.

"Show yourself!"

There was a crash followed by a string of highly inventive curses. The tension eased from Duke's body, and he lowered his weapon.

Cash stumbled out of the woods, leading a horse by the halter. "There you are. Tarnation, I've been looking for you everywhere. Ma's fit to be tied y'all didn't turn up last night. I told her you'd probably decided to hole up in the hotel in town now you're hitched and all, but she's bound and determined to have you back home where she can keep an eye on you."

Duke snorted. "You'd think I was still in short pants."

Henrietta giggled at the image of the tall man running around with bared knees. She turned away and tried to compose herself. She rolled down the sleeves of her blouse and fastened the buttons at her wrists, then shook out her skirts, still damp from her earlier plunge.

"So did the preacher fix y'all up?"

"About that..."

Henrietta whirled around. "Yes, everything's all settled."

Cash squinted his eyes. "Settled?"

"Settled, married, hitched. You know." She looped her arm in Duke's, ignoring his confused look.

"Well, that's great then. Congratulations, big brother. And my sincerest condolences, ma'am, for getting saddled with this big, brooding oaf."

"At least I don't traipse around the woods loud enough for a rustler to hear me two counties over," Duke said to his brother while stealing a glance at Henrietta.

"I didn't want to..." Cash gave him an exaggerated wink, "...interrupt things."

"You *are* interrupting."

Cash held his hands up. "Apologies. I'm on a mission."

"From Ma? Well, congratulations, you found us. So, you can run along home now."

"Duke," Henrietta said. When he looked down, she offered him her most brilliant smile, the one that had the men in Philadelphia quivering in their boots. "We were about to leave anyway."

"You should listen to your wife." Cash smiled wide and offered Henrietta a small bow. "Besides, Aster, I'm far better company."

"We were in the middle of something," Duke said. He cast her a meaningful glance.

She swallowed loudly and turned away. Her courage from a few moments earlier had evaporated. She wasn't ready to admit just how out of control of her actions she had been the night before. Her mind was still foggy, but she remembered the feel of his skin beneath hers, the warmth in her belly as she'd kissed him, the way her body had moved slowly and sensually of its own accord.

And she remembered how good it had felt.

She blushed. Maybe it had been the peyote, loosening her from the tight strictures that had defined and controlled her life before she'd journeyed to this wild land. Of course, by the time she'd come to her senses shortly before dawn, all the rules of society had come crashing down on her. But the desire she'd felt remained. Even the rigid muscles beneath her hand excited her, tempting her to run her fingers up his arm to his shoulders, to the hollow in his throat, to the scruff of new beard covering his face.

She shuddered.

Duke misinterpreted her reaction. "Are you still cold? Why don't you sit here by the fire while Cash and I pack up." He left her to snatch his duster, still lying on the ground. He shook it, releasing leaves and twigs, then draped it over her shoulders, swallowing her.

She watched as they gathered their meager belongings and packed them into the saddlebags. Only after the horses were haltered and saddled did she remember her discarded clothing by the riverbank. How could she have forgotten her gloves? True, her blouse did cover most of the burn, but there was always a chance someone could spy the scar's ragged edges peeking out of her sleeve at her wrist.

Duke fetched her things and helped her don her jacket, his hands gentle as he slipped the sleeve over her burn. That one show of kindness was her undoing.

A Bride In Truth

Duke

Duke stripped off his sweat-drenched shirt and cast an eye toward the horizon. It was a few hours before supper, plenty of time to cut down another tree. He wiped his hands on his trousers before picking up the axe again. He and Wyatt had already felled half a dozen pines for the frame of the horse barn. Cash had taken off again, but Duke had long ago given up relying on his little brother for anything involving physical labor. Wyatt pulled his weight, but his heart was in the mountains, and even family offered too much strain for a man who craved solitude. Duke needed Shaw, but he needed the money from the cattle sale more.

He swung the axe at the tree, angling it upward to widen the notch in the trunk. A few more thwacks and he'd have another to haul back to the ranch. Normally, he relished each swing, the sweat, and the grueling labor required to run a family ranch. The more backbreaking the task, the more his mind settled into the familiar nothingness he wrapped around himself that kept the memories at bay. But his mind betrayed him that day, straying to the woman who had sat near him, heard his grief, and hadn't walked away. Her words echoed in his head.

She remembered. What had she meant by that? He wanted to ask her. Hell, he wanted her to do it again—to straddle him, to kiss him, to thread her fingers in his hair. He wanted her.

"I think it's dead," Wyatt said, rousing Duke from his trance.

"What?"

"The tree. I think you killed it and made a hell of a mess doing it."

Duke looked down at the tree trunk and the hacked off branches surrounding it. He must have continued working long after his brain had stopped focusing on the task at hand. "Here or back at the barn, still needed to happen."

"Yeah, but if we'd cut off the branches *there*, we wouldn't have them to haul back as well."

Duke nodded and started the grueling work of looping a rope around the fallen tree trunk, tying it to the workhorse's pommel, and dragging it the half mile to the construction site. He fell in step with the horse and stole a glance at his brother a few yards away from him, guiding his own horse through the stubby grass, avoiding rocks and cacti.

"What do you think of her?"

"The girl?" Wyatt asked.

"Who else?"

"It don't really matter what I think. You're the one married to her."

Duke glared at his brother. Wyatt wasn't much of a talker on the best of days, but he could have tried to make an effort.

"Yeah, I know. But what do you think of her?" Duke asked again.

"She's hiding something."

Duke faltered and grabbed a fistful of the horse's mane to keep from falling. He swallowed a curse. "Go on."

"Why did you marry her?"

"I wanted a wife."

Wyatt barked a laugh. "If you say so."

"What the hell is that supposed to mean?"

"You want us to believe you decided months ago to get yourself a woman. So, instead of looking around Lincoln County or even Santa Fe, you figured you'd get a mail-order bride from Boston or Providence or wherever. And then it was your *eloquent* writing that convinced her to come down here, by herself?"

"She traveled with a vicar and his wife," Duke muttered as they arrived at the site of the new horse barn.

"That's not the unbelievable part." Wyatt untied the log and looped the rope onto the pommel for the ride back.

"I can read and write, jackass," Duke said as they started the return journey.

"You don't want to tell me what you're up to, fine. You're a grown man and can do whatever the hell you want. You asked. I answered. We done now?"

Duke held his tongue as they finished the workday. If Wyatt had suspected they were pulling a fast one, had everyone else? And why were they so convinced no woman would want him?

Henrietta

HENRIETTA SAT BACK on her heels and admired the sheen on the pine floors. Who knew that scrubbing and waxing could lead to such great satisfaction? She'd started at the corner of the family room and had worked her way horizontally across the floor, moving chairs and tables as she went, ensuring every inch was cleaned and polished perfectly. She pressed her knuckles into her lower back and rubbed at the knot which had formed hours earlier, but she hadn't wanted to stop to rest, not when so much needed to be done. If Duke wanted her to cook and clean for him, she would do so to the absolute best of her ability. And she had.

She allowed herself a small smile as she stood and perused the results of her work. The loud growl of her stomach insisted it was well past midday and time to break her fast. Bridget had packed lunches for the men, leaving the two of them to see to the housecleaning without 'grown lads interrupting them every minute o' the day when there's work to be done.'

"It looks mighty fine to me," Bridget said as she walked up to Henrietta and handed her a slice of bread and a hunk of cheese wrapped in butcher paper. "But it's past time for a break. Best take in some sunshine. Ye need some color in yer cheeks, lass."

Henrietta beamed under the faint praise for her day's labor. "I won't be long."

"Take yer time. I plan to take a wee nap before starting on the supper."

Henrietta thanked her and dug into the makeshift sandwich, careful not to drop crumbs on the spotless floor. Over the past several days, she'd dusted, polished, and swept every inch of the ranch house, admiring wooden carvings of rearing horses, old photographs of the Gildownies, and more than a dozen landscapes of the mountains of New Mexico Territory. There was only one room she was hesitant to enter, one door that remained firmly closed every time she'd passed by. When she'd asked Bridget, Duke's mother had said it had been Judith's special place.

Every fiber in her being urged Henrietta to slip inside and to learn more about the woman whose passing had left an open wound in Duke's heart. She told herself it was respect that kept her from turning the knob, but that was a lie. It was simple fear. Fear of a dead woman.

Henrietta decided to venture out of doors instead. There were a dozen or more horses grazing in the pasture, but she paid special attention to the Appaloosas, mentally forming a list of all her questions on their origins, their unique traits, and the economic advantages to breeding the unusual horses. She next visited the site of the new horse barn, where Duke and his brothers spent so many hours each day, but the men were nowhere to be found.

Duke generally rose before sunrise and returned to their rooms long after sunset. Only the briefest brush of his hand at the dinner table and a pleasant inquiry into her day convinced her he hadn't completely forgotten about her.

It wasn't enough. Not nearly enough. She kicked a stone, sending it scurrying across the rocky terrain behind the frame of the new horse barn and into the woods beyond. She was about to turn back to the house when she heard splashing coming from somewhere in the trees. Lifting her skirts so they wouldn't snag on the thick vegetation, she picked her way through the woods until she came upon a pile of men's clothes with a creased and faded Stetson on top.

Perhaps she should have turned around, but her curiosity was piqued. She tried to creep forward with stealth, but she was a city girl and unused to moving in silence.

"Hello?" a deep voice sounded nearby, followed by loud splashing.

"Duke?"

Silence, and then a soft, "Aster, is that you?"

Henrietta gasped as she peeked around a tree and caught a glimpse of Duke's bare, bronzed chest rising out of the still waters of a pond. She ducked back and leaned against the tree, the rough bark of the trunk pressing painfully into her. She should go back to the house immediately. And she would. Of course she would...after another glance. She bit her lip and poked her head around the tree, but the pond was empty. Its placid waters didn't show even a ripple.

She took a tentative step forward, leaving the relative safety of her hiding spot. Swinging her head from side to side, she surveyed the countryside for the man the world named her husband, but there was not a soul in sight.

"There you are." Duke's voice was low and soft in her ear.

She whirled around to face him, only to stare straight at his glistening, wet, bare chest inches from her nose. As she took a step back, she tripped over a branch. Only his firm grip on her arm kept her from falling into the thick brush.

"Are you all right?" he said as he righted her.

"I think so."

She tried to avert her eyes but couldn't fight the temptation to look down to see if he were truly completely naked. Her eyes traced his thick chest to a narrow waist and to the half-buttoned underpants plastered to his skin, barely concealing the bulge between his legs.

"What are you doing out here?"

"Hmm?" She was unable to tear her eyes away from the fascinating shape of his body. She should be embarrassed—she would be later, certainly. Now, though, it was all she could do to keep her hands tightly gripped on her skirt when all she wanted to do was to run her fingers along the sharp planes of his body. Her face flushed as her imagination ran wild.

"Aster?" Duke laid a hand on her forehead. "Are you overheated?"

"Umm." She forced her gaze back to his face, but that was just as dangerous. His thick, dark auburn hair, normally hidden by a cowboy hat, was wet and tangled, and she had an intense desire to run her fingers through his locks. His eyes, dark brown, with burnished flecks of amber and gold, filled with concern.

"There's a pool nearby. Why don't you take a dip?"

She blanched at the idea of stripping naked in front of him. "Absolutely not."

"Damn it." He slapped his hand against his forehead. "You can't swim. I forgot."

"Oh, it's not that..."

He gripped her arms gently, his face lighting up. "Oh, but this is perfect. I'll teach you. The pond's not deep, and I'll be there the whole time."

"I...I don't have a bathing costume." She looked around the forest as though there might be a modiste nestled in the trees.

"You don't need one."

Her eyes widened. "I am not taking off my clothes!"

He scrunched up his face in confusion. "Why not? I sleep a foot away from you every night, and I've never once tried to take advantage.

Besides, all you need to do is slip off your shoes and your dress—anything that will weigh you down in the water."

Her stomach roiled. She was so stupid. Here she was imagining he was as attracted to her as she was to him, but the truth had been staring her in the face the whole time. He didn't remember meeting her in Philadelphia because she meant nothing to him, less than nothing. He wanted a housekeeper and a way to get his mother to stop meddling in his life, not a woman to hold dear or to marry in truth.

She fought to keep the hurt and embarrassment buried deep inside. He was still in love with his late wife, and she couldn't blame him for that. It was best to put any romantic notions firmly aside. This was a business transaction—nothing more and nothing less.

She plastered on a brilliant smile. "Why not?"

Ten minutes later, she stood by the pond's edge in her bare feet with her toes sinking into the warm, soft, wet sand. Henrietta was struck by a vivid memory of chasing Rosalie along the Cape May beaches when they were young. A smile slid across her face. She'd been so happy then.

"The petticoats will have to go."

She shot Duke a suspicious glance. "Why?"

"They're like an anchor pulling you under."

She was already stripped down to her corset, exposing her burn in its entirety. Would it be that much more indecent to stand in her bloomers than in her petticoats? Besides, now that the idea of learning to swim had taken her, she wanted to do it right. All those summers of traveling to New Jersey where dozens of girls her age had danced among the waves, she and Rosalie alone had been strictly forbidden from leaving the beach. She knew why, of course. And she'd never faulted her parents for it. Just like she couldn't blame them for the rules restricting her riding or trying anything else remotely dangerous.

Once back home in Philadelphia, she would abide by the rules and do everything expected of her, but here in New Mexico, she yearned to live without bounds. So, she slipped off the petticoat and took a tentative step into the pond, only to pull her foot back with a squeal.

Duke started forward, his face a picture of alarm, but she held up a hand. "It's cold."

He sank back into the water and smiled. "You'll get used to it."

She held her breath and plunged her foot back into the frigid water. Shivers wracked her body, but she forced her other foot in. "Why is it so cold?"

"Spring fed. The quicker you come in, the better," Duke encouraged.

She threw him an incredulous look as she shifted her weight from one foot to the other. Inhaling deeply to find her resolve, she took a step forward and then another, wincing with every move deeper into the icy pond, but she'd never been one to back away from a challenge. She wrapped her arms tightly around her body and tried to still her chattering teeth, moving steadily forward until she was thigh-deep in the pond a foot from Duke.

"You're doing great," he said. "Are you afraid?"

She shook her head once.

"Good. So, the main thing to remember when you're in the water is to be calm, to use gentle, fluid movements. The more you thrash around, the more difficult it is to stay afloat. Does that make sense?"

She nodded, hugging herself tighter. "Still cold."

He closed the gap between them and ran his hands up and down her arms. He was trying to warm her up, and she supposed it worked because heat flooded through her body from his touch. She had to fight her instincts to lean into him. *This was a business transaction.*

"Does that help?"

She sighed. "A little."

"Ready to learn?"

She nodded, too paralyzed by fear to speak.

He grabbed her by the hand and led her toward the center of the pond, where the water reached almost to her chest. He was right. She didn't know whether she was numb from the cold or whether the sunshine warmed the water in the middle of the pool. Either way, she was not nearly as chilled as she had been earlier.

"Do you trust me?"

She peered into his eyes and saw only the kindness he'd shown her time and again since she'd started this journey. She bit her lip and nodded her head.

"I want you to just lay back. Don't worry, I have you." He placed a hand on her back and another on her shoulder and gently pushed her the way he wanted her to go.

She bent her knees and leaned back against his arm, her gaze fixed on his. Her heart thundered in her chest. She'd lied. She was afraid, but not just of the water. Her fear stemmed from the desire to be with him and the certainty he felt nothing in return, not even when she lay in his arms with only a corset and drawers separating them.

"Relax and let your legs float up, just like you're lying in a bed or in a field."

She lifted one foot and then the other and immediately sank. She kicked out but couldn't get a foothold. Water rushed up her chest toward her chin. She flailed her arms and fought to pull herself up out of the water. She grabbed hold of Duke, clawing at him to keep from going under.

"Easy, easy," he said as she clung to him, all embarrassment at her near nakedness long gone.

His soothing words and his strong, muscular arms around her pushed through the fog of terror, urging her to escape. Gradually her heart eased its frantic pounding as she focused on the sweet, clean air filling her lungs and the warble from birds in the trees surrounding them.

"Better?"

"Mm-hmm," she said, though she kept her arms wrapped around his torso.

"Ready to go again?"

"Again?" She tried and failed to keep the panic out of her voice.

"We'll take it slower. I won't let go."

"Promise?"

"I won't let anything happen to you," he said.

Duke gradually eased her back into the water with one arm under her back and the other under her knees. Still, she refused to let go of him despite his coaxing words and easy manner.

"Do you know how I learned to swim?" he asked in a soothing voice, one he probably used to calm a frightened colt.

She shook her head.

"My brothers and I were playing on the cliffs overlooking the river, closer to Ruidoso. Wyatt picked me up and threw me off the cliff into the middle of the river."

She loosened her grip enough to peer up into his face. "Why?"

He smiled. "Said I was aggravating him. I probably was, too."

"You could have drowned!"

"Yeah. For a minute, I thought I was a goner."

"What happened?" she asked.

"As I was thrashing around trying to figure out which way was up, I remembered a leaf."

"A leaf? Why?"

He lowered his arm, and water lapped against her scalp. She panicked and kicked out, but his grip was firm on her back, holding her.

"A leaf drifts into the river and though it might sink down to the bottom, within moments it floats to the surface."

She focused on his warm and gentle voice and fought to control her wildly beating heart.

"I realized the secret to swimming is to become a leaf. Stretch your arms and legs out wide and let the current take you."

"I don't understand," Henrietta said in a shaky voice.

"A leaf doesn't fight the river. It surrenders and floats right to the top."

She reluctantly released her hold on Duke and spread her fingers wide, and let her hands drift up to the surface of the pond. "A leaf," she murmured as she closed her eyes and imagined she was the leaf floating down a stream.

"I'm going to let go now."

"No!" Her eyes flew open. She felt the water closing in, seizing her legs and dragging her under.

His arms were around her instantly, gathering her close. "I've got you."

She held tightly to him as he carried her to shore and set her down on the grass. He tried to pull away, but she held fast. Her chest ached as she fought to regulate her breathing. Duke lifted her onto his lap, wrapped his arms around her, and whispered soothing words in her ear. Gradually her panic subsided, leaving her weak and breathless in his arms. She thought he might let go, but he didn't, and she was glad of it.

"I'm sorry," he whispered, "so sorry."

She leaned back just far enough to see the pained expression on his face. Without pausing to consider, she kissed him. He tried to pull away, but she threaded her fingers in his hair and pulled his head lower, deepening their kiss. Warmth radiated through her body as she rubbed her breasts against his bare chest. She wanted more, so much more. She opened her mouth and touched his lip with the tip of her tongue. His arms tightened around her, and he groaned in her mouth, then he disentangled himself from her with an apology. Before she could gather her senses, he'd set her on the ground and fled into the woods.

Heat rushed her cheeks, and she mentally kicked herself for throwing herself at a man who clearly didn't want her. She should give up her stupid mission and run home to Philadelphia and live the life her parents had planned out for her.

Only she couldn't go back. Not yet. The memory of that last moment with her father, when she'd confronted him and he'd dismissed her with barely a nod, stoked her anger and had set her resolve. Henrietta had made her plan that day to leave home, to defy her parents for the first time in her life. Perhaps she should have handled things with Jonathon and her family better, but at the time it had felt like the only choice left open to her.

It was why she'd set off for New Mexico Territory. The need hadn't changed. A child's future—perhaps even her life—might be at risk, and only Rosalie could help. No more thoughts of Duke and a life that could never be.

Duke

HE CURSED HIMSELF AS he studied Judith's grave marker. What had he been thinking, asking Aster to take her clothes off and swim with him? He'd been so sure he could pretend to be the doting husband while keeping his distance. He'd been a fool. He'd wanted her. He'd needed her. He still did, truth be told.

He crouched next to the grave and ran his fingers along the smooth engraving on the marker. He'd chiseled the words himself.

Beloved. Forever.

What would Judith think of his fake marriage? On the day she died, he'd promised her he would be faithful until the day he left this earth. Five short years after her funeral, his mind, his body, and maybe even his heart betrayed her.

"Stupid." He slammed the heel of his palm into his forehead.

"I've always thought so."

Duke rounded on Cash, who'd slipped into the graveyard behind him. "Where've you been?"

"Around," Cash said. The man reeked of alcohol and rosewater.

"Strange you're nowhere to be found when there's work to be done," Duke said accusingly.

Cash shrugged. "You're the strange one, standing out here in a graveyard when you've got a new bride—and a mighty fine one at that..."

Duke glared at his brother. "Stay away from her. I'm warning you."

Cash shook his head. "You just can't let it go, can you? No matter how many times I apologize."

Duke shoved past Cash, knocking against him, hard. "Some things are unforgivable."

He stalked to the paddock. Maybe some time with the horses would ease his foul mood. It wasn't Cash he was angry at, though his brother had hurt him in the past more than he thought possible.

He never should have agreed to this scheme. And yet, as he leaned his head against Dapple's neck, he let himself imagine what it would be like if Aster were his bride in truth.

For Love Alone

Henrietta

Henrietta had felt Duke's eyes linger on her throughout dinner. Despite her determination to push him from her mind, his sheer presence filled her with unexpected giddiness as she tripped over her words, spilled her glass of wine, and almost fell on her backside when she pushed her chair back with more force than necessary.

"Are ye quite well, lass?" Bridget asked after the men had left the table for the never-ending chores on the ranch.

Henrietta looked down at the shattered remnants of the water pitcher at her feet. "Oh, I am sorry. I'll replace it as soon as we go back to town. I saw a painted ceramic one at Tunstall's Mercantile the day I arrived. Of course, it had a painting of a rooster on it. Do you like chickens? I don't, truth be told. I got pecked when I tried to feed one when I was a child and ever since I've kept my distance..." She drifted off as she realized her simple comment had turned into an unintelligible ramble.

Where was her mind these days? She'd never been prone to flights of fancy, though she *was* a romantic soul. How could she not be, with a mother as passionate as she was about Russian literature and the melodrama of Tolstoy?

She bit the side of her cheek hard enough to draw blood to keep herself from spilling more of her childhood than she'd intended. Twice now she'd caught herself referring to her cousin Rosalie and had only been rescued by Duke's quick redirection of the conversation, but

Bridget was perceptive and, without Duke's steady presence, Henrietta was sure to make a fatal mistake.

"'Tis not mine, dearie, but yers."

"What?" Henrietta paused, broom in hand.

"The pitcher, lass. This is yer house, yers and Duke's. He bought out his brothers and sister years ago. Oh, I do hope I'll be welcome to live here in my dotage, but 'tis not mine. I've never desired it, not even when my husband was alive."

"I didn't know."

"Is that a fact, then? And yer husband never mentioned it in all those letters?" Bridget eyed her appraisingly.

Henrietta shook her head and focused on sweeping up the shards of glass.

"Good. I'm pleased he's found himself a bride who married him for love and love alone." Bridget nodded, a satisfied smile creeping across her face.

Henrietta blushed and muttered something incoherent as she scooped the glass into a dustbin. She ran out of the room, with an offhand word about checking on the injured man, Arthur. The other two Regulators were long gone, leaving only this one man who might trade information about her to save himself.

She hastened to the wash basin to clean up before checking the man's wound, then caught herself as she started to roll up her sleeves. A quick glance confirmed he was indeed awake; his eyes focused on her every movement. She forced a small smile, though it likely resembled a grimace, and lathered the harsh lye soap. She had a momentary, desperate wish for her sliver of lavender soap in the other room. There was no help for it. Cleanliness was essential to prevent infection, so she dunked her hands into the water, soaking her sleeves almost to the elbow.

She dried off and assumed her best impression of her childhood physician—cool and efficient. She needn't have worried. The man was far more interested in her bosom than her drenched arms. She pursed her lips and didn't comment, though she may have been a tad rougher than normal in her ministrations.

His eyes tightened, but he didn't make a peep as she cleaned and dressed the wound. There was no clear sign of infection, at least not that she was able to discern. There was no pus, no angry red swelling, though the stitches were far from healed.

"When do ya think I'll be able to ride?"

She shook her head. "I'm not certain, maybe a few more days?"

"I reckon they'll be here soon," he grunted as he tried to lift himself off the mattress.

"Who?"

She touched his shoulder, and he collapsed back onto the bed.

"Probably the whole damned army." His face twisted as he saw her reaction. "Beggin' your pardon, miss."

"Why would the army be looking for you?"

"I winged one of 'em."

"What do you mean?" she asked slowly.

"I shot him, got him good, too. Doubt he'll be walking soon unless he found his own angel to help him."

She frowned at the man's forwardness, but she was far more concerned with the implications of his starting a war with the US Army. Her uncle had been a colonel, and having known him, she was certain the soldiers would not give up until they found the perpetrator. No wonder Duke hadn't wanted to offer the man refuge.

She tried to give the injured man a reassuring smile as she gathered his dirty dinner dishes, but her mind was far from easy. Guilt bubbled inside her as she realized how much risk she'd put them in—this family who'd shown her nothing but hospitality. She had stolen, lied, and betrayed her fiancé, her parents, and now Duke and his family, and for what? *Rosalie wasn't even there.*

She placed the dirty dishes into the kitchen sink and worked the hand pump until water flowed out in a stream. She relived every moment of the past month as she scrubbed viciously at the dishes and considered her next steps. By the time the last dish was dried and put away, she'd made her decision.

She would place herself in Duke's hands, tell him everything, and plead for his mercy and for his help. Then she would turn herself in to Jameson. Mind made up, she folded the kitchen towel into neat squares and placed it on the counter, straightening it to line up with the edge.

Taking a deep breath to quiet the flurries in her belly, she walked to the bedroom to gather the stolen goods to present Duke with the whole picture. She fought every instinct to protect the secret which, she was certain, would cause her family far more pain than her disappearance. She'd done that calculation weeks ago when she'd made the discovery, and nothing had fundamentally changed except her own failure. She clenched her hands, her fingernails cutting deeper into her palms in a familiar, comforting gesture.

She crossed the room to the nightstand and stopped short. Her reticule was missing. Hadn't she left her handbag on the table by the bed? She turned up the lamp and dropped to her knees to search the floor around the table, under the bed, and in the corners of the small room.

It had to be here. Had someone taken it? Was there a thief in the house?

Henrietta ran through the list of suspects in her mind, dismissing one after the other. The injured man's friends had been here earlier, and they were notorious outlaws. Would they have come into her bedroom and taken her purse, hoping to find money to aid in their escape? It was feasible. But no, she'd had her handbag since they'd left. She distinctly remembered Susanna pointing it out on the table in that cursed hotel.

She'd been so out of sorts that day and so busy in the days afterward that she must have left it somewhere else. She sat on the floor, closed her eyes and did her best to retrace her steps since leaving the hotel, though recalling part of that day and night made her blush.

"Drat!"

The last time she'd seen her handbag was when she'd dropped it on her pile of discarded clothing at the riverbank to skip stones. There was nothing for it. She'd have to retrieve it. She rushed out of the room, down the hallway, and headlong into Duke's brother Wyatt.

"Whoa, there." He took an exaggerated step back and fixed her with a pointed stare.

"Sorry."

"Where are you off to?" Wyatt was tall and lean like Duke, but their similarities ended there. Each interaction with Wyatt had left her feeling like a mare rejected at an auction—pretty enough, but, on second glance, not worth the price.

"Um...nowhere. I got turned around."

His eyebrows shot up. "In the house?"

Her eyes darted left and right, everywhere but at the giant blocking her escape. "Um." She forced a silly giggle. "I'm looking for Duke."

"He'll be in shortly," Wyatt said curtly.

She gnawed on her bottom lip and avoided his gaze. "Well. Goodnight then."

When he made no attempt to move out of the way, she whirled around and dashed back into the bedroom, pulling the door closed behind her, and crossed to the window to peer out into the dark.

Duke

THE NIGHT WAS COOL, brisk even, despite being early summer. God, he loved it there. He still remembered Pa's pride when they'd first ridden the property and had pointed out the mountain stream, the most precious of all resources in the West—the source of life, guaranteed survival, and the promise of a future. When Pa had taken them to the giant oak tree with its limbs so heavy they stretched to the ground, Duke knew this would be the site of their homestead.

They'd made so many plans that day, the two of them, while the rest of the family picnicked. Martha and Ma had been eager to get out of the sun and go back to civilization. Keith had never been an outdoorsman and was content to escort the women to Lincoln after their lunch. The rest of his brothers had shown an interest of sorts, but Duke had been the one who understood at a primal level the desire to build a life there.

Would Pa be proud seeing his dreams come to life?

It was the question that drove Duke's every decision. What would Pa think of the mess Duke had made, embroiling himself in Aster's machinations? But Duke knew the answer as surely as he'd known where Pa would build the new horse barn, which horses would make the finest stud, and which cows would be the most fertile.

He'd have said, 'Live your life with integrity, knowing the Lord watches your every action and sees the truth in your heart even when it's hidden from everyone else.'

Pa had raised him to be honest, but more importantly, he'd taught him to respect and honor women above all. Duke felt a new level of shame when he thought of how he'd avoided his Ma and Martha since Judith's death. Not because they'd been cruel. No, they were never that.

They accepted a truth he couldn't face. Childbirth was the greatest danger to a woman, and there was not a damned thing a man could do to protect them from it. And there was the rub. He liked Aster. Truth was, he liked her more than he wanted to admit, but he couldn't be responsible for another woman's death. Not ever.

It was time to face the music, with Aster's approval or not. He doffed his hat and smoothed down his hair before entering the house. The living room was empty save for his Ma, rocking in her chair near the window, knitting needles in constant motion, plunging and looping. She finished her stitch before she glanced up at Duke.

"Where is everyone?" he asked.

"Wyatt went upstairs an hour or more ago and Cash is..." She pursed her lips and whipped the yarn around the end of her needle. "Who knows where yer brother has run off to."

"And Aster?"

"The lass? Oh, she is a dear one, my boy. So fierce and determined. A bit like myself, if ye don't mind my saying. Rosie will be mighty glad to meet her. I have a feeling they'll be fast friends. Now I put my mind to it, they do resemble each other a bit."

"About that, Ma...."

"I canna tell ye how happy I am. And I know yer Pa is looking down on ye with so much pride that ye've given it another go. Now I know what ye're going to say." She held up her hand. "I was wrong for pushing ye so, and ye might have the right of it. Though if ye say that to another soul, I'll have yer hide. I should have trusted ye to find the right woman. All these years, working yerself to death with no one to warm yer bed at night."

"Ma," he said, taking a step toward her, "that's what I wanted to talk to you about. About Aster."

"Ach, look at me, son." She set her knitting down to wipe her eyes with the ever-present handkerchief. "I'm a right mess. It's just I'm so pleased. I'd given up hope."

"Please don't cry. I can't bear that." His heart ached when he thought of how much his Ma had endured in her life, but she'd only ever wept when her children were hurt.

"Now, none of yer fussing at me. I'll do as I please. I dinnae need yer leave."

"I didn't mean that." He shuffled uneasily from foot to foot.

"I can trust the lass to take care of ye while I go to yer sister's. Her time's coming soon, and she'll need her Ma."

He twisted his mouth in what he hoped was a smile as he imagined his baby sister facing that greatest trial. "Of course. Martha needs you."

"Aye, she does. Ye all do. Thank Heaven I'm here to set ye right now and again."

"That's true." He turned to leave the room, not trusting his own eyes to stay dry. He stopped as he reached the bottom of the stairs. "I do love you, Ma."

"Well of course ye do."

He shook his head and climbed the stairs. He would have to tell his mother the truth, but not tonight. The muscles in his shoulders were tight, his back was sore, and he longed to soak in the tub rather than the quick scrub and rinse in the rigged rain barrel shower out back. If it hadn't been for Aster in his bed, he'd probably have skipped bathing all together. As it was, he was dead on his feet.

Even the hard floor by the window tempted him onward. A pillow and a blanket was all a man needed. He turned the handle slowly and opened the bedroom door, certain Aster was long abed, but was met with an empty room lit up as bright as day.

"Aster," he called, knowing full well she wasn't there. He scratched his head, his hair still damp from the shower. The bed was wedged tight to the window. Why would she have rearranged the furniture without him? He strode to the bed, intending to move it back into place, and stopped abruptly. One end of the bedsheets was tied to the back leg of the bed and the other was looped over the windowsill.

Betrayed

Henrietta

Henrietta stole a glance at the man riding next to her, clearly visible in the early dawn hours after a night of slow, careful travel across rocky terrain. He'd been right to be cautious, and she should feel grateful for his presence. She was grateful, truly, but he wasn't the man she wanted to spend the night with. That fateful night she and Duke were together, alone, out here in the wilderness, made her cheeks heat with embarrassment.

Cash had found her saddling her mare Ginger earlier and had insisted upon riding with her once she'd made it clear she intended to ride out with or without him. Despite his initial warnings, he'd soon slipped into his naturally easy demeanor. She shouldn't feel guilty—she had looked everywhere for Duke, had even slipped back up to the house to peer into the first-floor windows, but had spied only Bridget in the living room knitting in her rocking chair. Yet the bile rising in the back of her throat was not nausea from hours rocking slowly in the saddle, but the bitter taste of shame.

She should have waited.

"There it is. The trail to the river." Cash nudged his horse onto a beaten path twisting beneath pine trees soaring to the sky.

The land changed dramatically in New Mexico Territory. Stark desert yielded to verdant valleys bursting with color and life. Deer grazing on tufts of grass lifted their heads and watched them as they rode past, curious and unafraid. Dawn brought with it vibrance and renewal, painted across the skies. She'd never seen such wide skies, stretching from horizon to horizon with only the mountains disrupting the view.

They picked their way through the woods to the remains of their camp. Had it only been a few days earlier that she and Duke had been here? She shook away the guilt threatening to seize her in its grip. She was on a mission. Find the reticule, ride back home, and tell Duke everything. She'd give him her trust, and together they would decide on the best path forward to protect his family and to help a child she'd never met, but had felt such a kinship to, that Henrietta had risked everything to help her.

Henrietta dismounted and passed the reins to Cash. "I'll be right back," she said as she picked her way through rocks and fallen logs toward the sound of rushing water. She fought the urge to scan the ground for thin, flat stones. There'd be time for that later.

She headed directly to the spot a few feet from the river where she'd left her belongings, but there was no handbag there. Her pulse leapt. *It had to be there.* She kneeled on the ground and ran her hands across rocks and scrub of grass and found...nothing. Leaning back, she closed her eyes and stilled her breathing, as she often had before playing piano in one of the many recitals she'd performed in as a child.

Determined and patient, she crawled forward and pushed rocks out of the way, methodically searching the ground inch by inch. She nudged a rock aside, exposing camel-colored velvet. It had been here all along. No thief had stolen it. No one had even known it was here or the secret it guarded.

Today would be different. She would share the secret and unburden her heart and her mind because she'd found someone to share it with. Someone who knew what it was to have your life upended in a single moment. It was like playing the wrong note on the piano, where the piece, perfect in its beginning, became forever flawed, dissonant, and disconnected from its original beauty. But unlike a song where she could simply start again from the beginning, her choice weeks ago had set her on a journey she could not stray from. And she couldn't go back.

With music, she'd always played solo. What if she'd played in a duet? Would a partner have lent her the courage to continue playing? She smiled and shook her head. There was no going back in time. Her mother would tell her to remember what Thoreau had written, 'You must live in the present, launch yourself on every wave, find your eternity in each moment'.

She clutched the reticule to her breast and rose to start the short journey back to camp. Perhaps she had time to practice skipping stones before they left. If nothing else, she could show Duke how much she'd improved. She scooped up every flat, two-inch stone she could find.

By the fifth stone, she'd begun to get the feel of the movement. Cash joined her by the eighth. By the fifteenth, her rocks were bouncing across the water three or four times before they plummeted. Still, Cash's throws were better, more consistent, though he seemed to think it was just as amusing when the rocks sank to the bottom on the first or second bounce. He found everything amusing, smiling and laughing, recanting wild stories of his gambling escapades, even women he'd met in his travels.

His voice faded into the breeze as she focused on the feel, the weight, the grip between her fingers. She cursed the dratted gloves she kept on. If Duke had been there, she would have stripped them off. He'd seen her scars up close and hadn't shied away.

As though her thoughts bid him near, his voice broke through her reverie and Cash's constant chatter. She smiled and prepared to show him how much she'd improved, though she wasn't nearly good enough yet, but Duke wasn't looking at her. His eyes were fixed on his brother, and they burned with anger.

"Morning," Cash said, his wicked grin growing wider.

Duke's lips were clenched in a tight line. Wyatt walked out of the woods, swung his head from one brother to another, and then grabbed

Duke's arm. Duke shook him off, charged Cash and punched him in the jaw, knocking his younger brother onto his backside in the river.

"What the hell?" Cash floundered in the water as he tried to regain his footing.

"You never could let anyone else have anything. Always taking what's not yours."

"What are you on about?" Cash glared at his brother.

A flicker of Duke's eyes in her direction broke through her shock. "Duke," she said in a placating tone as she moved toward him. "You don't understand."

Duke glanced at her, and the coldness in his gaze stopped her in her tracks. "I understand plenty."

"No, you don't. I forgot something, and Cash offered to help me," she said.

"I'm sure he did, stealing you away in the middle of the night." His voice was flat and unyielding.

She threw the stone down at her feet with a smack. "You're an idiot," she breathed as she stalked past him.

He didn't reach out, didn't try to stop her, and didn't follow. That hurt more than his assumption that she'd allowed herself to be seduced by his brother.

She ignored Wyatt's scowling face and mounted her horse, her reticule fastened tightly to her wrist. She'd started this mission alone, and if that's how it would end, then so be it.

Duke

A DRIPPING WET CASH rubbed his jaw, then spat a wad of blood onto the rocky ground. He opened his mouth wide a few times, then said, "Feel better now?"

Duke clenched his fists and took another step forward.

"Whoa." Wyatt grabbed Duke's jacket and pulled him away from their brother.

"Aster left her handbag out here and she was in a panic thinking someone was going to steal it," Cash said.

"If that's true, then why didn't she come to me?"

"She did! Said she'd looked everywhere but couldn't find you. Did you really think I was running off with your new bride?"

"I wouldn't put it past you," Duke said under his breath.

Cash barked a short laugh. "I made one mistake, and you'll never let me forget it."

"You betrayed me."

Cash shook his head. "It was a kiss."

"She was my wife!" Duke took another step forward, only to be caught by Wyatt.

Cash took a deep breath. "I was an eighteen-year-old kid, and I was drunk."

"You're always drunk," Duke snarled.

"At least I'm having a good time drinking with my friends. I don't sit alone in the dark nursing a glass of whiskey as if it's my damned salvation," Cash said with a sneer.

"That's enough," Wyatt said, stepping between his brothers. "What Cash said is true. Aster was looking for you. I saw her."

Duke gaped at his older brother in disbelief. "Why didn't you say that before?"

Wyatt lifted an eyebrow. "You weren't in a listening mood."

Cash took off his jacket and gave it a good shake, spraying water at his brothers. "And as far as what we were doing...most of the time she talked about you. Wanted to practice skipping stones so she could show off for you. I don't know why she bothered."

"I...uh...I don't know what to say." Duke took off his hat and ran his thumb along the crease in the top.

"You know what's funny?"

"Cash," Wyatt warned.

"No, he needs to hear this. You wonder why we were all shocked when you brought a wife home? 'Cause none of us, not even Ma, could believe a girl as sweet as Aster would marry you."

Duke staggered back as though he were the one who'd been struck. "Is that true?" he asked Wyatt.

His older brother shrugged. "You...you changed when Judith died. And look, man, I don't blame you. But you pushed us away, all of us, even Martha, who was just a kid. You're so angry and bitter all the time."

Duke nodded. "Got it."

"Come on, brother." Wyatt tried to pat him on the shoulder, but Duke shrugged him away.

"So, you're saying I'm a jackass?"

"Yeah, pretty much." Cash laughed, then winced and grabbed his jaw.

"Shut your trap." Wyatt glared at their younger brother, then turned back to Duke. "Nah, you're just a man who got dealt a bad hand, but you've got a second chance."

"And you're screwing it up," Cash said.

Duke threw his brother a glare, but his words stung. Because they were true. He and Aster weren't married; they weren't anything, yet he'd still acted like a jealous fool.

She was right.

He was an idiot.

Wanted

Henrietta

Henrietta snatched her hand back when Susanna tried to give her a sympathetic pat. It was instinctual. Henrietta had her gloves on. She always did, even when it was just the ladies in the room. The harsh truth was that women could be far more vicious than men, with their side-long glances and their loud whispers.

She tried to cover her strange behavior by retying the bonnet under her chin. If Susanna noticed, she didn't mention it. They sat side by side on the wooden bench on the arcade outside the hotel. One glance at the dining room had been enough to turn Henrietta's stomach with a dizzying memory.

"You were right to come to me," Susanna said with a gentle smile, her lips red enough to be rouged.

"I..." Henrietta tightened the reticule around her wrist for the third time in an hour. She regretted sharing the incident at the river with her new friend. It felt like a betrayal of sorts, though she couldn't imagine why. "Do you think I should have stayed?"

"I might have." Susanna cocked her head to the side and grinned. "It would have been exciting to see men fighting. Brothers at that."

Henrietta shook her head. "No, it was horrible watching Duke's family tearing itself apart over a stupid misunderstanding."

"Your family."

"What?" Henrietta shot her friend a questioning look.

"They're your family now."

Aster bit her lip and looked everywhere but at her friend. Perhaps she should confide in Susanna. How easy it would be to give her troubles to someone else, someone who would make the difficult choices for her. Until a month ago, she'd never decided anything more serious than the dress to wear for a party, not even the man she would marry. Did she want to be that woman anymore?

"Aster?"

"Sorry. I was a million miles away."

"In Boston?" Susanna asked.

"Where?"

"Didn't you say you were from Boston?"

Did she? It was hard to remember what she'd told whom, but she wouldn't have mentioned Boston. She'd spent only a few weeks there, and that had been years ago.

Henrietta smiled triumphantly as she recalled the story she first invented for the Martins. "No, not Boston. Cranston. It's in Rhode Island."

"That's right. Do you miss it?"

"Cranston?" Henrietta's smile faltered slightly. "No. My family is gone."

"Oh dear, how thoughtless of me. But surely you have friends you must miss desperately."

"Yes, but now I have you," Henrietta said. "I can't tell you how much I appreciate you listening to me ramble on about all my problems."

"I think it's a matter of perspective. I wish I had two men willing to fight over me."

Aster shifted on the seat. "Yes, well, I'm not sure it had much to do with me."

"Of course it did. Why else would a man spend all night tracking you?" Susanna's voice dripped with envy, catching her off-guard.

"Did," Henrietta paused as she considered Susanna's wistful expression. "Did something happen to you?"

When Susanna looked away, clearly trying to avoid her gaze, Henrietta continued, "Did a man...hurt you?"

Susanna smiled bitterly. "You needn't concern yourself with me. I was a different woman. It was a different life."

"I'm sorry. If you ever want to confide in me, I'm here."

They sat in companionable silence, each caught up in their own memories. Henretta's brief anger with Duke was long gone, leaving only sadness in its wake. She was the cause of so much trouble for him and his family. She'd asked him to shelter her, to lie to his family, to offer refuge to outlaws, and now she'd been the cause of an actual fistfight between them. She couldn't do this anymore. She wouldn't.

Henrietta stood quickly. "I shouldn't be here."

Susanna yanked on her hand, trying to pull her back down to the bench. "Of course, you should. Stay here with me, make him come to you on his knees, offering the world to get you back." She lowered her voice. "Hold out for jewelry."

Henrietta was happy her friend had wrenched herself back from whatever painful memory she'd been snared in. "No. I'd best go back. But thank you."

"I'll be here if you change your mind."

Henrietta looked at her oddly. "Isn't your uncle coming to fetch you?"

Susanna's eyes were big, black orbs. "I didn't tell you. He's been ill.

"Oh, Susanna, that's awful. Here I am going on and on about my problems, and I didn't even bother to ask after you. Will you forgive me?"

Her friend nodded, then offered a weak smile. "I'm sure all will be well. It was nice to turn my mind to something else."

"I shall come back to check on you." Henrietta grabbed Susanna's hand and squeezed it hard. "I promise."

As she headed down the arcade to where she'd left her mare, Henrietta heard the distinct, booming voice of Mr. Martin emanating from Tunstall's Mercantile and Bank. She waited for a small herd of cattle to pass, flanked by a few cowhands, before crossing the street. How long did it take to sell a few cows? Surely, Rosalie would be heading back to Lincoln before long. She shook her head. Either way, Henrietta would soon be rid of this burden, and Duke and his family would be rid of her.

"Mrs. Martin," she called to her friend as she entered the store, but Mrs. Martin was so intent on her shopping she didn't hear Henrietta approach.

The woman was bent over a counter covered in baby gowns: white, blue, and pink. Henrietta's heart lifted as she considered how lucky this child was to have such a doting grandmother. It wasn't until Henrietta pointed out a particularly fine shirt with delicate smocking that her friend looked up at her, clearly startled.

"Oh, my dear, how have you been?" Without waiting for an answer, she continued in a loud voice, "Mr. Martin, it is Miss Blue."

"Miss Blue," the vicar bellowed. Several townspeople looked up from their shopping to see what the commotion was about.

Henrietta smiled wanly, hoping Jameson was long gone. If he were anywhere in town, he would have heard Mr. Martin shouting her name. She hadn't seen the agent since that first day in town. Perhaps he'd latched onto some other unfortunate woman to harass.

"I suppose you have good news to share?" Henrietta asked, gesturing at the baby clothes.

"The best, though the poor child is quite small, not like our own dear boys. Isn't that right, Arnold?"

"What was that, Bertha?"

Mrs. Martin continued on without answering the poor vicar, chatting about the limited offerings of yarn, the benefits of swaddling, the need to be up and about as soon as possible after giving birth. When she paused to take a breath, Henrietta asked about their son.

"Oh, he's quite well, and completely taken with the child, holding the babe for hours at a time. It feels just like yesterday when my own children were young and we were the ones pacing back and forth all night long."

"Quite strong!" Mr. Martin yelled.

"Indeed. He is strong. Why, I was just saying to my daughter-in-law, a wisp of a girl, how the boy would likely grow even taller than his father, though it is hard to imagine it now. How time does fly." She swiped at a tear on her cheek. "Look at me. All sentiment. What must you think of me, Miss Blue?"

"I am delighted—"

"What?" Mr. Martin asked.

"I said," Henrietta yelled, "I am thrilled for you both."

"Yes, yes, Bill's a fine name, but not for our boy!"

Henrietta nodded and smiled as they regaled her with stories of the child's antics, though he couldn't have been more than a few weeks old. She let her mind drift as the two bantered, gazing around the store where Rosalie worked. She could almost imagine her cousin standing behind the counter, pointing out the vast array of buttons laid out in tin boxes or fishing lemon drops out of an enormous glass jar.

Henrietta perused the store for a pitcher to replace the one she'd broken when her gaze landed on several posters placarded on the wall next to the door. One page flapping in the slight breeze streaming through the open doorway caught her attention, freezing her to the spot. It read, 'Wanted for Murder. $1,000 Reward.' Under the words was a rough, hand-drawn sketch of Arthur, the injured man in the guest bedroom at Twisted Oak Ranch.

Begging her leave with promises to visit the fort as soon as possible, she crossed the busy store to stand in front of the posters. Casting a furtive glance around her, she ripped the paper off the wall, folded it quickly, and stuffed it into her purse.

Henrietta wasted no time finding and mounting her mare and pressing her leg against the horse's flank. She'd ridden her entire life but never on a mount this responsive to the barest touch. Duke must have spent hours training the mare. Henrietta had the strangest longing to watch him, to learn from him. He clearly loved horses as much as she did.

She nudged Ginger again, and the horse sprang into a bouncy trot. As the town sped by, she spied a man in a loud suit walking down the arcade on the other side of the street. The darned detective hadn't left town after all. She slumped in the saddle as if that might hide her from the agent, but she needn't have worried. His gaze was firmly fixed on something or someone behind her. Despite the traffic, she pressed her leg against Ginger's flank harder, urging the horse to a lope.

She would turn herself into the man, but not until she'd made amends to Duke and his family. And not before she warned them of the storm coming.

Duke

IT WAS EASY ENOUGH to pick out her trail through the broken underbrush and trampled grass. She'd made no attempt to hide her passage, nor should she have. Aster was entirely blameless. Duke's anger was all internally focused, as it should have been from the moment he'd discovered her missing. There was no need to give her the attention due a wife, but she'd deserved better than his careless disregard and then his childish reaction when she'd done no more than her right as a free woman.

And maybe that was the problem. He'd fallen so easily into the role of distant husband when she wasn't even his wife. And she'd shown only kindness—to him, to his family, and to the feckless Regulators who'd descended upon them in the middle of the night.

He used the solitary ride through the wild country to calm his jangled nerves, breathing in the sweet smell of a wildflower summer. The hills were blanketed with soft pink buttercups, showy goldenrod, and the woman's namesake, blue aster. The delicate violet petals clustered together atop a plant hearty enough to survive the scorching heat and months without a single drop of rain, followed by fierce snowstorms.

He reined in Dapple and dismounted near the field of flowers. She was surely a woman who'd grown up surrounded by lilies, irises, and hothouse roses. He was confident she'd been pursued by more intellectual, wealthier, and probably far more sensitive men than him. Who was he kidding? She'd no more look at him than at the witch's hair vine, which wrapped itself around healthy plants and strangled the life out of them.

And yet, he still knelt in the field of wildflowers to gather a bouquet of yellow and blue asters, careful not to tread on the crimson Indian paintbrush and the delicate Sierra Blanca lupine. Duke considered the flowers in his fist. Would a woman like Aster appreciate the lovely, wild tangle of blooms? Or would she see only a sad, wilted bundle of weeds, knocked down by wind and pelted by rain?

He didn't have long to wait for the answer. A few miles outside of Lincoln, he saw the dust kick up around a horse and a familiar figure as she rode into view. Her face mirrored his own fear and determination. Without a word, she slipped out of the saddle and waited for him to do the same. He hid the bouquet behind him as they walked side by side, guiding Ginger and Dapple down the hard-packed dirt road toward Twisted Oak Ranch.

"Aster, I wanted to say I'm awful sorry about earlier. I had no right to fall into a jealous rage. I guess the pretending just felt a little too real."

She peered up at him, then ducked her head, a rosy blush heating her cheeks. "I'm sorry, too."

"You weren't the ass."

She smiled. "No. That was all you." She tossed the reins against her palm and cast him a sidelong glance. "I'm sorry I caused an argument between you and your brothers."

"Don't be. It's been brewing for a while now. Cash and I have never seen eye-to-eye on much of anything."

"I don't know what it's like to grow up in a houseful of children. When my Aunt Louisa died and Rosalie came to live with us, I felt so ashamed because I was happy while Rosalie was so sad and forlorn. With her arrival, I gained a sister and a best friend. We couldn't be more different, much like you and Cash."

"I can't imagine you and Rosalie getting into a fistfight."

She giggled. "No, but we did have our tiffs, mostly about going to parties. She detested them."

"And you?"

"I loved them. They were a dizzying whirlwind of color and music, and conversation. And the dancing, I loved the dancing. When I waltzed, I felt like I was floating in a dream."

"I bet you never had trouble finding a partner."

"No," she said, frowning. "No, I never had trouble. Though it helps when your father is one of the most influential men in Philadelphia."

"If I'd known that, I might have asked him to invest in the ranch." He attempted a light tone, but that was difficult with the financial stress of growing a business from nothing.

"Did Rosalie never mention it?"

"I don't think your family was too pleased when Shaw came and stole her away."

She pursed her lips. "My father *was* upset. Her marriage caused a bit of a scandal since she was engaged to another man. My father may be the head of the family, but my mother is its beating heart. She is a romantic soul, but barely a week went by before he was asking after my errant cousin."

"I don't know Rosalie well, but I know my brother loves her. He would die for her."

"He almost did," she said with a shiver. "Oh my goodness, I almost forgot." She opened her handbag and pulled out the creased paper she'd taken from town. She shook it out so Duke could see the sketch of the very man they'd helped a few nights earlier, a man who had put Duke and his entire family in harm's way.

He took the page from her, forgetting for a moment that he still held the bouquet in his hand.

"Oh, are those for me?"

"It's nothing. Toss them if you like," he handed her the flowers and focused on Arthur's image on the page. They'd run out of time. The man had to leave.

She buried her nose in the blossoms. "They smell like the forest after a rainstorm. Thank you."

"They reminded me of you."

"Because of the name I gave myself?"

"If you like." He cleared his throat, suddenly uneasy in the presence of this woman who delighted in racing horses, smelling wildflowers, and skipping stones.

"I had to come up with a name in a hurry. When I saw a woman holding a bouquet on the train, I remembered the nickname Rosalie gave me when I was young. Aster. She said the color reminded her of my eyes."

He stole a peek at her face and then looked away again. He could get lost in those eyes. "She's right."

They walked along in silence, content with each other's company. It would be twilight by the time they reached the house, and the skies were already tinged pink.

As if hearing his thoughts, she said, "What makes it that color?"

"I don't know, but it makes me think of summer picnics and lazy days fishing and horses chasing each other across the plains. How about you?"

"It looks like freedom."

He nodded. "I reckon you're right."

She sighed deeply and cast a worried glance at him. "I saw that Pinkerton agent in town today, and I made a decision."

He stopped, turned to face her, and swallowed hard. "You want to turn yourself in?"

She fidgeted with the reins and refused to meet his gaze. "Yes, but that's not all."

"Then what is it? I know I behaved like a bastard earlier, but you can trust me. I promise."

Her eyes glistened with tears, and he swore his heart stopped.

She said, "I'm counting on it."

Truth

Henrietta

Henrietta sat down on Duke's duster and watched while he unsaddled the horses and led them to the little mountain stream. They were in a clearing surrounded by fir and pecan trees and cottonwoods. Butterflies floated around her, seeking the sweet nectar from the Indian paintbrush and wild beebalm. Bees buzzed around her own cluster of asters, and she waved them away.

Her heart pounded restlessly in her chest as she watched Duke caring for the horses, checking their legs and hooves, whispering sweet nothings in their ears. What would it be like to be treated like that? With care, with compassion, to be the one he shared all his secrets with? She unbuttoned her gloves and tugged them off, one finger at a time. He'd trusted her with his deepest sorrow. And now she would share her own secret.

When he crouched a few feet away from her, she scooted over on the coat and patted the ground next to her. He sat down and stretched his long legs out, then leaned back on his elbow.

"I don't know where to start." She peered at his face, shadowed by the wide brim of his hat.

"I've always heard it's best to start at the beginning, but I reckon you can start wherever you please and I'll still be here."

She smiled sadly. "It's not really my story, but I'll do the best I can." She took a breath before continuing, "I told you Rosalie moved in with us after her mother passed."

He nodded, his warm brown eyes lending her strength.

"Her father, my uncle, was devastated. I don't think he ever fully recovered from my Aunt Louisa's death. He was so dedicated to his family, but when he lost his wife, he disappeared into his work in the army. And, Rosalie, well, she was left to survive the best she could." Henrietta paused in an effort to still her mind.

"I can't imagine."

"The reason I mention all of this is to let you know Rosalie lost both her parents that day, and in many ways she still sees them as a nine-year-old would."

"She idolizes them?" He took her hand, and heat and strength poured into her from the simple gesture.

"Exactly, and with her father gone now as well, she'll never see them as they were, with all their wonderful qualities, yes, but with their flaws as well. And we all have flaws."

"I know I've got my fair share."

She smiled and squeezed his hand. "Shortly before my wedding..." He pulled his hand back, but she held firm. "I went to my father's study to ask for money to buy something—I don't remember what—it doesn't matter. He wasn't there, but his safe was open so I thought I'd take what I needed and leave him a note...I am *not* a thief."

His lips twitched, but he held his tongue.

"In my father's safe I found a letter from my uncle. I could tell right away that it was from him. He'd written from campaign often enough for me to recognize his writing."

She broke off and stared at the tops of the trees and the swallows darting from branch to branch. How lovely it would be to have the freedom to flit and fly wherever she pleased. "I read the letter. It was a horrible breach of privacy, and I regret it every day, but the envelope was open, and I thought...well, I have no excuse. I was just curious why it was in the safe."

She drew in a long, ragged breath, then said the next words in a rush, "He must have written it before Rosalie came to Lincoln to visit. He spoke of the illness that had gripped his lungs. Consumption." She swallowed hard.

Duke nodded in sympathy. "A foul disease."

"Yes, it is. It took my Aunt Louisa and my Uncle George from us." She licked her lips and searched for the right words. "My uncle spoke of a child in Texas he'd been supporting for years, though he wouldn't say why."

She broke off, suddenly shy and embarrassed to be speaking of such private matters. "I had the impression that the child was his illegitimate daughter."

Duke didn't appear to be shocked by her words, which helped her gather her resolve to continue the story. "My uncle begged my father to continue to look after the child, perhaps even invite her into our home. When I asked my father about the letter, he dismissed my concerns and told me not to trouble myself with it."

"But you wouldn't let it go?" Duke asked, tracing slow circles on the back of her hand, sending shivers up her arm.

She shook her head. "Normally, I would have. I'm not," she frowned, "I'm not a strong person."

Duke barked a laugh and then apologized quickly. "I beg to differ. I wager you'd best any man I know in an arm wrestle."

Henrietta felt the tightness in her chest ease as she imagined a line of men waiting to test their strength against hers. "Not that kind of strength. Up until that moment, I'd never had a single argument with either of my parents, not even when my father had refused to attend Rosalie's wedding."

"I don't recall much of my visit to Philadelphia." Seeing Henrietta's crestfallen face, he continued quickly, "I was pre-occupied with finding financial backing for the ranch. But I seem to remember your father being at the church that day."

"Yes, well, that was my mother's doing, not mine.

"Ah. Ma's can be mighty forceful."

She smiled weakly, struggling to compare her calm, refined mother with the fierce Bridget. "We fought. It was terrible." She looked up at him to gauge his reaction, and he nodded for her to continue. "I told him that if he wouldn't send for the child, then I wouldn't marry the man he'd chosen for me."

"So, you're not in love with...?" He sat up slowly and interlaced his fingers with hers, brushing his thumb along her knuckles, sending a tingle up her arm.

"Jonathon? I thought I was. But as the wedding day neared, the less sure I became." She tore her gaze away from him and stared into the trees. "You must understand, I've always done what was expected. *Always*. And my parents want this marriage. He's from a good family; he's well respected, and he has a promising future in politics. There's nothing inherently wrong with him. There's just no..." She met his gaze again, blushing.

"Spark?"

She nodded, then cleared her throat. She had to finish her story before she lost her courage. "My father flew into a rage. I've never seen him that angry."

"Were you frightened?" He sat up, his muscles tensed.

She shrugged. "Maybe a little, but I was angry too. Angry from all the things that had built up in me over the years, all the things I was forbidden from doing, all the times I'd smiled and gone along with whatever was demanded of me. All the times I'd done what I was told to do without ever being asked what I thought or felt or wanted."

"What happened?"

"I was sent to my room as though I were still a little girl." She laughed derisively. "While I sat there stewing, I made a plan. At dinner, I was pleasant and appeasing as always. When my mother took me for my dress fitting a few days later, I went with no complaints. But all the while I planned my escape."

She took a deep breath. "On the day of my wedding, I traveled to the church with my parents. I went to the small alcove to pray while the guests were seated. Once I was alone, I snuck out of the church, hired a buggy and went home." She hesitated. "I'm not proud of this next part of the story. I want you to know that."

Duke inched closer. "We've all done things we're not proud of," he said quietly.

"I retrieved the bag I'd packed the night before and went to my father's study. It was easy enough—all the servants were busy preparing the wedding feast. I tossed his papers around to make it seem like there had been a scuffle, and I tore off a piece of my wedding dress and left it on the desk. There was a large marble statue I used to snap the handle off my father's safe. Along with the letter from my uncle, I took a dozen other pieces of correspondence and quite a bit of money."

She bit her lip and glanced at Duke, expecting to see disappointment in his eyes, but found only a sad understanding. "I traveled across the country to find Rosalie. If the child is her sister, she'll know what to do. I didn't take the money for myself. You need to know that."

He nodded. "I never believed you were a thief."

Her chest swelled with those simple words. "The child needs the money more than my father does. He has bank accounts full of cash."

"Why are you telling me this now? Don't get me wrong, I'm grateful you are. But I reckon there's a reason," he said.

"I don't want to lie anymore. Not to you. I hate myself for coming between you and your brothers. And I hate that I put your family at risk by insisting you shelter outlaws. You've had enough heartbreak in your life. I refuse to cause you more."

He touched her cheek, his calloused fingers so gentle against her skin. A tremor of excitement flooded through her body.

"You're the best thing that's happened to me in five years," he murmured, rubbing his thumb along her bottom lip.

She leaned into his touch, wanting to be closer, craving more. An image—no more than that—of sitting astride him, her tongue in his mouth, flashed before her. Heat rushed into her cheeks. She pulled away and covered her face with her hands.

"I'm sorry," he said. "I thought...it doesn't matter."

She peered at him through her fingers. "I told you I recalled that day, and I thought I had remembered everything, but..." She bit her lip. "I just recalled something else, and I'm mortified."

He gently pulled her hands away from her face. "Nothing happened. I promise."

"Only because you kept your wits when I had completely lost mine. You must think I'm a...oh I can't even say it."

"I think you're brave and kind and so, so beautiful. You take my breath away."

"Oh," she breathed.

"I was a jealous fool for chasing after you in the middle of the night. I have no right to expect you to feel the same way about me. I'm a bitter, angry man." He snorted. "Just ask my brothers."

"They're wrong." She inched closer to him and reached out to touch his face, to feel his skin.

"That tickles," he said as she brushed her fingers along the whiskers on his jaw.

She smiled and chucked him under the chin, but he captured her hand and brought it to his mouth, kissing first her fingers, then her palm, and then the inside of her wrist. Her pulse jumped wildly, sending shivers up her arm.

"My scar..."

"Beautiful," he murmured, continuing his exploration of her arm, tracing the ragged edge of the burn with his mouth.

His light touch brought excruciating pleasure to the delicate, sensitive skin. She longed to strip away her blouse so he could continue his journey of soft, warm kisses and his itchy whiskers on her bare arm, her shoulder, her neck. She craved his touch on every bit of skin which had been hidden away from the sun, from her friends, even from her family.

"Duke?"

"Yes?" he said, not ceasing his kisses.

"I think you're beautiful too."

He rocked back and let out a laugh loud enough to send the birds skittering away. "Come here."

She edged closer, and he pulled her onto his lap, placing his hands on her waist. This time when she tilted her head up, closed her eyes, and puckered her lips, he kissed her. It was even better than her wild, fleeting memories.

When she opened her mouth, he touched the tip of his tongue against hers, sending tremors of sweet agony through her body.

Duke

HE PULLED HER TIGHTLY against him as he helped Aster out of the saddle. He leaned down and brushed her thick chestnut hair away to give him better access to the nape of her neck, to kiss her along her hairline. She leaned back, pressing back against him, sending a desperate need through his body. Reluctantly, he tore himself away from her. She faltered, then regained her footing.

"I have to see to the horses." He stared at her lips, so full and lush, bruised from their fervent kisses.

"I'll wait for you," she said, peering up at him through lowered lashes.

He couldn't resist. He leaned down and pulled her into his arms once more, crushing her to him. She eagerly responded to his kiss. So lost in her, it was several moments before men's whoops broke through his befuddled state.

He released her and threw a dirty look at his brothers standing on the front porch. Cash had an annoying smirk on his face. Wyatt looked thoughtful but pleased.

"Which one of you idiots wants to help me with the horses?"

Cash begged off and made a production of grabbing his jaw. Wyatt shook his head at his brother's antics, then ventured down the steps toward them.

Aster squeezed his hand and gave him a worried look. He smiled and whispered, "I'll be right there." She nodded and lifted her chin, her face once more a mask of calm determination. She smoothed her skirts and adjusted her bonnet, then strode into the house, pausing only long enough for Cash to open the door.

They'd decided on the way to tell his family who she was, if not exactly why she'd come, or why they'd been masquerading as a married couple. The lies were eating at Aster. He knew it was the right decision to trust his family, but he'd be lying to himself if he said he hadn't enjoyed the closeness thrust upon them.

He nodded to Wyatt as they led the horses to the old barn, too small by half for the current stock.

"Seems like you made things right with your gal," Wyatt said.

Your gal. Two words that held a life-shifting meaning for him. Duke wanted Aster to be his, completely and openly. She'd chiseled a tiny fissure into the walls he'd built around his heart. One more blow and the barricade would shatter. Terrifying.

Wyatt pulled the barn door wide open, flooding the space with light from the late afternoon sun. Duke led the horses inside and looped their reins around a post, then uncinched Dapple's saddle. The horse nickered and danced, eager to be home, in sight of the feedbox overflowing with sweet hay.

"Easy, boy." Duke hefted the saddle off and strolled past the stalls, each one occupied, the comforting scent of horses, hay, and manure filling his nostrils. He headed to the tack room, only to come to an abrupt stop at the door, then pivoted and headed back to the full stalls and the unfamiliar horses in them, noses deep in feeding troughs.

"Wyatt? Who's here?"

"Yeah, was gonna tell you. That army captain friend of Shaw's is here with a few men looking for the Regulators who shot up some soldiers the other night."

"What?" He threw the saddle on an empty post and rushed out of the space. "Why didn't you tell me straight off?"

"It's fine. Ma's plying 'em with her cobbler and a heavy pour of applejack to wet their throats."

"How could you let Aster walk into that?" Duke ran past his brother back to the house.

Damn. All it took was Mellon putting two and two together—a new bride and a missing cousin. True, the two women didn't share much of a resemblance. Aster had thick, brown hair with a hint of gold, where Rosalie was a blonde. Still, when he looked closely, he saw the same set of jaw, the same defiant tilt of the head, and their voices shared that quick, clipped speech from the East Coast.

He slammed the door open with an car-splitting crash. Five heads swiveled in his direction, but his eyes were on Aster's ashen face, her baby-blue eyes wide and frightened.

"Shut that door and wipe yer feet before tracking in all that dust from the road. I raised ye better than to bust into a room, making such a fuss." Ma sat in her rocking chair with her hands wrapped around a full glass of applejack.

"Pardon, Ma." He closed the door behind him carefully.

She sniffed and took a swallow of the deceptively sweet and smooth liquor. There was enough alcohol in that tumbler to have most grown men under the table. He tried to make eye contact with Ma, but she'd already turned back to Captain Mellon and a slovenly man whose blue coat was covered in gold filigree. Mellon's glass was untouched on the coffee table, while the other officer's glass was practically empty.

Duke leaned against the back of Aster's chair and placed his hand on her shoulder. She gripped his hand, and he could feel the shaking even through the glove. "What's this all about, Mellon?"

"Going homestead to homestead searching for the killers I told you about," the other man said after draining the last of his glass. He held it out to Ma without even glancing her way, as though she were his servant, not the matriarch of the family serving him her finest brew.

"And you are?" Duke said, not bothering to hide his instant dislike for the man.

"Colonel Nathan Dudley, at your service." The man with rheumy eyes stood at attention, wavering slightly. Clearly, this wasn't his first drink of the day.

"Duke Gildownie. I reckon you've met everyone else."

The man grasped the back of the sofa and directed his gaze at Aster. "I met your wife." He bowed slightly, then, off balance, slid back to the cushions.

"When did all this happen?" Mellon said. "I saw you a few days ago, and you didn't mention anything about a mail-order bride. I mean no offense, ma'am."

Aster shook her head but didn't make a peep.

"You had a lot on your mind." Duke kept his tone flat and neutral, but Mellon abruptly sat back on the sofa, recalling whatever it was that had preoccupied him that day.

"Time for business," the Colonel said. "We are hunting a group of killers. With your family's history of supporting the Regulators, I wanted to search your property personally."

Duke cast a glance at Wyatt, who'd slipped into the room without a sound and now leaned casually against the front door. A quick turn of his head was all Duke needed to know they hadn't hidden the wounded man. They were at great risk. Aster's hand clenched his so tightly, he thought he might come away with bruises by the end of this conversation.

"Then you'd best get to it," Duke said.

Mellon and the Colonel started to stand when Duke continued in a drawl, "If you have a warrant, that is."

"We're talking about a murderer!" The Colonel's face turned as red as Duke's prized sorrel stud.

Wyatt pushed off the door and sauntered up to the group with his hand casually resting on the Colt revolver in his holster. His other brother chuckled. Both Duke and Wyatt shot Cash a dirty look. Ma simply refilled Dudley's now empty tumbler.

"Maybe. But I don't know you," Duke said. "And I sure as hell don't trust you. I was the one who pulled my brother Shaw out of that jail you had him in, illegally, I might add. I got no love for you or for your damned army."

Colonel Dudley downed the applejack, then slammed the tumbler down hard enough to shatter it, sending glass flying. Aster flinched and clenched his hand even tighter.

"We'll be back. With the sheriff." The Colonel stood and only wobbled slightly, grabbing hold of Mellon's shoulder to steady himself.

"You do that," Duke said through gritted teeth.

Ma rose and walked the Colonel to the front door as if their visit had been a pleasant afternoon between friends. Mellon hung back and waited for the two soldiers and Duke's brothers to leave.

"A word," the captain said, casting a glance at Aster, who sat paralyzed in her chair.

Duke nodded and strode to the other side of the room. "What's this about?"

"I don't know what you're playing at, but I'd bet my bottom dollar that 'your wife' is the missing girl from Pennsylvania."

Duke stared at him in stony silence.

"I spent too much time with Rosalie to not see the similarities between them. I can only assume the girl's safe with you."

Duke nodded and folded his arms in front of him. "Why are you telling me this?"

"Dudley may be a drunken ass, but he's not stupid. He'll put it together when he sobers up."

"Not saying you're right," Duke said. "But if you are, what would you recommend?"

"Assuming you haven't actually married the girl, keep playing the game and get rid of whoever it is you're hiding in this place. Dudley and Jimmy Dolan will have the place swarming by dawn."

Duke stuck out his hand. "You have my thanks."

Mellon grasped his hand and sighed. "Your family will be the death of me."

Duke smiled and glanced at Aster, watching the two of them warily from her perch, and his Ma, glaring at him from the front door. "You and me both."

Haunted

Henrietta

She should never have come here, never have forced herself upon a man who was still grieving from an unthinkable loss, never have invited death into his home. And that's what she'd done. She recognized that horrible Colonel Dudley from Rosalie's stories. He'd led the hunt for Shaw, ultimately arresting and torturing him for doing what any man would do—protecting the woman he loved.

She clenched her fists hard; the familiar pain allowed her to focus on the physical sensation, to calm her thoughts, and to wrestle her fear under control. The damage had been done. The only thing to do now was to move forward, to help Duke in whatever plan he'd devised. He'd been so strong, so defiant, and so darned clever. He'd been the voice of reason and clarity when chaos threatened to consume them. Even now, speaking with the captain, his eyes lingered on her, lending her courage.

She smoothed her skirts and stood, suppressing all the wild imaginings in her mind, and went to Duke. Despite her fear, her skin tingled with anticipation of his touch. She looped her arm in his and leaned into him. He looked down at her, his thick hair falling across his forehead. In the dim light, it looked a plain, dark brown, but in the outdoors where he thrived, his hair shone a burnished auburn. She had a vague memory of leaning over him and tangling her bare fingers in those locks and felt a desperate longing to do it again, to make the dreamlike image real and true.

The captain nodded to her as he left the home, pausing only to thank Bridget for her hospitality. How different he was from the Colonel. Why was it that men with less talent, less integrity, and less capability rose to the highest echelons?

Bridget stalked across the room, not bothering to hide the storm raging inside her. "We need to get that man out of here now." She held her hand up to forestall any argument. "I'll no have him put ye at risk, not now we've got a lass here we have to protect."

Duke grimaced. "Ma, we need to protect you too."

"Bah. I've no fear of that sodger coming in here, insulting me while drinking me out of house and home."

"I do," Henrietta said. "He holds great power, Mrs. Gildownie."

"Call me, Ma, dearie. 'Twould be my heart's desire to hear ye say it."

Henrietta felt a flutter of apprehension wrapped in the strangest desire to be part of this large and complicated family. "Ma," she whispered. And in that moment, it didn't feel like a lie. She didn't want it to be a lie.

"Two more daughters in the space of a month! I'll have to get on my old knees tonight to offer my thanks to God above. I'd given up hope, but never stopped praying this day would come. Ach, ye'll love our Rosie girl."

Bridget cocked her head to the side and considered Henrietta intently. "Ye do have a look about ye. Can't quite put my finger on it, but ye remind me of Rosie somehow."

It was her opening. She should tell Bridget now, but when she opened her mouth, the words caught in her throat. She didn't want to lose this woman's affection, and, truth be told, she didn't want to lose the fragile bond she'd forged with the man next to her.

The moment for confidence passed when the door flew open and Cash bounded toward them. "We got to get that man out of here."

"Mellon said they'd be back by dawn," Duke said, giving voice to her terror. She'd brought this upon them, and there was not a thing she could do to stop it.

"I'll saddle the horses," Wyatt called over his shoulder as he headed for the door.

"We'll help. Ma, can you and Aster get him ready to go?"

"Aye. Come with me, lass. We'll need to change that dressing and get it wrapped up tight."

Henrietta nodded and left the comfort of Duke's side, following Bridget out of the room and down the hallway to the bedroom where the Regulator lay, still immobile after only a few days of recovery. She tried to summon concern for the man, but fear for Duke and his family consumed all her capacity for compassion.

HOURS AFTER THE MEN had left and Bridget had retired to bed, Henrietta haunted the rooms of the ranch house, picking up abandoned dishes, straightening cushions, and collecting discarded articles of clothing to launder. She couldn't imagine resting her body, not when her mind darted from one terrifying image to another. Was the cruel Colonel Dudley lying in wait for them with guns drawn on the hunt for vengeance against the Regulators? Duke had said he would return once they were safely off the family land, but what if his horse had bolted and he was thrown to the ground? Was he even now alone and injured?

She couldn't have closed her eyes if she'd tried. Instead, she wandered from room to room until finally she ventured into a small room tucked at the back of the house, one she'd never dared enter before. It hadn't been forbidden, not exactly. Henrietta just had the gnawing fear it was a private place meant for Judith and Duke alone.

Tonight, she was on her own without anyone to see her, to hear her, and the lure of that closed door was as tempting as any apple in Eve's garden. She gripped the handle tightly, expecting the door to be locked, but it swung open without a sound. Henrietta ventured silently into the dark room, with only a single candle to light her way, casting ghostly shadows. A piano stood against the wall in the center of the formal parlor, filled not with rocking chairs and knitting needles, but with high wingback chairs of blue chintz. A glass-fronted cabinet boasted an assortment of fine bone China and a handsome silver teapot.

This was a woman's room. Judith.

Henrietta ran her fingers along the back of the settee, her eyes fixed on the cottage upright piano standing proudly against the far wall. She ignored the lure of the instrument dragging her across the room and instead focused on the picture frame sitting on top of the piano. It was too dark to make out the details of the photo, so she lit the candles in the candlesticks on either side of the keyboard.

The woman's face emerged from the gloom, beautiful, captured forever in her youth. Judith couldn't have been more than twenty years old when the photograph was taken. Her features were as delicate as a French porcelain doll, and her hair was coiled into an intricate design, adorned with flowers. She looked off to the side with a small smile as though the person she saw there was the most important in the world. Duke's wife had been a truly beautiful girl.

Henrietta placed the photograph back on the piano and wondered about this woman, Judith, who Duke had been so desperately in love with. Had she sat here in the same room, at the same keyboard, and played piece after piece? Had she loved listening to the brothers debate the quality of one particular stud over another? And would she despise knowing Henrietta had slipped into her life without invitation and with a lie in her heart?

Henrietta pressed her hands against her stomach to still the turbulence in her belly. She was an interloper here, in this woman's parlor, sitting at this woman's piano, and yet she felt an affinity with

Judith, taken before her time. Not for the first time, she wondered how Judith and the baby had died.

She removed her gloves opened the piano lid, and placed her hands atop the cool ivory keys. Without playing a sound, she moved her fingers up and down the keyboard, recalling the quick rhythm and smooth runs of a Bach minuet, but Bach had never been her favorite. The tempo was too even and held too little emotion. And yet, she'd played more Bach than any other composer. There was something soothing about the steady rhythm, the strict control of the crescendos and diminuendos, the expected resolution into G major.

She'd mastered Bach. Could play it in her sleep. In fact, there were years when she had fallen into dreams with her fingers tapping out the melody on the bedsheets. She'd soon expanded into Beethoven and Mozart. Although the music proved far more challenging, she knew constant repetition would soon bring her the perfection she'd come to expect from herself, even if it meant she practiced the same piece for weeks and weeks on end until her mother had begged her to play anything else.

The Romantics had been her downfall. How could she play a piece like Chopin's Fantaisie-Impromptu or even the simple works in Schumann's Kinderszenen, when every note could be held for an indefinite amount of time depending on the pianist's own desire? What if she chose wrong?

And yet, there in the darkened room, she felt the pull of Chopin and began to play a nocturne. With each run, each trill, her excitement built until her fingers tripped over a key and played a C-sharp by mistake. She continued the piece, recalling her tutor's instruction to never stop in the middle, but it was too late. The mistake had been made. She couldn't finish. So, she started at the beginning. Again and again, growing more and more frustrated as the night dragged on.

Duke

HE PUSHED OPEN THE front door just before dawn, dead tired and eager for a few hours' sleep, even though it meant bedding down on the hard wood floor. Halfway to the stairs, he heard a faint melody drifting from the parlor, a room he'd frequented only when he'd needed to feel Judith's presence, to beg, too late, for her forgiveness. He drifted through the house with his boots on, mindless of the trail of dirt he left in his wake.

The music propelled him forward to the closed door of the parlor he'd built for his late wife. As quietly as he could, he turned the brass handle and pushed open the door to find Aster bent over the piano, her fingers moving up and down the keyboard in a blur. Judith had been a fine pianist, but she would never have thought to attempt a piece of music as rich and complicated as this. He wasn't surprised by Aster's talent. She was a genteel lady, with access to the best tutors that money could buy. She was as out of place here as he had been strolling down the streets of Philadelphia. Duke had been a fool to think she might have been happy here, that their pretense of a marriage could be anything else.

He started to slip out of the room when the music paused. Aster cursed and began to play the piece again from the beginning; he thought. She played on, rocking back and forth over the keys as her fingers whirled from one side to the other until she stopped again.

"Damn it," she muttered. "Stupid, stupid, stupid."

As she started again, he could see dried, salty tears on her cheeks.

"Aster?"

Her fingers froze, a breath above the keys.

"It was sure pretty. I don't think I've ever heard anything quite like that."

"It was horrible," she said in a voice so soft he barely heard the words.

"What are you talking about?"

She twisted on the bench to look at him, her face cast in shadows from two candle stubs on either side of the piano. “It doesn’t matter. Did everything go as planned? Were you stopped?”

“No. I mean, yes. Everything is fine. I left Cash and Wyatt with Arthur deep in the Mescalero Reservation. They’ll make it to the hunting cabin by this evening.”

“Oh.” She glanced at the windows and the heavy drapes blocking the light. “Is it morning already?”

“Almost.” He ventured forward, hat in his hand. “Did you not sleep at all?”

She looked down at her hands, still resting on the keys. “No.”

“Why?” He took another step closer.

She shrugged. “I was worried.”

“I’m sorry.”

Aster whipped her head back to him, her forehead wrinkled with concern. “I’m the one who’s sorry. I brought all of this down on you. I kept thinking...what if something had happened to you? Or to Cash, or Wyatt, or even Arthur? It would have been my fault.” She drew a ragged breath. “All of it.”

“It was just a long night on the road.”

“Another sleepless night because of me.” Her pale eyes glistened in the candlelight.

“I’ll survive,” Duke said with a chuckle.

She smiled, and his heart quickened in his chest. Did she have any idea how breathtaking she was, sitting there at the piano, with her thick hair flowing down her back, her hands so graceful as they sat poised on the keys as if at any moment she might begin again.

“Will you play something else for me?”

She dropped her gaze and shook her head. “I don’t play for anyone anymore.”

“Why not?” He approached her. Despite their earlier kisses, he was hesitant to touch her, for fear she might bolt like a startled doe.

Her lips turned down at the corners. "When I was young, I thought—I dreamed—I might be good enough to perform the masters. But I wasn't. I'm not. I was foolish to even try."

"I'm no musician, so my opinion means less than nothing."

She patted the seat, and he slid next to her on the bench and laid his hat on the floor.

"Your opinion matters a great deal to me," she murmured.

He fought the urge to wrap his arms around her, to carry her to the settee and to make love to her then and there with no thought to the future. He cleared his throat and tried to ignore the soft curve of her breast brushing against his arm. "I've never heard anything so lovely. You're like the Pied Piper. I'd follow you anywhere."

She blushed and lowered her eyes, then murmured a dismissal.

"I wish you could see yourself through my eyes."

She smiled, her lips quivering. "You don't see me as I really am."

"Don't I?" He brushed a stray lock of hair from her face.

She shook her head.

"I see a woman who traveled across this vast country alone, hunted by a relentless hound. And you didn't do it for yourself, but for someone else."

"And I hurt a lot of people when I left."

"I know. And I'm sorry for that. I can see how much it's troubling you." Her hair hung loose across her shoulders, and he yearned to tangle his hands in the silky locks.

"Duke?"

"Hmm?" He stared at her lips, so lush and full it was all he could do to not taste them again.

"She was so lovely." Aster gestured to the framed photo of Judith.

"She was the prettiest girl I'd ever seen," he said with a wry smile, remembering the instant he'd laid eyes on her at the picnic. She'd been so young. He tore his mind away from the memory that haunted him day and night without ceasing.

Aster nodded, a serious expression on her face. "I feel her here, in this room."

He drew in a labored breath but couldn't find the words. Judith was here, in this room, in this house, everywhere he looked, always. *Haunting him.*

"Would she mind me here, do you think, playing the piano?"

He shook his head, unable to find his voice.

"She was practical that way?" Aster asked.

"Yes," he said hoarsely. The sad truth was that Judith hadn't cared for the piano or the parlor or the house he'd built for her. She hadn't wanted any of it.

"Duke." Aster touched his hand, and all thoughts of Judith slipped away. God forgive him, he burned for the woman sitting next to him on the piano bench.

"How did she die?"

It was like he'd been struck by a bullet, straight into his chest. Aster's words wrenched him back to that moment in the wilderness. Judith's agonizing cries for him still echoed in his ears.

"It's past time we got some sleep." He choked out the words, then strode from the room so he wouldn't have to face his betrayal in another woman's eyes.

Where There's Smoke

Henrietta

Duke was gone by the time she woke, long after the sun had reached its zenith. Henrietta had waited hours for him to come to their bedroom after they parted the night before, but she must have nodded off before he'd slipped inside, if he'd come back at all. The sunlight streamed through the open window, the beauty of the day mocking her misery, enveloping her as completely as the fog. It was time to face the truth—Duke was in love with Judith and would be forever. And why wouldn't he be? He'd built this home for her, had shared his dreams of the ranch with her, *had loved her*. And she'd borne him a son. Henrietta saw the woman's touches everywhere around her, from the wedding ring pattern on the quilt she lay beneath to the cheery gingham curtains to the engraved silver-handled brush on the dresser.

This was Judith's home, and Duke was her man, body and soul, forever. He was a handsome man with a kindness almost painful to watch knowing the loss he'd survived. And the ranch spoke of the man's ambition. If he'd wanted to marry, he would have had a dozen women vying for the position, each one more lovely and talented than she, with no horrific scar marking her as damaged, worthless.

He'd kissed her. He'd even seemed attracted to her at their makeshift picnic by the cool stream. But once his ardor had cooled, and he'd seen her as she truly was, she'd come up short, as she always had, as she always would. Today would be the day she'd give herself up to

Jameson, release Duke from the deal they'd made, and return home. He would be patient and sympathetic when he gave the letter to Rosalie. Somehow that sure knowledge made leaving him hurt even more.

But she'd never been afraid to embrace pain. By the time she'd dressed and packed her few possessions into her worn carpetbag, she'd buried her disappointment deep inside. The woman in the mirror reflected the confident and pleasant persona she'd created for herself years earlier, leaving all her turbulent thoughts hidden beneath the calm surface.

Henrietta seized the carpetbag and left Duke's bedroom for the last time. She missed her parents. It would be good to go home, back to the routine of visits, charity work, and parties. If Jonathon would still have her, she'd soon be hosting her own social events in the District of Columbia. It wouldn't be a bad life. Perhaps not the one she'd let herself daydream about when she'd first felt that stirring of attraction for Duke, but it wouldn't be unhappy.

She'd no sooner reached the bottom of the stairs than Bridget hurried to her, wiping her hands in her apron. She looked pointedly at Henrietta's luggage.

"Bridget—"

"Ma." The small, fierce woman raised an eyebrow as if to dare Henrietta to disagree.

Henrietta pulled herself up straight. "Duke and I have something to tell you."

"Well, ye canna."

"Pardon?" Henrietta asked in confusion.

"He's no here."

Henrietta's heart lurched, and she dropped the carpetbag. "Where is he?"

"Riding the property with that ugsome fella from the army and a half dozen others."

"Why? I mean, of course I know why, but when did he leave?" *And why didn't he wake her before he left?*

"A few hours back. The house is full of them sodgers. I've had a time of it keeping them from charging into yer room and rassling ye out of bed." Bridget pursed her lips as she eyed the case.

"Oh, thank you," Henrietta stammered.

"Aye. 'Twould be better to set yer case back in yer room before they come running up the stairs." Bridget gestured toward the carpetbag but didn't question her further.

Henrietta did as she was bid and rushed back down the stairs to help Duke's mother deal with the invasion of her home by uninvited guests. She took a deep breath and adopted a placid expression before entering the living room.

A disparate group of men sprawled across the furniture and teemed about the living room, strolling in and out of the room as if they owned the place. She recognized the captain she'd met the day before. He stood by the front windows with his arms crossed, looking as miserable as she felt. There were a few more soldiers interspersed with a dozen or more rough-looking men with gun belts hanging low across their hips. A man missing his two front teeth offered her a gaping smile as she entered the room. She tried to hide a shudder and sought the relative safety of the captain and another soldier.

"Ma'am, may I present our surgeon, Major Martin."

She tried to smile, but despite years of practice, she couldn't still the turmoil writhing inside her.

"Miss Blue?" The surgeon's voice was deep with a tinge of melancholy, as though he would rather have been anywhere else. That made two of them.

"Mrs. Gildownie," Captain Mellon corrected the other soldier.

"Forgive me, ma'am. My parents send their greetings."

She squinted at the man and tried to remember his name. "Who?"

"My parents. You traveled with them from Santa Fe."

"Oh, the Martins. Yes, of course. How are the vicar and your dear mother?"

"They are well. I thank you for asking."

She waited for him to continue the conversation, but he seemed content to end it there, and the Captain was no help either. She sighed. "And the baby?"

"He's a healthy boy, despite being premature. I delivered him myself a few weeks past."

"Your mother was so delighted when I last saw her in town." Henrietta said, remembering the woman's excitement at welcoming their first grandchild into the world.

"Yes," Major Martin said.

Silence. Goodness, this was far harder than it should be. Of course, she could mill about, but the men's leers and loud, rude whispers about her 'rump' were enough to keep her close to the officers.

"And your wife?"

"Who?" The Major looked genuinely confused.

"Is your wife well? After delivering the baby?" She tried to keep the exasperation out of her voice, but it was difficult.

"Oh, no. I'm *Henry* Martin. You're thinking of my brother, William. His wife is quite well. Thank you."

"I didn't know."

"Know what?"

This time she didn't try to hide her frustration. "That there are two of you. You and your brother."

"My parents didn't mention me at all?" Despite the Major's even tone, she thought she detected a slight twitch near his eye.

"Um." She was saved when Duke and the drunken Colonel walked through the door, followed by a man with slicked back hair and a confident air. The ruffians stood straighter and looked to him for guidance.

Captain Mellon grabbed her arm as she started toward Duke. She looked down at his hand, and he dropped her arm immediately, but not before hissing, "Jimmy Dolan. Be careful."

Jimmy Dolan. Rosalie had mentioned him only briefly, but in those few moments, her cousin's eyes had shone with true terror.

"Excuse me." She nodded her head and headed toward Duke, trying in vain to still the flutters in her belly. Why did this man make her feel like nothing else mattered? The others faded away when he turned his gaze on her, the tightness around his eyes easing.

She ignored the men she stepped around as she made her way through the crowd. When he slipped his hand into hers, she felt the shields she'd built around her heart crumbling. She'd been mad to think she could walk away and feel nothing, build a life with another man without thinking about the one she'd leave behind.

He leaned down to whisper in her ear, his breath hot on her neck, sending shivers of excitement down her spine. "Good morning, sleepyhead."

She grinned despite being surrounded by danger. "Why didn't you wake me? I would have ridden out with you."

"I would love that on another day. I want to show you everything, but today's not the day. And you were sleeping so peacefully, I couldn't bear to disturb you."

"Is everything well?" She cast a quick glance at the other men and slid closer to him.

"It will be." His jaw tensed and relaxed.

"Well, now, how about that drink?" Colonel Dudley said, slapping Duke on the back. Duke frowned, and she could see him fighting to keep his temper under control.

She squeezed his hand and said, "I'll put some coffee on."

"I was thinking about that fine apple brandy," Dudley said.

Henrietta's mouth fell open and her eyes darted at the dozen or so men in the room. The last thing they needed was a houseful of drunken brutes. "I don't think we have enough."

The slick gentleman stepped in front Dudley and grabbed her free hand.

"Your man failed to introduce us, but I'll forgive him the oversight. I, too, am struck dumb by your beauty. James Dolan at your service." He smiled, flashing a toothy grin, a single gold filling glimmering in the light from the window.

"This is my wife," Duke said between clenched teeth.

His words gave her strength to shake the man's hand, but not enough to offer any sort of welcome. The Colonel might have the full power of the military, but this man was the true viper in their midst.

"As I said before, there are no criminals hanging about the place, and we've got work to do." Duke slipped his arm around her waist, pulling her further away from the man, Dolan. "We'd like you and your men to leave."

Dolan nodded. "Well, now, that's not very neighborly." He looked past them at the men lounging on furniture, leaning against the wall, and a few sprawled on the floor. "Search the house."

The men stood and shoved each other with noisy grunts and wicked laughs as they filed out of the room, spreading through the house. Duke flinched at every creak of the floorboards, every squeal of a door, and every crash. Her heart ached at the pain she saw in his eyes as these men, these criminals, swaggered through the house he'd built, knocking carvings of horses and hand-wrought pottery to pieces on the floor.

Her lips trembled, but the whispered words were important. "I brought this on you, and I'm so incredibly sorry."

"Not your fault," he said under his breath. "None of this is your fault. I knew better than to shelter the man. I just couldn't say 'no' to..."

"To me?"

He kissed the top of her head, a mere brush of his lips on her hair, but the slight touch sent tingles along her scalp. She leaned in closer, longing to touch him, fitting neatly beneath his arm as though he was built for her and she for him.

She noted for the first time that Bridget was noticeably absent from the room and had been for a while. "Where's your mother?"

"Cleaning," he whispered in her ear.

Of course. While the men had been fixated on her, Bridget had slipped away to the guest bedroom to get rid of any evidence. However, an ear-shattering 'whoop' from the hallway told her they'd found something.

One of Dolan's men ran into the room, holding a bit of cloth covered in blood.

Duke

DUKE CURSED UNDER HIS breath. He should have cleared that room top to bottom the night before, but his thoughts had been in such chaos, all he had wanted to do was watch the stars while allowing the remainder of the night to sweep away all the pain of the past.

He opened his mouth to speak—to admit the truth to Dolan and to offer up himself—but was struck dumb when Aster giggled and covered her mouth with her hand.

"You've found my lady things. Are you married, Mr. Dolan? Of course you are, a fine man such as yourself. They are a nuisance, but the cloths are a required part of a woman's life."

Major Martin nodded sagely. Even Captain Mellon blushed faintly and turned to leave the house, saying it was past time to get back to the fort.

The Colonel didn't budge, his eyes focused solely on Dolan. That man's eyes lit up as Aster spoke, his gaze fixed on her impressive bosom.

Duke casually slipped his hand beneath his jacket to rest on the hilt of his Colt. He was no shooter. That had been Shaw's calling, but he and all his brothers had been raised around guns, and he reckoned he could outdraw the bastard.

Hell, what was he thinking? He could no more take on a dozen men than drive the herd through a blizzard.

"Well, you are a fine-looking woman, even with your lying mouth," Dolan said with a sneer.

Aster's eyes widened at the insult, but Duke wasn't surprised by the man's insolence. Anyone who didn't see a predator when they looked into Dolan's eyes would shortly feel his bit, likely a bullet in the back.

"Where are you hiding him?" The Colonel's face was red and splotchy. Maybe luck would be on their side, and his heart would explode.

"He's long gone, Dudley. Come on, men," Dolan strolled out of the house, giving orders to search for tracks. "The bastard's bleeding. Should be easy enough to pick up his trail."

Duke didn't relax until he counted every last man leave the house. Only then did he take stock of the damage they'd wreaked on his home. Furniture lay broken, curtains torn off rods, dishes and glassware smashed, but the women were safe, and he thanked God for it. Aster's face was ashen, and she shivered despite the warmth of the day. He pulled her into an embrace and rested his head against hers, breathing in sweet lavender, clean and fresh. Despite the ruin of the house, he was deeply grateful for her. Just her.

She gasped and stiffened in his arms. He thought at first she'd been harmed somehow, but he could detect no obvious injury on her person.

"What is it?"

She pointed out the window. He pivoted quickly and flung her behind him, imagining a rifle trained on her, but there was no man with a gun.

No men at all. Just smoke.

Sparks Fly

Henrietta

Henrietta grabbed her apron and ran out of the house toward the sound of frantic stomping and bloodcurdling screams. By the time Duke flung open the wide doors of the horse barn, flames were already shooting twenty feet into the sky. There was no time to fill a bucket of water—the horses were dying, trapped in their stalls, enveloped in thick, putrid smoke as fire devoured their sweet hay.

Henrietta covered her nose and mouth with the apron and darted into the immense structure right behind Duke. She fought her instinct to run, to save herself, and the terror that gripped her whenever she remembered that pivotal day when her life had changed years earlier. During a game of tag, she'd run into the kitchen and headlong into the stove that fateful morning, dumping a full pot of boiling water down her body, leaving her forever scarred.

Instead, she forced herself to the first stall, feeling along the door until she reached the smooth metal of the latch, already hot beneath her gloves. Her fingers stumbled over the latch in her desperation to swing open the gate. The sorrel inside bucked against the door, almost striking Henrietta in the head in its desperation to escape.

Finally, Henrietta was able to unlatch the door. She jumped back to avoid the horse as the mare raced past her and out of the barn. Henrietta could only hope the horse didn't stumble and break a leg in her panicked escape. She moved from stall to stall as the flames leapt higher. Her face burned from the heat, and despite the cloth over her face, her lungs screamed their protest at the hot, acrid smoke. She felt her way from stall to stall, unable to see through the dense gray cloud surrounding her.

A thunderous crack tore through the air, and a roof beam crashed down in front of her in a torrent of sparks and ash. Her skirt caught fire, and she froze. This was how she was going to die, consumed by fire, her body covered in burns. She couldn't cry for help. She couldn't breathe. All she could do was wait for the inevitable.

Her feet were swept up from beneath her and she toppled forward, but before she fell, she was lifted high and carried out of the inferno. She was thrown to the ground, knocking some sense back into her head. She sucked in a mouthful of clean air and was consumed by racking coughs. Her stomach heaved and bile filled her mouth. She leaned over and retched until her body ached from the strain.

Cool water slid over her bare flesh. Someone tore off her clothes, but she didn't care about her nakedness, not when her lungs screamed for air. A glass was thrust into her hands, and she gulped the water down only to cough it back up. She heard Duke's soothing voice, but she couldn't make out the words. She struggled to pull air into her chest, each breath burning her throat.

Duke smoothed back her hair, his hands so gentle despite his size. He breathed in deeply and blew out his breath slowly and loudly until her breaths mimicked his. Gradually her heartbeat slowed, and the panic that had consumed her subsided.

"Get the lassie inside. I'll see to her." Henrietta barely heard Bridget's calm voice over her pounding heart.

Duke lifted Henrietta off the ground, holding her close to his chest. She rested her head against his shoulder and closed her eyes, not opening them again until she'd been gently placed on the bed. He stood and shuffled from foot to foot as his mother followed them into the room with a fresh pitcher of water in her hands.

"Off with ye. See to the horses." Bridget shooed him out of the room, slamming the door in his face.

"Ach, lass, what were ye thinking, racing into a burning building with nary a thought to yer own safety?"

Henrietta tried to speak, but her throat rebelled. She licked her lips and croaked, "The horses."

"Aye. There's the horses, but ye're far more precious." Bridget poured fresh water into the washbasin and moistened a cloth. "Do ye think my boy would survive the loss of another wife?"

"I'm not—"

"No, ye're no dead, but only because he carried ye out before the roof came down. Did ye no ken how dangerous it was?" Bridget sniffed and wiped Henrietta's forehead with the damp cloth.

"They're his whole life, the horses."

"Nae, lass. Ye're his whole life."

But she wasn't. She'd struck the match that set everything he loved on fire.

Duke

CASH RETURNED IN TIME to help shovel the last of the dirt into the mass grave. Two mares, a stallion, and a foal's charred remains lay beneath their feet as a testament to the cruelty of men.

"Sometimes I really hate people," Cash said, leaning against the shovel.

"Yeah." It had been two days since the fire. Two days of sifting through the embers, trying to salvage as much as they could from the wreckage. A few harnesses, a tack box, and two singed saddles. Duke had tried to find gratitude every time he pulled something from the destruction, but there'd been so little. So, he gave thanks that his mother and Aster had been saved and that his brothers hadn't been there.

Wyatt or Cash would have drawn a weapon, and the grave he'd dug would have been for one of his brothers, or for both of them. There was a special place in hell for Jimmy Dolan and his crew of killers.

"Did you have any trouble with Dolan or the army?" Duke asked.

"Nah, I could hear 'em coming a mile away. Easy enough to slip away."

"And Wyatt?" Duke patted down the dirt with the back of his shovel.

"Left him at the cabin griping about babysittin' an idiot who got himself shot. Then I spent a day laying a new trail for Dolan and Dudley to chase."

Duke nodded, then headed back to the ruins of the old barn, his little brother tagging along. "I reckon we'll have our work cut out for us trying to get that new barn up before the snows come."

"We need Shaw and Keith, both," Cash said.

"Yeah, I was fixing to head into town today or tomorrow. It's just Aster—"

"Was she hurt? Why didn't you say?" Cash glanced back at the house.

"I don't know. She was scared. Hell, we were all scared, but she tore into the barn like an avenging angel, working as hard as me to get the horses out." Duke could still see her standing frozen there in the barn, her dress caught in a halo of fire.

"She's got courage. I'll give her that."

"Yeah," Duke leaned the shovel against a charred upright. "Unfortunately, she's got it in her head that this," he waved his arm about, encompassing the devastation, "is all her fault."

"That's hogwash."

"Try telling her that," Duke snorted.

"I will, but first, we gotta get word to Shaw up in Santa Fe. What's that fancy hotel he's staying at?"

"The Grand," Duke muttered, then threw his brother an embarrassed look. "Only I told Aster I didn't know how to reach them."

"Why?"

Duke hung his head. "No reason."

"I don't see how it would matter to her one way or the other, but maybe it's time to come clean with your wife."

Duke nodded. "About a lot of things."

HE FOUND HER IN THE parlor with her fingers poised over the keys, as though she'd forgotten why she was there. She turned to look at him when he opened the door, a blank expression on her face.

"Aster?"

"Hmm?"

How to begin? At least she'd been honest with him, even in her deception. She'd trusted him with her secret, had shared her most painful memories of losing her siblings and her disagreement with her father. Duke hadn't exactly lied, but failing to tell the whole story felt more like a sin than if he'd simply made up a story exonerating himself from his crime.

He longed to be the man she saw when she gazed at him with such open trust. A few moments more, and then he would confess everything. "Will you play for me?"

She smiled and ducked her head. "No."

"Please?" And then he did the unforgivable and preyed on her false sense of guilt. "I just want to forget for a while."

Her smile faded, and she nodded, tears welling in her eyes. "What would you like to hear?"

"Your favorite song."

"Schumann?" she asked.

He nodded. He had no earthly idea who that was, but if this was the last moment they shared in this wonderful deception, then let it be filled with the sounds of her greatest joy.

She twisted on the bench to face the piano again, closed her eyes, and pressed the first key. As if in a trance, her hands moved slowly, languidly across the keyboard in a lilting, haunting melody, one moment a lullaby, the next an elegy. He was not a man given to wild fits of emotion, but the song gripped his heart, so perfectly fitting for the fear and pain of the last two days as he'd buried his horses and his dreams.

He didn't bother to wipe away the tears dampening his cheeks. His life was laid bare in the tune, the hopes and the tragedy. When the last dulcet tone sounded, echoing in the room like the final toll of the church bell, he didn't move, didn't breathe.

"Child Falling Asleep," she murmured, still facing the piano.

"What?"

"The name of the song."

He nodded, but couldn't understand how such a simple, innocent name could possibly describe what he'd just heard, what he'd felt.

"Schumann imagined a child struggling against sleep at the end of a day filled with play."

"It's about an ending," he said.

"Yes," she said softly, her fingers still resting on the keyboard.

"It's beautiful," he said. *She* was beautiful, sitting there, her face alight with passion, her brilliant crystal blue eyes glowing in the light.

She turned and smiled so sweetly that he felt his resolve weaken. He broke their gaze and stared down at his boots, covered in dust and ash—that was his life, not this glimmer of a bright future he'd deluded himself into believing.

"Aster..." He cleared his throat and sniffed, looking everywhere but into her eyes. "I haven't been completely honest with you."

"No?" She stood and glided across the parlor until she stood directly in front of him, blocking his escape from the room and from this conversation.

"You asked me if I knew how to reach Shaw and Rosalie."

"Yes." She slipped her hand into his. "Duke, you're shaking." Her face fell. "Has something else happened?"

He swallowed hard. "I lied. I've known where they've been the whole time."

She flinched and withdrew her hand. "No. No, you would have told me."

He shook his head.

"Why didn't you say?"

He shuffled his feet and stuffed his hands into his pockets. "In the beginning, I guess I was just being a jackass. And then..."

"Yes?"

She peered at him with such open trust, he wanted desperately to be the man she believed him to be. But he wasn't. "I liked being with you. I liked pretending you were my wife, and I didn't want it to end."

"Oh." Her face softened. "I still wish you'd told me the truth."

"I should have. I should have done a lot of things differently." He rocked back on his heels. "And now, well, now I can't hardly live with myself. You deserve so much better than me."

"It was just a white lie. I've done far worse. I've brought nothing but chaos and violence into your home."

"That's not all," he said slowly.

"What do you mean?"

He met her gaze and felt the shame sheer down to his boots. "You asked me how Judith died."

"You don't have to tell me. It was wrong of me to ask, bringing up something so painful. There's not a minute that goes by that I wish I hadn't said it. I'd give anything to take it back."

He cleared his throat and then blurted out the words he'd refused to admit to her, to his family, to himself.

"I killed her."

HE REFUSED TO LOOK away from the horror in her face. There was a tiny part of him that had longed to see the revulsion he'd felt all these years reflected in someone else's eyes.

"I don't believe you," she whispered.

He snorted. "It's true. I wish to God every day it wasn't, but I can't hide from the truth any longer."

"What..." She cleared her throat. "What happened?"

"Judith was so delicate, so frail. And I dragged her out here to the back of beyond, away from her family, her friends, everything she'd ever known. She was so unhappy, but I thought she'd get over it. Ma always said, 'Life's not for the weak.' And I reckon she's right. Ma was opposed to the marriage. She saw what I refused to see—Judith wasn't built for the hardships on a homestead. I thought if I built her a house." He gestured around him. "This house. She'd be happy."

"And she wasn't?"

"She wanted to go home." He met her gaze with tight eyes. "But I *loved* her, and I didn't want to be alone. She was my wife." His voice cracked.

She touched his cheek with soft, gentle fingers, burning his skin with her innocence, with her loving heart.

"And she was pregnant," he said with a shudder. "I promised I'd take her to her Ma's when the time came, but I kept thinking she'd change her mind if I bought her pretty things or if I built her a parlor like the one in her childhood home."

Aster smiled. "It is lovely."

He closed his eyes and willed his mouth to form the words. "I was out riding fences with Wyatt. We'd had a few head get loose, and I was determined to find the breach. We were gone two days, and when we got back, she was nowhere to be found."

He was grateful Aster didn't speak, didn't offer her understanding or comforting platitudes. He'd heard enough to last him a lifetime.

"I reckon she'd had enough, or maybe she'd felt the first pangs of labor and decided to go home. I'll never know. She wasn't a horsewoman, not like you." He glanced at her and had to avert his gaze, seeing such love and compassion, and he didn't deserve it. He didn't deserve her.

"We found her a few miles from the ranch. She'd been thrown from the horse and had been calling out for me for hours. I delivered the baby on the hard ground of the desert, surrounded by rocks and cactus, with the sun beating down on her."

He inhaled a ragged breath and spit out the rest in a rush. "Our son, George, was born dead. And Judith died an hour later, there in the wilderness, with the babe in her arms."

His throat tightened and his chest heaved, choking off the rest of the story—that he'd wanted to take his own life, but had lacked the strength to fight off Wyatt as he'd held Duke down. And that every day since, he'd sat with a single glass of whiskey and had considered trying again. Until a woman, a slip of a girl, with pale eyes and chestnut colored hair, had thrown her arms around his neck and kissed him, igniting a spark of life he thought had died forever.

No, he couldn't tell her that. He didn't want her pity, not when he'd let himself want so much more.

"I swore that day I would never marry again—"

His words were cut off when the door to the parlor swung open, slamming against the wall.

Sacrifice

Henrietta

Henrietta patted Susanna's hand and tried to calm the woman's nerves while struggling to control her own after her conversation with Duke. Susanna had been through far worse and deserved her full attention. The poor woman had been assaulted on the road, held up by bandits, on her way to Fort Stanton to visit her uncle.

"How'd ye get away?" Bridget asked, handing her a glass of her applejack.

Susanna drained her glass in a single swallow. Her thick waves of black hair were tangled with leaves and tiny twigs. Her cap was missing; her crimson frock was covered in dark streaks and deep tears, and her face was smudged and scratched.

"I'm just glad you were able to find us here." Henrietta dabbed a damp cloth on the cuts, wincing each time she touched her friend's face.

"How *did* you find us?" Duke asked, his arms crossed in front of him.

"Mind yer manners, boy. And make yerself useful by seeing to her horse." Bridget turned to her youngest son, sprawled on a chair across from Susanna, ogling the woman with open interest. "Go with yer brother. There's work to be done before the sun sets."

Cash grumbled, but stood, only leering slightly at the black-haired beauty before following Duke out of the room. The door hadn't even shut behind them when Bridget said, "I can't abide an idle man."

"Shall we send for your uncle? Only if he's stationed at Fort Stanton, it may pose a bit of a problem for us," Henrietta said reluctantly.

Henrietta had no desire to run across Colonel Dudley or the miscreants who'd caused so much damage in the name of justice mere days earlier.

"Oh no, thank you. He's been so ill, I'd hate to add to his distress." Susanna's voice quavered.

"He'd be a mite more distressed if he's expecting ye and ye don't turn up on his doorstep," Bridget said matter-of-factly.

Susanna's face blanched as she absorbed Bridget's words. "Oh no, he's not expecting me. I thought I'd surprise him. I feel such a fool for thinking I could travel through this wild country on my own."

"Perhaps you should stay here until you're well enough to ride back to Lincoln. I'm sure Duke or Cash would accompany you. As you could see when you rode in, we've had our share of run-ins with outlaws lately." Henrietta's eyes widened as she realized how forward she'd been. "If that's fine by you, Bridget."

"If I've told ye once, I've told ye a thousand times over, call me Ma. And it's yer house, not mine."

"When did you get married?" Susanna said, pouting slightly. "I thought for certain you'd invite me to the ceremony."

"They got married nigh on a week ago when they were in town."

Henrietta's hands shook, and she looked around for something to do, some way to stay busy. Lighting on Susanna's empty glass, she said, "Can I get you something else to drink. Perhaps I can make a pot of tea? Or coffee? I think you prefer that."

"No, thank you," Susanna smiled sweetly. "Were you able to find the pastor then? I hear he's been in San Patricio this entire month."

Bridget frowned and pierced Henrietta with her hawklike gaze. Henrietta was a coward through and through and couldn't face the disappointment in Duke's mother's eyes.

"I'll see to your room, shall I? I'm sure you need rest after such an overwhelming experience," Henrietta said, rising quickly.

Susanna's forehead was furrowed, but she smiled and nodded her thanks. If Henrietta thought she could escape Bridget's questioning, she was sadly mistaken. Duke's mother stalked her as she rushed out of the room, down the hallway, and into the small bedroom where Arthur had recuperated.

"Sit doon. We're due fer a chat, lass."

Henrietta gnawed on her lip and fidgeted with her skirt as she sat down on the bed. Bridget moved to stand in front of her, blocking the exit.

"I dinnae take ye fer a cheat and a liar, so ye'd best tell me the whole sordid tale."

"Perhaps we should wait for Duke as it concerns him as well?"

"Nae, lass." Bridget crossed her arms and jutted her chin up, tapping her foot impatiently. "I'll no leave until I've heard it all, start to finish."

"I'm not a mail-order bride," Henrietta blurted out while mentally calculating how difficult it would be to slip past the woman and out the window. She'd done it before.

"I take it ye're not a bride at all?"

Henrietta hung her head. "No."

"Then why all the play acting? Do ye care for my boy or no?"

Henrietta jerked her head up. "I do. Very much. I...," she broke off, searching for the words to describe her complicated feelings. "I hadn't intended to."

"Well, that's something."

"What?" Henrietta asked.

"At least all yer calf eyes at each other weren't another act. Push over so I can rest my bones and start from the beginning. Who are ye and what are ye doing here?"

Henrietta told her. Everything. Her wedding day, her discovery of something Rosalie desperately needed, her decision to leave everyone behind for an arduous journey cross-country, hounded by a Pinkerton detective. Everything. Except for the contents of the letter. Everything. Except for the turmoil of emotion which seized her whenever Duke gazed at her with his warm, kind eyes.

"And when ye find Rosalie and give her whatever it is she so desperately needs, what then?"

"I don't understand what you mean." Henrietta's head was still bent forward, her fingers clenched in her skirts.

"What's next for ye, lass?"

"I hadn't thought..." she said stupidly. And it was true. She'd barely had a moment to think about the future, not when each day brought new challenges.

"Well, ye'd better start thinking on it and right quick."

"I suppose I'll have to go home. My mother deserves that at the very least. She is likely sick with worry, and I'm the cause." *And Duke hadn't asked her to stay.*

"Best to face up to it, then." Bridget sniffed and rose from the bed, rubbing her back as she did. "Ach, past time we tidied up this room for yer friend. She probably thinks we got lost on the way to the bedroom. Hand me those bedsheets."

Henrietta pulled the sheets from the wardrobe, and between the two of them, they soon had the bed put to rights, the pillows fluffed, and the window flung open, allowing the fresh, breezy sunshine to flood into the space. It was good to stay busy, to allow her thoughts to drift away as she focused on the job at hand.

As Henrietta reached for the doorknob, Bridget laid a hand on Henrietta's arm. "Ye'd best tell Duke yer plans. Break it off now, before his heart is too far gone. We nearly lost the boy when Judith died. I'll no let that happen again, not even for a bonny lass like yerself."

SHE'D INTENDED TO TELL him, to face him after dinner, after everyone had left the table to retire to their own rooms, when they were finally alone. Of course she'd planned to, though every part of her being railed against it.

Love demands sacrifice.

That's what Rosalie had always said.

But was this love? How could she be sure? She'd thought she loved Jonathon, and yet those feelings had evaporated quickly as their wedding day had approached. Perhaps she'd read too many Russian novels, full of reckless, wanton need and lust. The flutter in her stomach when Duke walked into the room, the desire to stand closer to him, to touch him and to be touched in return. Was that what Tolstoy had meant? Had she ever felt that for Jonathon?

No, she'd never felt this way before.

But that didn't mean Duke felt the same, and it didn't mean there was a future for them. *He swore he'd never marry again.* He was a captive of the past. She'd seen it when he'd spoken of his wife, of the way he'd fought to keep her, of the home he'd built for her, and of the dream they'd shared. And there was no competing with a ghost.

He was as wary of her as she was of him at dinner; his speech too formal, his careful distance from her. She didn't blame him. The soot stains on his shirt and trousers told the tale of a man whose life had been completely upended. Even the passion she felt for him, and she would be lying if she said she didn't feel a hunger for him even when sitting amongst his family at the table, even that had been one-sided. She had always been the one to initiate, and he'd always been the one to put a stop to it before it had gotten out of hand.

Her stomach churned as she planned the conversation. Simple, but honest. She hadn't tried that approach yet.

She had planned to speak with him. But when the meal was finished, he pushed back from the table and returned outside despite the late hour, to continue the arduous task of sorting through the rubble, of caring for horses who had nowhere to escape the heat of the day or the brisk wind at night, of the backbreaking work to ready the timber for the new barn. She tried to catch his eye before he left, but he barely looked her way.

So, when Susanna asked for her help to retire, claiming an aching head, Henrietta gladly took her friend's arm and escorted her out of the dining room, down the hall, and to the small first-floor bedroom.

"I'll let you settle," she said once Susanna was safely ensconced.

"Wait one moment, will you? I'd like a quick girl chat."

Henrietta fidgeted with her skirts, her thoughts still swirling with the upcoming discussion with Duke, but Susanna had had a horrible time and needed a friend. Henrietta smiled and nodded and closed the door of the bedroom for privacy.

Susanna plopped onto the bed and settled her head on the plump pillows. She stretched her arms above her head as a cat might, and yet again Henrietta was struck by the woman's beauty. It was no wonder Cash had flirted with her all evening.

"Would you fetch my handbag from the table there?" Susanna asked.

The beaded chatelaine bag was surprisingly heavy, but then again, Henrietta herself often carried a half-dozen indispensable items in her own reticule. She passed it over and sat down in the small chair next to the bed where she'd spent many hours nursing Arthur.

Susanna sat up, opened the handbag and withdrew a handkerchief, a small coin bag, and a revolver. Henrietta stood quickly and backed away from her friend. "Why on earth do you have that?"

Susanna smiled sweetly. "Protection, of course."

"But if you had a weapon, why didn't you use it against the bandits?"

"Well, that is a clever question, isn't it? I never thought of you as particularly intelligent, but I'm forever surprised."

Henrietta's mouth fell open.

"Do shut your mouth. You look like a guppy. Forgive me, I was only going by what I was told."

"I don't understand." Henrietta's legs wobbled, and she sat down again.

"No, I suppose you don't. Perhaps this will help." Susanna pulled a folded and creased paper out of her handbag and shook it loose. There, in front of her, Henrietta saw a rough drawing of herself below large block letters that read, 'REWARD'.

"Are you a bounty hunter?" Henrietta asked, dumbfounded.

"Me? Oh heavens, no, though I suppose we are in the same line of work. I believe you met my colleague earlier. Mr. Jameson. You could hardly miss him. Which is why we're such an effective team."

"You work for the Pinkerton Agency?" Henrietta paused, "But you're a woman."

Susanna's serene expression faltered slightly, hinting at a bit of steel just below the surface. "Yes, well, that has its advantages, as I've mentioned many times to the agency."

"So, what now?"

"It's time to go home, Henrietta. Do you mind if I call you by your given name? Or would you prefer to be called Miss Beedy or Aster? Or my favorite, Mrs. Gildownie?"

"I don't care," Henrietta said through gritted teeth.

"Well, then, Henrietta, you shall tell your dear *husband* and the rest of your family that you are so concerned for my frail health that you've decided to stay the night by my bedside. And when the household is quiet, we shall slip out into the night."

"Lucky we're on the first floor." Henrietta stared at the window as though it were somehow responsible for the situation.

"Not luck, dear. Mr. Dolan is quite friendly, and a few well-placed coins ensured he gave me a very detailed rendering of the place. It is pretty here, if you can look past the smell of manure and the ashes."

"Your *friend*, Mr. Dolan, is responsible for those ashes," Henrietta said, balling her fists.

"Is he? Well, then, we wouldn't want him to return in the morning to burn down the rest of the place. And he will. My partner, Mr. Jameson, holds an arrest warrant for your man, and Mr. Dolan seemed only too willing to form a posse to bring the criminal to justice."

"An arrest warrant for what?"

"Kidnapping, of course." Susanna held a hand to her mouth to suppress a laugh. She cleared her throat and continued in a more serious tone. "But that needn't happen. If you leave with me tonight, without any violence or threats to my person by these villains, then the warrant will disappear." Susanna snapped her fingers for emphasis.

Henrietta's heart was in her throat as she choked out, "May I at least write Duke a letter, saying goodbye?"

"That's a wonderful idea, but I shall have to read it, just to ensure my own safety. I'm sure you understand."

Henrietta nodded curtly.

"Now run along and fetch us some nightclothes. I, for one, would like a few hours' sleep after such an arduous journey."

Henrietta stood stiffly and walked to the door.

"Oh, and if you breathe a word of this, I cannot promise your new family will be safe. Mr. Dolan seems quite keen on violence. It is I alone who insisted on a civilized approach."

Henrietta's hand shook as she turned the doorknob.

AFTER A HALF-DOZEN attempts filled with suggestions from Susanna, the letter was complete and delivered to the parlor, to the one place she was certain he'd visit. Henrietta left it propped against the silver-framed photograph of his wife, Judith. Their departure went undetected, a quick and silent exit through the window, far easier than climbing down the trellis from Duke's second-floor bedroom. Even so, she couldn't help but smile when Susanna tripped and fell on dagger-sharp yucca fronds next to the charred remains of the barn. Henrietta knew better than to let someone else saddle her horse, but when she moved toward the burnt saddles and harnesses, Susanna stopped her and said they'd walk a mile or so and meet up with the men in her party who had horses readied.

Henrietta cast one long glance back at the two-story wooden house she'd called home and the people inside who'd invited her into their family. Her heart lurched in her throat and her knees wobbled so much she was afraid she might collapse there on the hard-packed dirt road leading away from the ranch, but she was made of sterner stuff and refused to allow Susanna to see any weakness inside her. It was only as she turned back to the woman that she spied it. Lying in the tall grass next to a fence post.

Without a word, she scooped up the prize and shoved it into her reticule.

Duke

HE LAY IN THE DARK, long after the rest of the household had drifted off to sleep. Every time he closed his eyes, he saw Henrietta's face, drawn and pale, as though even the few moments she'd spent alone with him had been an agony. How could he blame her? He'd revealed himself for who he was—a miserable, tyrannical husband whose wife had died due to his negligence. Once Susanna was out of their hair, he'd confess to his family, he'd help Aster move permanently into the extra bedroom, and he'd leave her be. He'd let his dreams of a life with her burn to a cinder like the rest of the world he'd built.

He heard a shuffling somewhere in the house, as though someone were pacing the halls. Briefly, he considered abandoning sleep. But no, he couldn't face his family or, God forbid, run into Aster in the dark, not when he'd finally admitted to himself that she and not the ranch, not the house, not the horses or the barn, was the only thing he truly wanted. Tomorrow would be a new beginning, one in which they'd return to what they should have been from the start: strangers. But tonight, one last time, he'd let himself dream it was her outside his room. That she'd open the door and walk to his bed. That she'd strip off her nightdress and climb on top of him. And that she loved him.

Hope

Henrietta

Santa Fe was dreamlike in the distance with its adobe structures floating in the clouds. For the millionth time, she imagined what it would be like to sit next to Duke, seeing this vision together, rather than shoved between Susanna and Jameson. Even after days of travel, with nowhere to run, surrounded by the wild country, the two continued to watch her as though she were an errant child who might wander away at any moment.

At least Henrietta had been able to write the letter to Duke. She hoped that in time he would forget her while still believing he was worthy of love from a woman far more beautiful, more accomplished, more perfect than she. And if she had to live her life alone or with another man, she could do so knowing there was a man in New Mexico Territory who would always hold a piece of her heart.

She cleared her throat and said, "I will offer you no further trouble if you'll allow me to visit my cousin Rosalie. I know she's here in Santa Fe."

"Absolutely not," Jameson said. "We've had a dozen detectives scouring this godforsaken country looking for you. The sooner we deliver you, the sooner we can move on to more important matters."

Henrietta turned to Susanna, who, despite her callous betrayal, had shown at least a modicum of compassion. Something must have happened to this woman to cause her distrust of men, but perhaps Henrietta could use that.

"Rosalie is my closest friend. I'd hate for her to hear some sordid tale about me from Duke and his brothers." Henrietta dropped her voice to a whisper. "You know how cruel men can be."

Susanna shuffled uncomfortably, then said, "Do you even know where she's staying?"

Henrietta bit her lip and cursed herself for not prying the information from Duke when he'd admitted to knowing how to reach his brother. "No."

"Pity," Jameson said.

Henrietta grated at the man's sarcasm. "You are detectives, aren't you?"

"And we already have a client." Jameson shifted his weight on the hard bench, shoving her into Susanna, who cast the man a dirty look over Henrietta's head.

"I can hire you then—I'm certain I can afford your fees for an hour's work—I have money of my own."

"The stage won't leave until tomorrow morning. Might as well earn a few more coins before heading back East," Susanna said.

Jameson grunted but didn't disagree.

The city of Santa Fe was situated in the foothills of the Sangre de Cristo Mountains. Susanna said the name translated to "Blood of Christ." Henrietta supposed the city, like most of the country in New Mexico Territory, was Mexican and Catholic. Although there were a fair number of English speakers, most people they'd driven past spoke in a mixture of Spanish, English and perhaps an Indian tongue. She would have liked to have met Duke's sister-in-law, Mary, who was Mescalero Apache. There was so much she wished she'd done in the few days she'd spent with Duke. She'd never ventured into the mountains, had never visited the Martins at Fort Stanton, and had never explored the ranch.

Henrietta's thoughts always returned to him and to the growing list of things she'd never do with him. Her chest tightened as she imagined his reaction to finding her gone. Had he cared for her, or had she always been a means of pretending his wife was still alive? The longer they were apart, the more Henrietta found that even that small part of affection from him would have been worth it.

He was like an intricate piece of music, one where every time it was played, she could explore a new phrase, an unexpected harmony, a new depth of emotion. She wrenched her thoughts away from what could have been back to the present and on the buildings they passed.

"What is that?" Henrietta pointed at a huge adobe, single story building fronted by dozens of carved wooden columns with wide doors spaced every few feet.

"It's the governor's palace. Didn't you pass through Sante Fe on your way to Lincoln?" Susanna gave her a quizzical expression.

"I did." Henrietta glared at Jameson. "But I hid in the hotel most of that time. I was being hunted."

Susanna laughed. "You certainly were entertaining prey to chase."

"How many women have you hounded these past weeks?" Henrietta asked.

"I narrowed it down to you and two others fairly quickly. I never believed the kidnapping story." Her lips twitched as she glanced at her colleague. "Jameson, on the other hand, ran quite a few rabbits to ground before realizing I'd been right all along."

Jameson cursed the woman, covering his ugly words with a cough.

"What gave me away?"

"What didn't? You forgot your name at one point, forgot where you came from, and then forgot the name of your fiancé. That was a nice touch, by the way, getting him to pretend to marry you. It took a while to discover he was related to your cousin's husband, what with the different surnames," Susanna asked.

Henrietta nodded, trying to recall each of her interactions with her false friend. Only one memory was hidden behind a fog. "That day at the hotel when we met for coffee..."

"That was brilliant, if you'll allow me to congratulate myself. I added a bit of peyote to the sugar bowl before you sat down."

"And if I hadn't used the sugar?" Henrietta asked.

Susanna raised a perfectly groomed eyebrow. "Of course you use sugar."

"Why do you say that?"

"A woman like you? You've been handed everything on a silver platter by a dozen servants. You never had to scrape enough coins together her to buy a loaf of bread." Susanna's tone was laced with derision.

"That's true." Henrietta couldn't help but wonder where this woman had grown up, though she now had an inkling of just how different their backgrounds had been.

"Besides, the milk was drugged, and there was a sprinkling on your cake as well."

"You're very thorough," Henrietta said.

"Thank you." Susanna smiled smugly.

Half an hour and five dollars later, Henrietta strolled into the lobby of the Grand Hotel, her boot heels clicking on the marble floor. She was flanked by the two detectives, but she didn't allow her jailers to steal her dignity. Head held high, she approached the concierge and demanded to see Rosalie McPherson.

Her mother had always instructed her to start as you wished to finish. If she intended to return home as an experienced woman capable of making her own decisions, she might as well act the part now. When the hotelier escorted her up the stairs, she inserted herself next to the man so that there was no room for Susanna and Jameson to do anything but follow a few steps behind.

When the man rapped on the door, Henrietta turned to the others and said, "I shall not need you with me. Wait here while I finish my business."

Jameson grumbled, but Susanna just cocked her head, fixed her with a calculated ebony gaze, and nodded.

All pretense disappeared as the door shut behind her. Rosalie was ever the same, her sharp eyes questioning the disturbance. Her tumble of blonde curls, half of which had fallen out of the hairpins, flew behind her as she rushed to the door. Seeing Henrietta's hesitation, Rosalie opened her arms wide.

"Henrietta? What are you doing here?"

Henrietta flung herself at the woman, wrapping her arms around her, practically knocking the smaller woman to the ground. She didn't bother to sniff back the tears pouring from her eyes.

Rosalie grunted and whispered, "You're strangling me."

Henrietta smiled through her tears and released her grip slightly. She'd always been stronger than Rosalie, much to her cousin's chagrin. "Sorry."

"What's this about? A man was here weeks ago asking if I'd seen you."

Henrietta cast an irritated glance at the closed doors. Of course they'd found the hotel easily; they had already known where Rosalie was staying. "Things would have been a sight easier if I'd known you were in Santa Fe from the beginning." She almost pouted, as she had when she hadn't gotten her way when they were children.

"Sit and tell me everything. Do you want a coffee? Or perhaps something stronger? I think I have some of Bridget's applejack around here somewhere, though I must warn you it can send you into a stupor if you're not careful."

"No, thank you. I need my wits about me," Henrietta sat on the settee and looked about the room. The furnishings were elegant, if not exactly new. There was an enormous canopied bed with a crimson coverlet that had her blushing, reminding her she'd intruded on the woman's honeymoon. A familiar pang gripped her heart as she imagined Duke and her spending a week in this room, without the fear of discovery, the pull of unending chores, or the ghostly figure of Judith forever between them. Her breath caught in her throat, and she had to focus on Rosalie's happiness to tear her away from the brink of despair, always lurking, tempting her closer.

"I don't have much time until they drag me away, but I had to see you. I came all this way because, um..." Henrietta broke off. Now that she was face to face with Rosalie, she couldn't bear to cause this woman more pain, not after all she'd lived through.

Rosalie pushed Henrietta's hair away from her face as she had when they were younger, when Henrietta had failed yet again at a particularly difficult piece of music.

"I found a letter from your father," Henrietta said slowly.

"From Papa?" Rosalie's face lit up with the news. "Oh, but that's wonderful. I miss him so much."

"Yes..." Henrietta hadn't the heart or the courage to share its contents, so she carefully removed the pages from her reticule and handed them over to her cousin.

Henrietta bit her lip and watched Rosalie carefully as she devoured the letter, her joy fading as she read and re-read the words. "No."

"I'm so sorry."

"Do you know what it says?" Rosalie's words were laced with barbs.

"I...I do."

"Is that why you came here? To hurt me with these lies?"

Henrietta's hands shook in her lap, but she remained silent as her cousin railed against her. It was only when Rosalie's lips started to quiver and the tears began to well in her eyes that Henrietta wrapped her arms around her, holding her close despite the woman's desperate need to escape the embrace.

"It can't be true." Rosalie said, gulping for air.

"Breathe," Henrietta whispered, the only words that had ever calmed her cousin when Rosalie was gripped in panic. She stroked Rosalie's hair and whispered all the meaningless nonsense one offers to a grieving friend.

Only once Rosalie's breathing evened and the tears had run their course did Henrietta release her. "I believe we could use that applejack now. I've grown quite fond of it."

Rosalie gave her a curious look as she poured two shaky, full glasses of the amber liquid. "Sláinte."

It was strange to hear the toast coming from anyone's mouth but Bridget's, but Henrietta smiled and wrapped herself in the comfort of her cousin's indomitable spirit. She took a sip and closed her eyes as the liquid slid down her throat, sweet and intoxicating.

"I have to find the child." Rosalie peered at Henrietta over the glass's rim.

"Maybe," Henrietta hedged, though she could tell from the fierce determination in her eyes that Rosalie had made up her mind.

"Still, we'll have to investigate. See if this girl even exists."

It wouldn't have surprised her if Rosalie had stood up and started packing her bags at once. She'd never been one to sit idly by or to consider the outcome of her actions. In that way, they couldn't be more different. Where Henrietta was methodical, intent on perfecting a skill, Rosalie would try anything, go anywhere, fail and pick herself up, and try again. She wasn't afraid of anything or anyone.

And she wouldn't have just walked away from a life she wanted. But she had. She had walked away. Rosalie had given up everything to save the man she loved. *Love demands sacrifice.*

"I wish I could go with you." Henrietta's voice was small and unsure as she continued. "And I wish Duke was here."

"Duke? I didn't think you would even remember him." Rosalie pierced her with her gaze. "You said you wished you'd known I was here. Where did you think I was?"

"Lincoln."

"You went there?" Rosalie asked.

"Yes."

"And you met Duke and Bridget there?"

Henrietta nodded, a single tear sliding down her cheek.

"Tell me everything."

And so, she did.

When she told Rosalie the contents of her farewell letter to Duke, her cousin's eyes grew wide. "You did not."

"What was I supposed to say?"

"That you love him, that no matter the odds or the distance between you, you'd find a way to return." Rosalie gripped Henrietta's hands tightly.

"He doesn't care about me," Henrietta said.

"Not possible. Any man with eyes and half his wits in his head would want you. Just think of all those idiots in Philadelphia throwing themselves at you."

"You know as well as I do they're only interested in a house on Rittenhouse Square and a link to Father."

"Exactly," Rosalie said triumphantly.

Henrietta's face fell.

"And that's why Duke is not like those fools. What man would pretend to be your husband, respect you enough to not force you into his bed as recompense, and care enough about you to lie to his entire family? And not a word about the money. Did he ever ask you for anything in return?"

"No," Henrietta said slowly. On pondering Rosalie's words, she landed on the one thing that cut the deepest. "Rosalie, I wanted him to make love to me. I practically launched myself at him multiple times, but he always walked away. I know I'm not...unattractive."

Rosalie lifted an eyebrow. "I'd agree with that, as would every man you've ever come across."

"Then why doesn't he want me?"

"Have you considered that maybe he wants more than a brief affair? According to Shaw, the only woman he's been with was his wife."

Henrietta looked away, the sour taste of bitterness filling her mouth. "Judith. Yes. I know all about her. She was perfect."

"I'd hardly agree."

"What?" Henrietta swung back around to face her cousin.

"You and I have so much to discuss and so little time, but I promise you this will not be the end of your New Mexico adventure."

A sharp rap at the door and a rattling of the knob didn't dissuade Rosalie. Once the woman set herself on a path, there was no force, natural or man-made, that could stop her from prevailing.

Duke

HE SLID THE PLANER along the wood plank, smoothing out the ridges to produce an arrow-straight piece of lumber for the new barn. They'd fashioned a crude lean-to shelter to offer a place out of the weather, but it wouldn't protect the horses from the onslaught of a summer storm. Wyatt had returned from the mountains the day before, giving Duke the consistent extra hand he needed. And Cash? He'd been remarkably helpful in constructing the new building. Keith had negotiated a fair rate for a loan from the McSween's, but the money would dry up quickly if Shaw didn't return soon with the proceeds from the cattle sale.

He should have sent a telegram to Santa Fe, but if Aster had gone there to find Rosalie, she might believe he didn't respect her decision to leave. And he did. He'd learned his lesson with Judith. He'd never force a woman to stay with him, not when she so clearly wanted to go. So, he did what he always did when he needed an escape from the pain—he labored from dawn till dusk, until his muscles ached, his stomach churned, and his body was so tired he fell asleep before his thoughts could take hold.

Some days it even worked.

The part that troubled him the most was that she left in the middle of the night without waking him, without saying goodbye. He pressed too hard on the planer and sent up a cloud of wood dust, causing Cash and Wyatt to erupt in a fit of coughing. Cash glared at him and took a step back, waving his hand in front of his face in an exaggerated attempt to clear the air.

Wyatt clapped Duke on the back. "Best head on in. Light's fading."

Duke shook his head. "Another hour."

"Won't make a difference in how fast we get the barn done. It's enough." It was rare for Wyatt to use his place as the eldest to force an issue. Truth was, he almost never had, preferring to stay in the background, watching and waiting as the rest of them squabbled, wrestled, and got into all sorts of trouble. But when Duke had needed him most, the day Judith died, Wyatt had been there.

"Right behind you," Duke said. While his brothers went into the house, he headed round back to the shower, eager to rid himself of the dust that coated him hat to boots. As he passed the parlor, he couldn't resist stealing a quick glance at the piano, where Aster had sat, where her fingers had flown across the keys in a display of passion that still made his pulse race and his heart jump. In the days since she'd gone, he'd done everything he could to avoid the room, unable to face yet another ghost of a love that wasn't meant to be.

The setting sun bathed the room in light. If he had pulled the drapes shut, if he hadn't walked past at that exact moment, with the sunlight streaking through the windows, it might have been months before he saw it—a flash of white against the dark mahogany instrument. He froze, unable to take his eyes off the unknown object. As though pulled by an invisible rope, he drew close to the window and peered inside, but he couldn't make out what the object was. He only knew it hadn't been there during that fateful conversation with Aster. It was an unspoken rule that no one entered that room.

He ignored his Ma, barely hearing her calls for him to remove his boots as he raced past her, through the living room, down the hallway to the closed door of the parlor. His hand shook as he gripped the door handle.

Not from fear. He'd already lost everything.

He shook with hope.

Goodbyes Are Forever

Henrietta

She peered out the third-floor window and judged the distance she'd have to jump to reach the nearest rooftop. It was possible. *Anything* was possible, but a broken leg would significantly hamper her movements.

"No one could make that jump," Henrietta said as she leaned out the window and felt for something to cling to. "It would probably be easier to climb to the roof."

"Either way. It doesn't matter as long as they believe you've escaped again. Come in from the window and hold still." Rosalie grabbed Henrietta's skirt and pulled until the worn fabric tore away from the hem.

There was another sharp rap and a thud as something heavy was thrown against the door. The hinges creaked under the strain.

"Off you go," Rosalie said.

Henrietta darted under the bed and scooted to the wall, folding herself into a ball. If they conducted a thorough search, they'd find her. But even so, she'd be no worse off than she was now. She tucked her head into her chest, closed her eyes, and focused on controlling her breathing.

Rosalie's shriek made her flinch.

"Henrietta, no!" Rosalie yelled. "Someone help!"

Henrietta heard the door crash against the wall, followed by rapid footsteps across the floor. "Where is she?" Jameson's voice shook with anger.

"Help her," Rosalie pleaded.

"Where is she?" Jameson repeated, louder.

"I tried to stop her."

Susanna's voice was low and calm. "Tell us where she went. Now."

"The window." Rosalie's voice broke as a sob seized her. Henrietta had to admire her cousin's acting skills. Rosalie had always been a consummate liar, coming up with the wildest tales of adventure, but her cousin had definitely honed her ability for deception over the past year.

"Is that a piece of fabric on that drainpipe? Which way did she go?" Jameson demanded.

"I...um...I...I don't know."

"You're lying," Jameson said.

"No, I'm not," Rosalie stammered. "I mean, I just want her to be safe."

"That's what we want too. I don't know if she told you, but Henrietta and I are friends. I care about her." Susanna's voice dripped with false sincerity.

Henrietta clenched her hands tightly together under the bed, anger seeping out of every pore. What did that woman know of friendship?

"She said..."

"Yes?" Jameson prompted when Rosalie broke off.

"She said she was meeting Duke Gildownie at the Palace of the Governors." Rosalie sounded defeated.

"The girl asked us about it the moment we arrived in town, remember?" Jameson said.

"Of course I remember," Susanna snapped, "but there's no way she set up a rendezvous. I never let her out of my sight."

"Um," Rosalie said meekly. "She mentioned something about a letter."

"What letter?" Jameson asked threateningly.

"I couldn't have them chasing after us, so I allowed her to write a letter to her man, but I checked every word. There was no mention of a meeting." Susanna's tone, normally so cool, so calm, rose in pitch.

Henrietta smiled when she imagined the two in a stand-off.

"My cousin is very clever with words. She used to hide coded messages all over the house as a game. I believe, and I'm surmising here, they used the same system to leave each other love letters," Rosalie said.

"We're wasting time here. The man might already be there, and then we're back to square one." Jameson stormed out of the room. Henrietta heard Susanna's softer footsteps trail behind her colleague.

"At least we know where she's headed," Susanna said, her voice faint.

Henrietta waited until she heard the door close, then counted to twenty before slipping out of her hiding place to congratulate her cousin on a truly impressive performance.

Duke

HE READ THE LETTER again, scrutinizing each word for any clue that she might actually care for him. He knew it was an exercise in futility, but he couldn't help but search for some hidden meaning, some hint her feelings had been more than an act for his family and for her pursuers.

Dearest Duke,

It has been my greatest pleasure meeting you. In the past few weeks, you've shown me the wonders of this great land, taught me the joy of skipping stones across the rippling water, and helped me learn to enjoy playing the piano again, which I did not think was possible. Although I must leave, I do so with a light heart for having known you. This memory will stay with me for my entire life.

My hope is that you will learn to forgive yourself and to love again, even if it means petitioning for a bride through Matrimonial News to share your life with.

With affection,

Aster

He traced the word "Dearest" and imagined her saying the word aloud in her sweet songbird voice. What was that song she'd sung outside Lincoln when she was high on peyote? *Goodbye, Liza Jane.* She'd warned him then.

Her goodbyes were forever.

"You fixin' to sit here sulking all night, or are you gonna come to dinner? We ain't gonna wait forever," Cash called from the open parlor door.

"Coming."

"What's that you got?"

Duke thrust the letter at his brother. "You were right. She's too good for me." He pushed past him into the hallway.

"Whoa! I sure didn't want her to take off."

"Doesn't matter." Duke charged into the dining room and yanked back a chair with a screech as it scraped against the floor.

Ma raised an eyebrow but didn't say a word for a change.

"Where's the fire?" Wyatt said.

Duke threw him a glare.

Wyatt held up his hands. "Sorry. Too soon?"

"Read it, Cash. Y'all might as well know everything."

"Nah, I don't think I will," Cash sat down and placed the letter on the table next to Duke.

"Ach, give it here. I'll read it."

"Ma, I really don't think you..."

His Ma stopped Cash's words with a single look as she snatched the letter off the table and read the note aloud. Wyatt looked down at his plate, clearly embarrassed to hear Aster's intimate words shared.

Cash looked thoughtful, an unusual expression for him. And Duke? He knew each turn of phrase, had imagined how her voice would have lilted at the end of each sentence, beseeching him for understanding.

Duke stabbed a piece of meat with his fork but dropped it again with a clatter. He couldn't eat. He needed a drink. More than one. He pushed back from the table, only to have his wrist encircled in his Ma's vice-like grip.

"Ye're not excused, boy."

"Ma..." Wyatt said, his eyes imploring.

"Aster's long gone. Naught to be done about it now, though I'm a mite disappointed in the lass. She could have waited till the morn to take her leave."

"It's passing strange," Wyatt said between bites of steak.

"Yeah. I mean, why would she take off in the middle of the night?" Cash asked.

"She's done it before." Wyatt frowned.

Cash's eyes darted to Duke. "But that was different. She got a bee in her bonnet about that little purse of hers being stolen."

Duke listened to his brothers, unable to speak, his heart in his throat, as they debated Aster's sudden departure. What did it matter when she'd left? She was still gone.

"And you say there was another woman here at the time?" Wyatt put down his fork, looking pensive.

"Susanna. Now, there's a woman for you. Black eyes as big as saucers and big—" Cash cut off at a sharp glance from Ma. He coughed. "Nice figure's all I was gonna say."

"One thing the lass said was true. Past time for ye to get married."

"You could try that Matrimonial News for real," Wyatt said.

Cash's mouth dropped. "You cannot be serious. He's gotta go after Aster. She's the girl for him. Can you imagine if he got saddled with another Judith?"

"Damn it, Cash." Wyatt slammed his fist on the table. "You never know when to shut your trap."

"'Tis true. Aster is better suited to his life here. I dinnae speak ill of the dead—"

"Then don't start now—" Wyatt began, but Ma cut him off.

"Judith wanted that shiny ring on her finger, but she never wanted this life on the range, and we all know it. She wanted an easy life in the city. Do ye no remember she demanded we sell the land so she could have herself a grand house in Santa Fe? I dinnae think she even wanted the babe."

"That's enough," Duke said, his voice no more than a whisper.

"She was no a bad lass and she dinnae deserve to die the way she did, but I'll no pretend she was a blessed saint."

"I agree with Ma."

Wyatt glared at Cash. "Big surprise."

Cash stood. "What? 'Cause I tell the truth?"

Wyatt pushed back his own chair and faced his brother. "Because you don't care who it hurts."

"And you do? If I remember, you took off right after Judith died, leaving me and Ma to pick up the pieces."

"Enough," Duke said again, his head in his hands.

"Sit doon, both of ye. I'll no have fisticuffs at the table. Judith has been dead five years now, and it's time yer brother settles doon with another lass. The question is whether it be Aster or someone else."

"I vote for Aster," Cash sat down heavily in his chair.

Wyatt's gaze was still fixed on Cash. "She made her decision."

"You never liked her." Cash continued to glare at Wyatt.

"I did like her. I still do. What I don't like is that she took off without a word."

Cash grabbed the letter from Ma. "She did." His face fell. "Though I still can't figure why she took off with Susanna in the dead of night, not unless something made her leave."

Duke jerked his head up. *Something made her leave.* Could his hot-headed baby brother actually have the right of it?

"Or someone," he said. Susanna Grimaldi. He knew everyone in these parts, but he had never met a Grimaldi before at Fort Stanton or anywhere else.

"What?" Wyatt asked.

Duke pushed back from the table.

"Sit doon!"

"Sorry, Ma," Duke said as he strode to the door. "I gotta go."

"Wait for me!" Cash stuffed a roll in his mouth and followed him out the door.

THE NEXT MORNING, AFTER spending a sleepless night in a campground near Lincoln, listening to Cash's snores, they rode into town. Duke peered up at the Murphy-Dolan Mercantile store. He'd never set foot in the place. They called themselves cattlemen, bankers; hell, Murphy even held the Indian Agent license. But they were more than that. They were a bunch of barnburners and rustlers, killers pure and simple, the kind of men Shaw had sought out, and the kind Duke had done his best to steer clear of. Until now.

Duke patted the Colt on his hip for comfort, though drawing would only get him killed faster.

"You sure about this?" Cash asked.

"Nope." He shoved the door open and stepped inside. At first glance, it was no different from any other trading post, filled with shelves of seed, grain, and foodstuffs, but no other mercantile was packed with as many rough-looking characters. Duke recognized four of the men as part of the group who'd terrorized the ranch.

Jimmy Dolan sauntered up to him, a sneer on his face. "Welcome, Regulator. Come to confess?"

"I'm not Catholic and you ain't no priest." Duke forced a tight smile to take the bite out of his words.

Dolan laughed. "Not in this life, anyway. You looking for supplies? I heard about the unfortunate accident out at Split Oak Ranch."

"Twisted Oak," Cash said angrily.

Duke put a hand on his brother's arm as a warning. Under no circumstances could they afford to further antagonize Dolan. Duke still counted himself lucky the man hadn't returned to the ranch after failing to find Arthur.

"I reckon I might need a bag of nails," Duke said.

Dolan nodded to a store clerk who hurried over with the merchandise. Duke fished a coin out of his pocket, but Dolan stopped him.

"Consider it a gift. I hear you've had a run of bad luck. Lost your barn, your horses, and your pretty little bride."

Duke took a deep breath and forced his grip to ease on the bag of nails. "About that. You got any idea where she might have gone?"

Dolan's lips twitched. "Well, I might at that."

"You wanna tell us?" Cash spit out.

Dolan smiled wider. "I reckon I do. She took off with Jameson and that black-haired vixen."

"Susanna? Why?" Cash took a step back. "And who's Jameson?"

"He's that Pinkerton detective who's been sniffing around. It's the darndest thing. The woman's one of 'em too."

"One of...what?" Duke asked.

"Pinkertons."

He didn't bother with goodbye. There was no time. He'd been skeptical of Susanna's story from the beginning—her missing uncle who'd failed to appear and her intense interest in Aster. The peyote incident took on a whole new dimension. He'd let that woman squirm her way into Aster's life and then spirit her away in the middle of the night.

There was nothing and nobody that would keep him away when Aster needed him.

A Lonely Widower

Duke

He'd tried a half-dozen times to lose Cash on the trail to Santa Fe, but the man was like a bad penny—always turning up, usually reeking of alcohol and covered in dust. Even so, Duke didn't mind the company, at least when his brother wasn't nattering on about some scheme or other. Duke had hoped Wyatt would be the one to insist he join him on the trip to Philadelphia, but his older brother had just shrugged, wished him luck, and said he'd work on the barn while the two of them took off, shirking their duty to the ranch and the family.

Duke smiled. For the first time in his memory, he didn't care about the ranch. Oh, he still loved the land and knew he had a mess of work to do when they returned, but the work would wait, and he wasn't sure Aster would. What if the telegram he'd sent to her in Philadelphia had been intercepted? Her Pa hadn't wanted Rosalie to marry a no-good cowman. What would he think if his own daughter agreed to it? Not that Duke would force her to if she didn't want him.

Despite his hopes and Cash's clear confidence in Aster's feelings, there was a sick, ugly fear deep in his gut that she'd slam the door in his face when they finally got to her fancy house in Philadelphia. He didn't remember much about that first trip and the visit to her home. He'd been focused on preventing his brother from killing Rosalie's fiancé. Now he racked his brain for any wisp of memory. If that afternoon was to be one of the few, fleeting, precious moments with Aster, he'd lost it forever.

"You reckon we got time for a drink in that there saloon? Maybe a hand of cards?" Cash pointed to an enormous wooden structure with a stream of men going in and out through the swinging doors.

"Do what you want."

Duke strode past the bar, barely hearing the tinny music floating in the air. He was lost in another memory—when Aster had heard another song from another saloon. He should have asked her to dance then, like she'd wanted, taken her in his arms on the street and swung her around until they collapsed into each other.

Cash cast one last longing look toward the bar before trotting to catch up with him. They'd left the horses to get some much-needed rest in a stable on the outskirts of town. Duke had grated at the easy pace they'd set, but it was plain foolish to run the horses into the ground. The Santa Fe Trail was no easy trek, not even for the two of them. He'd brought Ginger with them. She was Aster's horse. Even if the woman turned him away, he'd still gift her the mare. He couldn't look at Ginger without imagining Aster astride the beast, bent low over the horse's neck, chasing the wind across the hills.

"Where we goin'?"

"Thought I might try to find Shaw and Rosalie at that highfalutin hotel."

"Think Shaw would appreciate us chargin' in on his honeymoon?" Cash shoved his hat back, his lips twitching.

"Hell, they've been on their damned honeymoon forever." Duke tried to keep the envy out of his voice, but one glance at Cash's wide grin confirmed he'd been unsuccessful.

They wandered up and down the busy streets teeming with newly arrived settlers, ragged from their long journey through the mountains. There were wagons in varying states of disrepair and bedraggled urchins playing hide and seek between the heaps of trunks and barrels spewing out of the Conestogas. How many of these wretches had been lost on the wagon train West, seeking a better life? He shook the thought away. He only had room in his mind, in his heart, for one thing, and he was on a mission to have it, no matter the cost.

"Dunno what these idiots expected to find here? Gold?" Cash jumped back to avoid getting smacked by a portly woman wielding a spoon at the children darting under her skirts, seeking a hiding place in a frantic game.

"Silver, maybe."

"You reckon?" Cash's face took on a thoughtful expression.

Duke sighed. Before the week was out, Cash would be up in the mountains chiseling rock, looking for ore and finding a whole lot of nothing.

"That's it." Duke pointed out the three-story hotel towering over the nearby buildings, nearly touching the sky.

"Let's go bust up their love nest!"

Duke shook his head but didn't try to stop his brother as he jogged to the hotel.

Henrietta

SHE WOULD HAVE MADE her escape if Susanna hadn't doubled back to the hotel and lay in wait for her with her small revolver clasped in her hand. Rosalie had wanted to fight, to make a stand, but one look at Susanna's angry face and the cocked weapon had convinced Henrietta to go along. She would not be responsible for anyone else being hurt by her actions.

To a passing stranger, Jameson's grip on her elbow wouldn't have seemed unusual, but to her it was a symbol of the chains tying her firmly to a future she no longer desired. When they arrived in La Junta, Colorado, after an arduous journey through the Raton Pass, they headed straight for the train station. Susanna went to fetch their train tickets while Henrietta and Jameson waited on the platform.

"I'm tired," Henrietta said.

"You'll have plenty of time to rest on the train."

She shrugged off his arm and strode to a bench on the platform outside the station. Smashed between those two on the stage, watched at night by Susanna, she'd felt like a misbehaving dog on a leash. Where was she to go in La Junta? And why? Duke had likely forgotten her, caught as he was in his memories of a life with another woman. Rosalie may have been convinced Duke loved her, but Henrietta wasn't as certain. With every passing mile since her doomed escape attempt, she convinced herself he couldn't possibly care for her.

Even so, she hadn't lied in her letter. He had changed her for the better. She would remember him until she died.

"Paper! Get your papers here!" A tow-headed young boy in short pants and suspenders expertly weaved through the crowd.

Henrietta fished a coin out of her reticule and called the boy over.

"Tribune? Nah, a pretty gal like you, you're bound to be looking for a husband in the Matrimonial News."

She twisted her mouth into a sad smile. "Yes, why not? I'll take a copy of both."

"Right you are, miss." The cheeky lad handed over a newspaper and a copy of the Matrimonial News.

Jameson stalked toward her, shoving people out of the way, including a particularly burly man with a bushy beard and a mass of wild hair, a gun belt hanging low on his hips. The man grabbed Jameson by the collar, lifting him onto his toes. Henrietta smiled as the nasty little man's face turned a brilliant shade of crimson.

She sighed and leaned back in her seat, determined to enjoy a few moments alone, at her ease without Jameson's paws on her or Susanna's piercing black gaze tracking her every move. She flipped through the Journal. A man named Edison had patented a contraption called a phonograph that played sound on its own, like magic. Unfathomable. A quick scan through the rest of the pages was enough to bring her up to speed on the society events of Topeka, Kansas, not that there was much to speak of. She opened the Matrimonial News and read personal advertisements from lonely men and women desperate for someone to spend their lives with.

Henrietta blushed when she read of a man, five foot five inches, seeking a tall woman with a bosom to rest his head on. There was a woman of thirty-five with a desire for the love of an older man, money no barrier. And a dozen other lonely hearts seeking a soulmate in forty words or less. She'd almost reached the last entry when it caught her eye.

Lonely widower, 28, six foot four inches, needs a brave, beautiful wife in a harsh land where the pink skies stretch across the horizon. Seeking woman who loves horses, plays the piano, and skips stones. Aster, wait for me.

Her hands shook as she read the advertisement again and then again. Was this real, or was this just a dream? She pinched herself and yelped. She was definitely awake. Could Rosalie have been right? Was she truly enough? For him?

But what had he meant, wait for him? Where? How would he find her? Had he meant Philadelphia at her parents' home? But her home was Twisted Oak Ranch, not Philadelphia, and she didn't want to wait. Not anymore. Not when the future beckoned.

She jerked her head up and scanned the crowd for her hounds. Jameson was still fighting off the mountain man. And Susanna? Henrietta peered around, expecting the black-haired woman to pop out at any moment, but she was nowhere to be seen. This was Henrietta's chance if she was the woman Duke believed her to be, one with heart and courage. She'd done it before, escaped, but she hadn't had this much to lose.

She took a deep breath to still her beating heart, clutched the Matrimonial News to her breast, and stole away. Henrietta darted through the crowds, skirted the station, and broke into a run as she reached the street fronting the building. If she hurried, she might have time to reach the depot and the stage before they even realized she'd gone. And if not, she had money. She'd hire herself a wagon driver. She'd buy a team of horses and ride through the mountain passes on her own if she had to.

Cimarron

Duke

He cradled his head in his hands as Rosalie regaled him with the rest of Aster's story. This was his fault. If he'd insisted she stay with him, if he'd confessed his feelings, if he'd married her in truth, she wouldn't be in the grip of these villains.

"Where's the fire?" Cash said.

Three heads swiveled toward the man. He held up his hands. "Whoa. Hear me out. If Aster's parents hired the detectives, then there's no problem, right? They wouldn't want her hurt."

"The woman threatened her with a gun!" Rosalie crumpled onto the sofa. "I sent a telegram to my Aunt Florence, but Shaw said..."

"I said the detectives might not even know why they're searching for her," Shaw finished for his wife.

Duke nodded. "I never met a detective I trusted."

"Or a lawman who followed the law," Cash said.

Rosalie's face paled as she clutched her husband's hand. "Do you think they'd really hurt her?"

"I don't know," Shaw said with a solemn expression as he surveyed the group. "I swear I scoured the place for her, but she was gone. Vanished. I sent a telegram to you. Did you get it?"

Duke shook his head. "We'd already left. How long ago was this?"

"Five days." Shaw wrapped his arm around Rosalie's shoulders. "All we can do is hope your aunt gets your telegram in Philadelphia and calls off the manhunt."

Rosalie nodded as though she'd heard him say this a dozen or more times already.

"I can do more than that." Duke's mouth was set in a grim line. "If I travel the Cimarron Pass, I can make up some time."

He swiped his hat off the coffee table, knocking something to the floor. He reached down and grabbed a stone, smooth and flat, perfect for skipping.

Rosalie watched him as he turned the stone over and over in his hand. "It's Henrietta's. She was holding it when the detectives came," she said.

Duke tucked the rock into his pocket. He didn't have time to replay everything he should have said or done. Aster was in danger and getting further and further from him the longer he sat here in this opulent room chatting. He stood and rushed to the door.

"Where you goin' now?" Cash called. "It's nearly dark and they've got days on us. One night here won't hurt nothin'."

"Stay if you want," Duke smashed his hat on his head.

"Wait for me!" Rosalie jumped up from her seat and raced to the door.

"Absolutely not," Shaw said.

Rosalie turned on her husband, her face flashing. "She's my cousin, and I let her go—"

"Rosie," Shaw said, touching her shoulder. "Duke has to move fast, riding all night, living rough."

"I can 'live rough'! I've done it before."

"Of course you can, but..." Shaw threw up his hands. "Ah, hell, Rosie. You can't ride well enough to keep up."

Rosalie took a step back as though she'd been struck. Her lip trembled, and Duke anticipated tears to start flowing at any moment, but his sister-in-law surprised him once again by jutting her chin out and saying, with a shaky voice, "That may be true, but I can't sit around while she may be in danger. I did that once and look what happened."

Shaw's voice took on a tender tone, one Duke had never heard from his brother. "The burn wasn't your fault. Henrietta doesn't blame you. She never has."

"*But I blame myself.* I'm the one who chased her that day," Rosalie's voice broke. When Shaw wrapped his arms around her, the woman collapsed in shudders.

Shaw threw his brothers a pleading look. Duke cleared his throat and said, "I'll get her back, I give you my word. I won't let anything happen to her."

Aster's face swam before him, and shame gripped him in its familiar chokehold. He'd been given a second chance, if he had the strength and conviction to see it through.

Henrietta

SHE WOULD DO IT RIGHT this time. No more lies. Well, at least not until she'd eluded the dogs hounding her. She practically stumbled upon the post office three blocks from the rail station. Mrs. Martin, the vicar's wife, would have said it was positively providential. Whether it was providence, fate, or God lending His hand, she'd take it.

Ten minutes later, a telegram and a letter were on their way to Rittenhouse Square.

I have escaped your detectives and am on my way back to Lincoln where I will be married. Stop. Please join us for the wedding. Stop. Henrietta

She'd done what she could. She'd addressed both pieces of correspondence to her mother, unsure how her father would react. In her letter, she'd layered in multiple references to Anna and her Count, posing the question of what would have happened if Vronsky had been a good man, a kind man, the kind of man who would have sacrificed his ambition for his love. If anything could sway her mother, it was taking a tragedy and giving it a fairy tale ending. Life would be so much sweeter if every love story had a happy ever after.

Perhaps her mother could convince her father to call off the detectives, but Henrietta was not about to take that chance, not when getting word to the agents on her trail would be difficult, if not impossible. Jameson and Susanna would head straight to the stagecoach station. If only there were another way through the Santa Fe Trail.

"You're blocking the road!" an angry voice called from behind her.

Henrietta jumped and looked around. She was standing in the middle of the main thoroughfare of the town. It was a wonder she hadn't been trampled by a dozen oxen. She darted back across the street to the post office she'd just left. If this place were anything like the offices in Philadelphia, the postmaster would be privy to all goings on.

She opened the door and marched up to the desk. "Excuse me, sir. Where could one hire a private company to cross the mountains into New Mexico Territory?"

The postmaster, dressed in a drab gray suit and matching vest, jumped at her voice. He'd been so absorbed in sorting the mail. "Pardon me, ma'am. I didn't know you were still...ahem...I mean, I thought you had gone."

"Yes, yes. But my question? About travel?"

"Most folk take the stagecoach," he said.

Obviously it was the best mode of transportation—she had just taken it from Santa Fe to La Junta and it would be the natural way to return. However, Susanna and Jameson were likely already at the depot or would be soon. She adopted her sweetest smile. "That's not really an option."

He peered at her over his glasses and looked her up and down, taking in her stained dress, her sunburnt face, and her disheveled hair. She lifted her chin and raised an eyebrow, daring him to comment on her bedraggled appearance.

He shrugged. "You could sign on with a wagon train."

"And how long would that take?"

"To Santa Fe?"

She nodded curtly.

"Six, eight weeks."

She sighed. "That will not do."

"You're out of luck then. If you can't afford a ticket on the stage—"

"I never said that," she snapped, then instantly regretted her tone. "I'm sorry, sir. I am grateful for your help. I'm tired and I need to reach my destination as soon as possible. I do have funds to pay."

"If you're in a hurry, then your best bet is to take the Cimarron Trail, but water is scarce, not a journey to take lightly. You'll need a guide, and a good one."

"And could you recommend someone to me, someone fair, reliable?" She casually opened her purse and withdrew a silver dollar.

"I believe I could."

"Excellent."

She smiled as she left the establishment for the second time in an hour with a skip in her step and headed down the block toward the guide and toward her future.

On the Rocks

Henrietta

Henrietta surveyed the ground for the perfect stone, as she had at every campground since they'd started their journey down the Cimarron Pass three days earlier. She sent a silent prayer of thanks for her guides, Joshua and Carter Nilsen, and her luck at happening upon their party just as they were about to leave La Junta with a small group of investors and bankers and their wives. That had been the one thing she'd been unwilling to compromise on—other women in the party. She had been on the frontier long enough to realize that women were a scarcity and it was best not to rely on the inherent goodness of mankind for her safety.

"So, take heed, ladies," Joshua said as he poked life into the dying embers. "In an Indian attack, surrender. The Comanches are more likely to take you home to their camps than to take your scalps."

Henrietta had heard this warning already a dozen times from a half-dozen men, from stagecoach drivers to rail conductors to guides. She tuned out the man's voice and surveyed the surrounding land.

The Cimarron River Valley was the most beautiful place she'd ever been, with its soaring mountain ranges in the distance and evergreens towering over vast meadows boasting a brilliant array of wildflowers. The skies themselves were a study in color worthy of any painter's palette. And yet, the wolves' howls at night, the far-off call of a mountain lion, and the sheer variety of poisonous snakes and scorpions were enough to keep her on edge, even in the fitful sleep she succumbed to each night.

The postmaster hadn't lied when he'd said water was scarce out here in the wilderness of the Cimarron Pass. Until that afternoon, she'd seen no sign of a creek or river. They'd had to rely on their canteens and the great barrels strapped to the side of the wagons. The sound of rapids from the Cimarron River was a balm to her soul. Just knowing there was fresh, flowing water mere footsteps away eased her mind. They'd been able to refill the barrels which had come perilously close to dry the day before.

Three more days and she'd be back in Santa Fe. She didn't dare hope Rosalie would still be there, but every day she inched closer to realizing her dreams. Duke loved her. She wrapped her coat tightly around her as the men in the group continued to regale one another with the horrors of an Indian raid, while the women shivered in the pale light of the fire. One of the women, Laurel, a small, pale creature, had smiled at her tentatively the first day, but she'd been so timid Henrietta had struggled to hold a conversation with her, despite her natural ability to chat with anyone. The other two women had looked askance at her—a lady traveling alone. She hadn't bothered to explain that she was on her way to meet her fiancé. She'd learned years ago that some women were more inclined to believe the worst in a person, no matter the circumstance.

Laurel's husband was a bear of a man, brash and bombastic. He was such a contrast to the young woman; it was a wonder they'd found each other. Every time his voice boomed her name, Laurel flinched and rushed to his side with fear in her eyes. More than once, Henrietta had considered intervening, but what could she have done, one woman surrounded by strangers in this wild country? Still, Henrietta did her best to be kind to Laurel, often sitting close to her as the day drew to a close, in a silent promise of friendship.

That night she dreamed of Duke, of his rare and fleeting smile, of his calloused thumb rubbing against her lip, and of leaning into his tall frame, enveloped by an embrace. And this time, when she pulled his head down for a kiss, he returned it with a hunger that matched her own. Heat rushed through her body as his hands slid down her back to her backside, pulling her closer to him. She woke in a tangle of skirts and blankets, flushed and excited.

The sun was a mere glimmer, a pale orange streak on the horizon when she opened her eyes. An hour before dawn. She turned onto her side and willed herself back into the dream, but sleep wouldn't come. A coyote wailed in the distance, a lone cry into the fading night. She might as well get up and start the coffee. Carter Nilsen was in charge of preparing their breakfast while Joshua got a few minutes of much needed sleep after night watch. The sludge the man fixed was no match for the sweet ambrosia Bridget had prepared.

Henrietta threw off the blanket and got up, moving quietly through the camp to avoid waking her comrades. Carter nodded at her from the far side of the camp and shifted his rifle in his arms. As she reached down to lift the coffee pot and an empty bucket from the supply pile near the wagon, she spied a set of hazel eyes watching her. Laurel shrugged out of her husband's embrace, barely interrupting his rhythmic snoring, and joined Henrietta on the path to the riverbank.

Once they were far enough away from the rest, Laurel said, "I've been up for hours."

"Are you feeling well?" Henrietta once again noted the woman's small frame, her pallid skin, her gaunt cheeks. Without a wide-brimmed hat protecting her face, she would probably turn as red as the lobster at home.

"I am," Laurel's small voice cracked ever so slightly as she said the words.

"Is there anything I can do?" Henrietta passed the coffee pot to Laurel to wash and fill while she managed the larger, heavier bucket.

"There's nothing anyone can do." A quick glance back at the camp was all Henrietta needed to know where the problem lay.

Henrietta dropped to her knees and dipped the bucket into the river, feeling the clean rush of the mountain-fed water, cold against her hands, the fine spray misting her face. She shivered despite the warmth of the night. This close to the river, all she could hear was an intense pounding as the water skipped and tripped over boulders the size of barrels. Laurel stared at the river as a lover might and leaned precariously over the rushing water. She wobbled, and Henrietta grabbed her arm to keep the small woman from falling. Laurel turned her eyes on her and opened her mouth. Whether to thank or curse her, Henrietta would never know.

There was a whoosh and a thud, and then Laurel fell into her, pushing both of them into the rapids. Henrietta opened her mouth, and water rushed in, choking her. She waved her arms frantically and forced herself off the bottom, coughing and gasping as her head broke the surface. In an instant, she was pulled under again.

Her feet found purchase on the rocky bed below. She pushed herself up and flailed wildly. Her chest burned. Her throat ached. She couldn't breathe. Couldn't see. She fought the water as she would an assailant, lashing out with fists and feet, but her skirts were heavy, and her limbs grew weak. The struggle seemed so futile. Her hand brushed against something smooth and hard. Stone. She grasped the rock. It fit so perfectly in her palm. Perfect. Like Duke. He was perfect for her, accepting her for all her many faults, loving her despite them, or maybe because she was flawed. Helping her discover her love of music again. As her body was buffeted by the current, she imagined his hands holding her, lifting her up.

What had he said? To swim, you must be a leaf and surrender to the power of the water. To fight was to fail.

She forced her limbs to stop their frantic motion and allowed the water to bring her to the surface. Sweet air filled her lungs before she submerged again. But this time, she waved her hands in wide, steady circles, like a ballet dancer moving from one position to another. When she reached the surface again, she continued the slow motion until she bobbed along the river, like a leaf.

Something soft brushed against her, and she lost her concentration, sinking, but she refused to panic, and sure enough, she soon rose to the surface. She searched for the object and found Laurel's body floating next to her. She reached out and grasped Laurel's dress, pulling her closer. After a few attempts, Henrietta was able to lift her head out of the water long enough to see the shore. She kicked gently at first and then harder, propelling them to the river's edge.

Laurel's body was so heavy and unresponsive, Henrietta thought at first she might be dead. She lowered her ear to the woman's chest and was rewarded by a steady rise and fall. The sun had not yet risen, leaving Henrietta to search her friend for signs of injury by running her hands along Laurel's small body. When she pushed back the woman's hair from her face, Henrietta found a bump the size of a plum. She continued her search and discovered an arrow protruding from Laurel's right leg, tangled in her skirts, stained crimson from blood, visible even in the dim light.

Her heart skipped a beat, and she ducked instinctively. She peered around the forest surrounding them.

Comanche.

Duke

A SCREAM FOLLOWED BY a boot in his side woke Duke from a deep slumber. He shot up, his Colt in his hand. He and Cash scanned the surrounding woods.

"Big cat?" his brother said in a low voice.

Another scream.

"That's no cat," Duke said.

It was a woman. A woman in trouble.

Cash kicked dirt onto the fire as Duke ran to the horses at the edge of the camp. They mounted and spurred the horses forward in the dim pre-dawn light. He'd known three things when they'd taken the Cimarron trail—it was quicker than the mountain route through the Raton Pass, water was nearly impossible to find, and Comanches roamed the hills.

He could almost hear his sister-in-law Mary telling him not to judge all members of a tribe the same, and he didn't. But for every Mescalero Apache he'd named friend, he'd found an enemy amongst the Comanche. The braves he'd run across hadn't wanted to barter or share a peace pipe. They'd only been interested in men's scalps and women to add to their tribe, and even that was not a given. He'd run across the hacked-up bodies of many a woman and child.

His hands tightened on the reins as terror threatened to unseat him. Cash was speaking to him, but he couldn't hear the words over the blood thundering in his ears. He urged Dapple faster, despite the risk to the prized Appaloosa.

It wasn't until Cash seized his arm and motioned toward a break in the woods that he realized the shouting had reached a fever pitch. He reined in the horse and dismounted, grabbing his Winchester. The two men crouched and edged closer to the brutal sound of war cries intermingling with fearful shouts and the roar of rifle fire. His heart skipped a beat as another woman screamed. To hell with sneaking up. He charged forward with his rifle at the ready.

Somewhere amidst the battle cries and the howls of terror, he heard his brother crashing through the brush next to him. The sun was just peeking over the horizon as they stumbled upon the campground. A warrior charged them, swinging his axe in a wide arc. Duke ducked and shoved his brother down, just in time to miss a blade lodging itself in his neck. He jutted his rifle forward and swept hard to the left in an attempt to trip up his attacker, but the man easily avoided it. The warrior jumped and kicked out. It was all Duke could do to avoid a moccasin in his face.

A blast sounded next to him, nearly forcing him back to the ground. His ear rang, and blood oozed out of his ear down his cheek. The warrior crumpled in front of Duke, his eyes wide with shock.

Duke didn't have time to thank his brother. He'd barely regained his footing when the next attack came, this time from a man wielding a Winchester much like his own. Duke fumbled with the Colt in his holster. He was no shooter, but he was quick enough to fire off two rounds at the brave. Cash and he moved deeper into camp, protecting one another as an onslaught of arrows and bullets flew at them from every direction. He couldn't hear out of his left ear, and his right wasn't much better, leaving him exposed. Duke swung his head from side to side, tracking men as they charged from the woods into the clearing. If it hadn't been the travelers in the camp firing at the Indians as well, he and Cash would have been easily overwhelmed.

As fast as the attack began, it was over as a whistle sounded and the Comanche melted back into the trees, carrying their dead with them. Duke wasted no time searching for Aster. Two women sat huddled together with three men surrounding them, blood pouring from multiple wounds. He couldn't hear the men's cries of outrage as he forced his way through their human barricade to lay eyes on the women. One look at the older gals was all it took to send him further into a panic.

He called out for Aster but could barely hear his own voice over the roar in his ears. One of the women pointed to a worn and faded carpetbag, the one Aster had used as a weapon when she'd been accosted in the Lincoln saloon. She was there, somewhere, maybe hurt, maybe....no, he wouldn't let his mind go there.

Someone grabbed him, and he shoved the man aside before realizing it was Cash. He was saying something urgently, but Duke couldn't hear the words. When Cash started dragging him away from camp, Duke realized he was trying to show him something. Twenty yards away from camp, they pushed through brush to discover a raging river, its waves crashing over fearsome looking boulders.

Cash pointed to something at the river's edge. Duke kneeled and pulled a coffee pot from the water. And then he spotted it. His heart stopped.

On the rocks. Blood.

A Priceless Gift

Henrietta

The sun was well above the horizon by the time Henrietta was able to pull Laurel's unconscious form into the cover of bushes. Despite the woman's small size, her skirts were sodden and heavy. Henrietta was strong; she always had been, but even so, it was a struggle to drag a grown woman across the rocky terrain. She collapsed next to her friend and took deep breaths, sucking in air laden with pine and earthy loam.

She closed her eyes and almost succumbed to the sweet pull of sleep when an angry shout roused her. She was on her feet in an instant, searching through the dense foliage for a weapon. Her hand seized on a dead branch, three feet long, almost too heavy to lift. She crouched over Laurel's still form, like a wildcat protecting its young.

A man blundered through the brush. She jumped up, screamed, and swung with all her might. Her attacker fell at her feet in a heap. She had no time to consider what she'd done before another man rushed forward. She lifted the branch again and almost connected with the man before she realized it was Duke. She dropped her weapon and leaped into his arms, mindless of the two prone figures at their feet.

Henrietta stifled a sob as she clung to his tall, lean form, wrapping her arms around him, holding onto him for dear life. His heart thrummed in her ear, steady and constant, as she buried her face into his chest. She closed her eyes and inhaled deeply. He smelled of wood smoke, and horses, and him...just him.

"Aster," he said softly. She held him tighter. "Aster," he said more urgently. "Aster, I can't breathe."

"What?" She released her grip slightly.

"I think you killed Cash," he shouted.

She pulled back and gasped. Duke's face and neck were covered in blood, thick and red. "What happened? Where are you hurt? Is it an arrow?"

"What? I can't hear you!"

She opened her mouth to shout, then realized blood was seeping out of his ear. She forced herself to calm down and mouth the words, "Are you all right?"

He nodded, then pointed to his ear. "I can't hear anything!"

She covered his mouth with her hand and looked around them into the dense woods.

She mouthed again, "But everyone can hear you."

He grimaced as he realized he'd likely be the one to call down the Comanche on them. She reached up and touched his face, covered in auburn whiskers. "I can't believe you're here."

He captured her hand and pressed it to his mouth, closing his eyes. "I thought...I thought I was too late."

She stepped closer and pulled his head down to whisper into his good ear. "There's nothing in this world that would keep me from you."

As if his trance had been broken, he gathered her into his arms and found her mouth with his own. His hands tangled in her hair as he pulled her close until every part of her body rubbed against him. His lips were insistent on hers, as if he was dying of thirst and she was a tall, cool glass of lemonade. The world slipped away. He was everything.

Henrietta nipped his bottom lip with her teeth and laughed when he groaned aloud, but her laughter ended abruptly when he thrust his tongue into her mouth. She molded her body to his and gripped his shoulders, desperate to tear down every wall they'd built between them. There was only the two of them and their need for each other.

A whimper sounded from far, far away, gradually growing louder until Henrietta withdrew from Duke's embrace to search for the wounded animal. It was only as she looked down at the ground that she remembered her friend, lying there, injured and in pain. Henrietta touched her lips briefly before returning to the reality of their situation. Laurel struggled in vain to push an unconscious Cash off her tiny body.

Henrietta's eyes widened in horror as she realized what Duke had meant by his words—*I think you killed Cash.*

Between the two of them, they were able to roll Cash's still form off the small woman. A loud snore from Duke's brother convinced her he might wake with a severe headache, but he would wake. She was far more concerned about Laurel, whose face was even paler than usual. Henrietta pushed up the woman's skirts to inspect the wound on her leg more closely.

An arrowhead protruded from the fleshy meat of her thigh. Blood seeped out around the shaft of the arrow, oozing down her leg in a steady stream of crimson. "We have to remove it," Henrietta whispered to Duke.

Laurel jerked up with an exclamation before falling back to the ground with a soft cry. Henrietta offered soft words of encouragement to her friend, but in truth she was terrified. They were in the wilderness, far from civilization, and possibly surrounded by Comanches. This was no place to attempt such a delicate medical procedure.

"Do you have a knife?" Henrietta asked.

"Cash can be a pest, but maybe just one attempt on his life today?" Duke said as he reached for his blade.

Henrietta couldn't help smiling despite the seriousness of their situation—her spirit was so high she thought she might float away. She used the knife to cut off a generous length of her petticoat, praying it would be clean enough from the long exposure in the river.

"I'll do a bit of scouting. Call if you hear or see anything." Duke took a few steps and then turned back. "Actually, maybe I should call if I need help. That was a mighty fine swing, Aster."

She copied her mother's fierce expression and nodded as though his words were no more than the truth. Still, pride swelled in her chest, far greater than she'd had after any piano concert.

Laurel cried out as Henrietta wrapped the makeshift bandage around her leg, even though she used infinite care where the bandage met the arrow shaft. When satisfied she had done all she could to help her friend, Henrietta turned her attention to Duke's brother.

TRAVEL WAS SLOW AS they made their way back to the campsite. They had floated several miles downriver in the rushing water. Although Cash's head hurt 'something fierce', he still found the strength to help Duke carry Laurel through the woods. The poor woman slipped in and out of consciousness, and Henrietta feared they would arrive too late to save her friend.

When they finally reached the camp, they were met by a gruesome scene from a horror novel. Blood covered both the dead and the living. The two guides, Joshua and Carter Nilsen, were digging shallow graves. Henrietta counted three bodies, all men, wrapped in blankets. And the two women who'd cast their sidelong glances at her? They were huddled together, shaking.

When Henrietta discovered the bloodied corpse of Laurel's husband, all she could do was hold her friend as the woman wept silent tears.

"There'll be time to grieve, dearest," Henrietta whispered in Laurel's ear. "But now we have to remove that arrow." She didn't say the rest of her thought—that her friend would soon join her husband if they couldn't stop the bleeding.

Cash squatted next to the fire and held a knife into the flame. Henrietta swallowed down her unease at the thought of how they were going to seal the wound, but there was no choice. There might have been sewing supplies in the trunks, but it would take time to sort through, not to mention the horror of rifling through the dead's possessions. Duke held Laurel's hand and whispered soothing words while Henrietta carefully removed the bandage, exposing the arrow. She sat back and pondered the problem.

"We'll have to cut the shaft below the arrowhead and then I'll pull it out through the entry hole," Duke said.

Henrietta blanched and glanced at Laurel, her wide eyes terrified but determined.

"She'll lose so much blood," Henrietta murmured.

Duke nodded, his face serious.

Henrietta's mother always said if something needed doing, it was best to begin without delay. Henrietta washed her hands in water from Duke's canteen and then in a splash of whiskey from his flask. She was tempted to take a swallow out of the worn and beaten container, but she needed her wits about her.

"Ready?" Duke said.

"No, but there's no other choice."

He nodded and began sawing away at the arrow shaft. Despite his firm grip on the shaft and his attempts to keep it still, the slightest jostle elicited a scream from Laurel. But the woman was stronger than Henrietta had given her credit for. Laurel clung to consciousness as the blade cut through the shaft.

Henrietta took the arrowhead from Duke, then handed him a piece of her petticoat to wrap around the shaft, now slick with blood, to get a better grip.

"Where are you from, Laurel?" Henrietta asked her friend, trying to draw her attention away from Duke's actions.

"New Orleans," Laurel said breathlessly, with beseeching eyes.

"I've always wanted to visit. My uncle was stationed there during the war, and he told me how beautiful it was. Magnolia trees and azaleas everywhere," Henrietta said, then bit the inside of her cheek. Laurel's family had likely fought on the opposite side during that particular conflict.

Laurel didn't seem to notice Henrietta's gaffe. "It is so lovely there. Sometimes it makes my eyes hurt." Her lip trembled. "I'll never see it again."

"Nonsense," Henrietta nodded to Duke. He gripped the cloth-wrapped shaft and yanked it out of her leg. Laurel wailed as blood rushed out of the wound.

Henrietta was partly grateful—the blood would carry the dirt and debris away. She focused on the upside rather than on Laurel's ashen lips and vacant stare. There was no time to waste. Henrietta poured the remains of the flask on the entry and exit wounds, then called to Cash, who rushed over with the fiery red blade.

He hesitated at the sight of so much blood.

"Give it here," Henrietta directed.

The leather handle was warm in her hand as she grasped the knife. She took a deep breath and pressed the blade to the exit wound. It sizzled as it seared Laurel's flesh. The pain was too much for the poor woman. Laurel fainted. Henrietta tried to ignore the smell of burnt flesh, putrid in her nostrils, as Duke turned Laurel's limp body over. Henrietta placed the still red-hot knife to the entry wound.

She washed both wounds with water and then inspected them for fresh bleeding. Although the skin was raw and puckered, there was no new blood. "Let's leave it open for a while to be sure," she muttered. Then louder, "Cash, you and Joshua should search for gauze or clean cloths to wrap the wounds."

She shook Laurel's shoulder and tried to rouse the woman to no avail. Duke's eyes mirrored her concern. Laurel could easily slip into oblivion if they were unable to keep her conscious. There was nothing for it—Henrietta squeezed Laurel's hand, then slapped the woman's face, hard enough to leave a mark.

"Laurel, come back to us."

A slight flutter of her eyelids was enough encouragement for Henrietta. After a few more minutes, Laurel opened her eyes.

Henrietta smiled wide. "Welcome back."

"Aster?" she whispered.

Duke caught Henrietta's eye. "Aster?"

She shrugged. "I couldn't imagine you calling me anything else."

"Are you still hiding?"

She shook her head. "I've told my parents everything."

"And?"

"It's up to them whether they accept my decision, and it's *my* decision. No one else's. For better or worse."

"Better," Laurel said softly, drawing Henrietta's attention back to her patient.

"So much better," Henrietta agreed. "Now we need to wrap your leg and get you fed. It's time to build back your strength."

Laurel nodded, but her eyes filled with tears. "I have nowhere to go."

"I guess you'll have to come with us, then," Cash said as he bounded up to them, carrying a roll of gauze.

Duke

AS TWILIGHT DESCENDED and the camp settled down to tend to their hurts and grieve their losses, Duke slipped his hand into Aster's and drew her away from the rest of the folk. They picked their way through the dense brush to the spot in the river where the Comanche had nearly stolen Aster from him.

The river, swollen with floodwaters from storms high in the mountains, raged, tumbling over rocks and fallen logs alike. In his mind, all he could see was Aster's broken and beaten body as she fought for her life.

"How did you do it?" He swallowed hard, fear bubbling in his gut.

"I survived because of you."

"Me?" He shook his head. "I don't understand."

"You taught me to be a leaf. If you hadn't, the river would have swallowed me up. And Laurel too."

A tremor seized him as he realized just how close he'd come to losing her forever. Just like Judith. But no. Judith had been running away from him while Aster had been running to him, and in that moment when he'd been unable to help her, she'd rescued herself. He hadn't been there for her. Before he could descend into the whirlpool of fear and self-recrimination, she wrapped her arm around his waist. In the dim light, he could just make out her brilliant smile. How could she be happy when she'd been minutes away from death?

As if reading his mind, she said, "I'm here. And you're here. And we're *together*."

She filled that one word with such certainty he could almost believe it was real, and God, how he wanted it to be real. He raised her hand to his lips and kissed her bare skin, free for once from the gloves she habitually wore.

"I love you," he whispered.

She stood on her tiptoes, reached around his neck, and pulled down his head so they were eye-level. "I love *you*, Duke Gildownie."

"Forever?"

"And always."

He searched her blue eyes and found what he'd always seen. Despite the lies and manipulations, she was true to herself and to him. She was the most honest person he'd ever known.

He brushed a trembling thumb across her soft cheek, still rosy from the day's ordeal. "I'm sorry it took me so long to find you. I..." He looked down at his boots. "I thought after I told you about Judith that..."

"That I'd what? Blame you?"

He nodded.

"What happened to Judith and George is heart-wrenching, but anyone with half a brain can tell how much you loved them. I know you would have done anything to save them."

He sighed and peered into the distance, his eyes glazing over, caught again in the memory that had tortured him for years.

"I don't deserve a second chance." He turned to face her again. "But I'm so grateful you've given me one. There is nothing I wouldn't do for you. If you want me to sell the ranch and move to Philadelphia, I will."

She smiled. "I found my life in New Mexico, in the pink skies and wild country, in its people, in its horses." She touched his cheek. "And in you."

He captured her hand and kissed it. He wanted to pick her up and take her deep into the woods, to make love to her all night long, but their first time needed to be special, beautiful, with no deception and no mind-altering peyote, after they stood in front of a preacher and their families, after they committed themselves to one another in church before God.

"Aster, will you marry me?" His voice shook as he said the words.

"I will," she said quickly.

"I don't have a ring to give you yet, but I thought you might like this." He reached into his pocket for the skipping stone he'd carried with him since Santa Fe. She accepted the plain, flat rock as though it were the most priceless gift in the world.

He leaned his head against hers and sighed. For the first time in years, he looked forward to what tomorrow would bring.

Everything

Henrietta

Rosalie fussed with Henrietta's hair, her dress, and her train like a middle-aged matriarch rather than a woman only three years older than she was. Every few minutes, her cousin erupted into tears—of joy, Rosalie assured her.

"I'm nervous," Henrietta finally admitted as she ran her fingers down the folds of pale blue satin. Rosalie's friend Selestina and her mother had sewn the wedding dress. It may have been the finest garment Henrietta had ever worn.

"What are you nervous about?"

Henrietta glanced at her cousin in the mirror. "I always thought my mother would be with me on my wedding day and that my father would be the one to give me away." Her eyes darted to Rosalie as she realized the possible slight to her cousin's husband. "I am incredibly grateful to Shaw for escorting me...I didn't mean..."

"I know, little Aster," Rosalie offered a smile and an encouraging pat. "It's not the same without them, but they will come around. They love you and they will love Duke too."

Henrietta nodded and inhaled deeply. "Well, then. I think I'm ready."

The next few moments passed in a blur as they loaded into the hired buggy for the short drive down Main Street to the little church where Shaw waited to greet them. Rosalie squeezed her hand before going inside to take her seat.

Henrietta inhaled deeply and smiled at Shaw. Even after a few weeks spent together, she didn't feel as though she knew him at all. Duke said he was an outlaw, a dangerous man, but she'd only ever witnessed him being exceedingly kind to Rosalie, a calming presence.

After the wedding, Rosalie would set off on her journey to find her sister. Henrietta's heart ached when she considered the turmoil her cousin felt.

She had her own turmoil today as she took Shaw's arm and started up the steps.

"Third time's the charm," Shaw said.

She looked at him sharply, only to find a sardonic grin on his face. A bit of the fear gripping her heart dissipated, and she was grateful to her soon-to-be brother-in-law. "Third and final time up the church steps," she said, forcing gaiety into her tone.

"I should hope so. Duke told me in no certain terms that I was not to take my eyes off you just in case you got it in your head to dash off."

The tightness in her chest lessened with each step to the open doors of the white-washed adobe structure with its thick oak doors, intricately carved with enormous crosses wrapped with vines of roses and lilies. How remarkable it was to find such detailed craftmanship in this dusty outpost in the wilds of New Mexico Territory, though perhaps she shouldn't be surprised. The man standing next to her was a testament to how an artist, an extraordinary talent, could lie hidden inside the most dangerous of men.

The cool, dim interior of the church was a stark contrast to the bright sunlight as they stepped inside. It took her eyes a moment to adjust to the soft candlelight and the sunshine drifting through the few stained-glass windows. She'd been here with Duke once before, had sat on a pew at the back of the church, and had met a woman who'd purported to be her friend. She caught herself scanning the crowd for Susanna's raven black hair, but the woman knew better than to show up at the wedding. Henrietta only hoped that her parents had called off the Pinkerton agents once and for all.

The thought of her parents and their noticeable absence had her belly churning again, and she stumbled, only to be caught by Shaw's firm and steady grip. She shook her head slightly to shake off the hurt and focused instead on the people seated inside the church. There was Rosalie, who she'd traveled across the country to find; fierce Bridget, who had tears streaming down her face; Cash, who boasted an enormous grin; and his solemn brother Wyatt. Rosalie's friend Selestina and her large family were present, along with Captain Mellon. Laurel, pale and wan, gave her an encouraging smile. Then there were the people who'd befriended her from the beginning, the Martins. Mrs. Martin beamed from beneath a pink bonnet with an enormous velvet bow tied under her chin. Next to her were Major Martin and the man she supposed to be his brother William, and his wife and baby.

The vicar stood near the altar next to the tall, lanky, incredibly handsome man she loved, the man with whom she would promise to spend her life, the man who she trusted with her dreams and with her heart. As though he could sense her nervousness, he held out a hand to her, as he always had, offering her strength and compassion and love.

THE DAY PASSED IN A whirlwind of well-wishers and partygoers, champagne and barbecue, and an enormous cake that Bridget and Rosalie had somehow managed to make without Henrietta's notice. The celebration was lovely, but overly long, ending well past midnight.

The stars were brilliant in the night sky streaming through their window when Duke and Henrietta finally escaped to their bedroom. As the door closed, she felt a sudden shyness overtake her. They'd spent so many nights here, slept less than a foot away from each other for weeks, and yet had never been together, not in the way they would be tonight.

"Are you nervous?" Duke said, leaning against the windowsill.

She nodded, unsure suddenly where to put her hands, where to look. She fidgeted with her skirts and tottered from one foot to the other, partly from the drink and partly from anticipation.

"I can sleep on the floor."

She searched his face for signs of jest, but despite the shadows, his face showed nothing but open concern for her. She crossed the room to stand in front of him, her heart racing in her chest. "No."

"No?"

"You will not be spending the night on the floor. I forbid it," she said seriously.

"You forbid it? What about all those words spoken earlier in front of the vicar? About obeying your husband in all things?" His lips twitched, but he made no move to touch her.

"And I shall, but only when you are not demanding stupid and outrageous things."

"So, you're saying that you will determine whether my requests are stupid and therefore worth following or ignoring?"

"Exactly." She moved to stand directly in front of him.

"And me sleeping on the floor is...?"

"Stupid and outrageous," she said.

"Well, you did call me an idiot. And I am whenever you're around. I forget how to think, how to breathe."

Her heart lurched. She leaned forward and tilted her head up. "Are you going to kiss me now?"

He peered into her face and said, "Would that be outrageous?"

"Why don't you find out?"

He cupped her face in his large and calloused hands, rough against her smooth skin. He leaned down and kissed her lips lightly before pulling back.

She pursed her lips to keep from laughing. "Do you call that a kiss?"

He shrugged, but despite his best efforts, he could not keep a grin off his face. "Can you do better?"

"I believe I can."

She stood on her tiptoes and laced her fingers behind his neck to lower his face to hers. "You're too tall," she said in a breathy voice.

"I'm sor—"

His words were cut off as she touched his lips with her own. This time when he tried to pull away, she opened her mouth. He moaned and pulled her tighter against him, all pretense gone as the desire of the past two weeks burned through his restraint. He thrust his tongue into her mouth, and a wave of heat flooded through her body. She was lost in the kiss, in the sweet and intensely intimate way his tongue darted in and out of her mouth in a steady rhythm.

When he finally pulled back to take a gasping breath, she was left shaken and quivering, and flushed.

"I want to make love to you, Aster. I want to hear you call out my name," he murmured, searching her face for permission.

"I want that too."

He sighed with relief. "Thank God." Before she could even take a breath, he swept her off her feet and carried her to the bed, setting her down gently before reaching behind her to unbutton her dress.

"How many of these damned things are there?" he grumbled as he pulled at the fabric.

"Let me," she said, placing her hands over his. With trembling fingers, she started to remove her gloves. "Will you..." She bit her lip and looked down.

"Will I what?" he asked, his eyes searching hers.

"Will you turn down the lamp?"

He glanced over at the lantern, then back at her in confusion. "Why?"

Embarrassed, she couldn't meet his gaze. "You've never seen the full scar." She swallowed and licked her lips, her mouth suddenly parched.

"Aster." He lifted her chin to look directly into her eyes. "There is not a single part of you that I don't love. Let me show you."

With trembling hands, he helped her undress, first her wedding dress, then layer after layer of undergarments, kissing and caressing her as he went, whispering how beautiful she was. Only then did he unbutton her long white gloves and slip them off inch by inch. "You're so lovely," he said as he kissed her palm.

"I want to see you too."

He laughed and said, "I'm not nearly as impressive."

"Let me be the judge." She tugged the tail of his necktie loose. He wasted no time stripping off the rest of his clothes.

He was all lean, knotted muscles, bronze from the waist up. She drew in a sharp breath as she saw just how impressive he was from the waist down. "Goodness."

He smiled as her gaze ran up and down the length of him. "Pleased, Mrs. Gildownie?"

She looked into his eyes, burnished gold in the soft light. "I am."

He brushed a lock of hair from her shoulder and kissed her burn, making her shudder as his mouth caressed skin that hadn't been touched by another since the physician had treated her wounds more than a decade ago. "So beautiful," he murmured as his mouth traveled the length of the burn from her shoulder to the middle of her back.

When his mouth found hers again, she was trembling with desire. When he placed his large palm on her breast, she whimpered and pulled him forcefully on top of her. It was exquisite torture to be touched, to be held, to be kissed. When his fingers found the sweet, sensitive place between her legs, she was nearly in tears from sheer need.

Gently he probed her folds with his fingers, all the while plunging his tongue deep inside her mouth. "Please," she whispered, dragging her fingernails across his back, though she wasn't sure exactly what she was pleading for.

When he nudged his manhood between her thighs, she thought she might die. And then he was inside her, moving so slowly, so sensuously, holding himself back. From somewhere in the still functioning part of her brain, she remembered there might be some pain, but she didn't care. She needed him deep inside her.

She wrapped her legs around him and urged him to let go, to make love to her without control, without the fear of hurting her. She was strong; she always had been. It was all the encouragement he needed. He groaned and pressed himself deeper into her. She flinched when she felt her maidenhood shatter, but the moment passed as waves of pleasure rolled through her body. Over and over, deeper and deeper, building to a crescendo, until she was on the precipice. And then her body tightened and released around him, sending her into the heavens.

"Duke," she called out as he continued to love her. Again and again, she cried out his name.

Duke

HE CURLED A LOCK OF her hair around his finger and listened to her breathing, her heart beating, her occasional sigh as she slept, curled up in his arms. He'd spent the last five years believing he did not deserve the happiness he felt in this moment, and yet Aster had unearthed every last secret he held in his heart and had not run from him. No, she'd run to him. She'd given up everything for him—a life in Philadelphia and a family she loved.

He had to make it right. She was too kind, too wonderful a person to have to sacrifice for him. However long it took, he would work to give her the life and family she deserved. He would never stop. If he could build this ranch from nothing, working all day every day of his life, he would do the same for her. More for her.

Because she was everything.

Perfect

Henrietta

She sighed as she took a bite of Bridget's biscuit, smothered in wildflower honey. Though Henrietta had stood next to her mother-in-law the better part of three weeks learning to mix the dough just right, she had to admit that Bridget's would always be superior. Over the past weeks, she'd come to the strangest revelation. It was not learning how to make the perfect biscuit that gave her the most joy, though that would have been amazing. No, she craved standing side-by-side with Bridget as her mother-in-law chatted with her, sharing her wisdom and her love.

"Heaven," Henrietta said as she finished chewing her first bite.

"I've a knack for baking," Bridget replied with a small smile as she lathered fresh butter on her own biscuit.

"I'll miss you." Henrietta reached across the table to grab Bridget's hand.

"Aye, you will, but my Martha's time is near, and I must be off."

Henrietta nodded and smiled encouragingly at her husband, whose face had become drawn and tight when Bridget mentioned Martha's imminent childbirth. "I'm sure you will see she's delivered safely," Henrietta said, more for Duke's benefit than Bridget's.

"Dinnae ye worry, lassie. Besides, by the look of our dear Rosie, I'll be needed back here shortly after the new year."

Henrietta's heart fluttered at the idea of her cousin being pregnant, especially now that Rosalie and Shaw were well on their way to Texas. "How do you know? Is it safe for her to travel?"

"She likely dinnae ken herself yet, but I have an eye for these things," Bridget said between bites. "And as for her health, even a woman heavy with child can do most anything better than a man."

Cash burst out laughing, only to receive a sharp reprimand from his mother.

Wyatt, though, was staring out the window, a half-eaten biscuit forgotten on his plate. "Expecting someone?"

Duke and Cash pushed back from the table and headed for the door to strap on holsters and grab rifles. The scent of smoke still lingered in the air long after the barn fire had been extinguished. The idea that Jimmy Dolan or the loathsome Colonel might return to wreak more chaos had Henrietta's teeth chattering and her stomach clenching. She couldn't sit back and wait for whatever destruction was coming.

Trying to master her fear, she followed the men to the door, unsure what to do, but determined to uphold her vows and stand with Duke no matter what trouble befell them.

Henrietta strode onto the porch to face whatever devil had come to call, but there was no devil in the form of evil men with hard faces and pitiless souls. To the contrary, the visitors were simply that—visitors—and yet they brought with them a whirlwind of love and hope...and fear.

She watched as the buggy pulled up to the house, and as a man climbed out. A man she loved, a man she thought had forsaken her, a man she had stolen from.

"Papa?" she whispered hoarsely, but he didn't hear her, turned as he was to help a lady descend from the vehicle.

Her father was roughly pushed aside as Henrietta's mother flew past him to greet her. Mama was not prone to effusive emotional displays, and yet today she wrapped her arms around Henrietta and squeezed her tight enough to steal the breath from her chest. She was whispering frantically in Henrietta's ear, something about letters and mail-order brides and Count Vronsky and Anna Karenina.

"So, which of you is Gildownie?" her father bellowed.

Three men answered yes, but only Duke took a step forward and reached out his hand. Henrietta managed to extricate herself from Mama's grip and dart to Duke's side, not sure whether she was trying to protect him or offer him courage to face Papa, who was intimidating on the best of days.

"I'm Duke Gildownie, sir."

"My husband," Henrietta interjected firmly.

Papa shook Duke's hand, though his face remained stern and impassive. "Horace Beedy, Henrietta's father."

"Who's Henrietta?" Cash hissed at Bridget, who quickly shushed him.

Papa peered at the ranch, the ruins of the old horse barn, and the skeletal frame of the new one. "You've had trouble?"

"Yes, sir."

"Best see to it that it doesn't impact my daughter." Only a tic in Papa's cheek hinted at the difficulty he was having with the conversation.

"Papa?" Henrietta called again meekly, still unsure of the welcome she would receive.

"It is good to see you, Henrietta. You've caused me no end of trouble. Your mother has been in fits worrying over you," he said in a stern voice.

"I know, and I am sorry for that." Henrietta darted a glance at her mother, whose eyes glistened with unshed tears.

"But I can't fault you for your decision to leave. I..." Papa sniffed and looked away from the crowd gathered on the front steps. "I may have erred with your cousin." His voice didn't soften, but his mouth quivered ever so slightly.

"Rosalie has already forgiven you for withholding the letter and the money."

Papa cleared his throat, looking unbearably discomfited. "And you? Do you forgive me?"

It nearly broke her heart to see the anguish on her father's face. "If you can forgive me for leaving without a word?"

He nodded once. It was enough.

HER FATHER WAS INTENT on riding the property with Duke to learn all there was to know about ranching in New Mexico Territory. After a brief rest, her mother joined Bridget and Henrietta in the family room for a cool glass of tea, which was soon replaced by a tumbler of applejack. Bridget contented herself with knitting in her rocking chair as Mama questioned Henrietta about the past few months' adventures.

"And the woman, the Pinkerton agent, drew a weapon and threatened you?" The horror on her mother's face would have been comical if not for the serious nature of the question.

"She did, but she was not nearly as horrid as her partner."

"Your father has lodged a complaint with the New York office." Mama took a long drink of sweet, smooth brandy. "You must believe that we never dreamed anyone would harm you. We only ever wanted your safe return."

"I know," Henrietta assured her mother. "You still haven't told me what prompted you to come. Did you receive my letter?" Henrietta frowned, swallowing down the hurt. "I thought you might have come for the wedding."

Mama fidgeted in her chair. "Your father..." She broke off to take another sip of brandy, as if searching for the right words to say. "Your father was adamant that you come home."

Henrietta's face fell, and she fought against the pain she felt every time she disappointed her parents.

Bridget's hawk-like gaze fixed on Mama. "Then what changed his mind, I'd like to know?"

"Duke's letters and telegrams, of course."

"His letters?" Henrietta asked in confusion.

"Heavens, sometimes we received two or three telegrams in one day, and the letters were so lovely."

"My boy wrote ye letters?" Bridget's face was a picture of disbelief. "Are ye quite sure 'twas Duke?"

"Why, yes." Mama scrunched her forehead as if considering the question. "We received four before we left, but it was a single line in a telegram that convinced your father to make the journey."

Henrietta leaned forward. "What did he write?"

Mama gripped her hand. "He said you've begun to play the piano again."

"I...I don't understand," Henrietta said.

"We'd given up hope. You are so talented, sweetheart, and then one day the music stopped, and the joy in your eyes slipped away. Why did you quit playing?"

Henrietta bit her lip and thought through her next words. "I realized I would never be...good enough."

"Good enough for whom?" Mama's gaze was fixed on hers, as though the whole world rested on what Henrietta would say next.

"For me. For you," Henrietta broke off. "All my life, I wanted...no, I *needed* to be perfect...for you and Papa."

"Why?" Mama's eyes filled with pain.

Henrietta's voice cracked, but she continued in a rush, "Can't you see? I'm the one who lived."

Her mother gripped her hand, tethering Henrietta to her.

"Dearest," Mama said, "you have been the delight of our lives. We've only ever wanted you to be happy and to find your place in the world."

"She's right," Papa said hoarsely from the open doorway as he stood shoulder to shoulder next to the man she loved.

"I am happy, happier than I've ever been. And I have found my place." Henrietta smiled, catching Duke's eye. "I know exactly who I am, here in New Mexico, with Duke. I'm right where I belong."

The End

Dear Reader

It has been my greatest joy bringing Duke and Henrietta's story to life. I've always been fascinated by the lure of second chances, the Lincoln County War, and many of the historical characters and events in these novels. I am not a trained historian and beg your forgiveness for any errors I have made in telling the story. If you enjoyed this novel and haven't yet read the first book in the series, *Cactus Rose*, please pick up a copy of Rosalie and Shaw's love story.

It would mean the world to me if you left a review on Amazon or on goodreads.

Please consider signing up for my newsletter to receive exclusive, free short stories, behind the scenes, and the latest updates on the series.

From the bottom of my heart, thank you for venturing into this world with me,

Lily

www.ingramcontent.com/pod-product-compliance
Lightning Source LLC
LaVergne TN
LVHW091130080826
845145LV00008B/2102

* 9 7 8 1 9 7 0 6 1 4 0 1 5 *